INTERVIEW WITH A Sadist

BESTSELLING AUTHOR
WS GREER

First edition published by Kindle Direct Publishing 2023

Publishers Note: This is a work of fiction. Names, characters, places, and incidents either are the product of the author's imagination or are used fictitiously. Any resemblance to actual events, locales, or persons, living or dead, is entirely coincidental.

Copyright © 2023 by WS Greer
All rights reserved, including the right to reproduce this book or portions thereof in any form whatsoever.

Cover design by Robin Harper/Wicked by Design
https://www.facebook.com/WickedByDesignRobinHarper

Interior Design and Formatting by Book Money Inc.

Important Note:

Interview with a Sadist is a BDSM romance. While all characters and situations are completely fictional, some scenes may imitate reality, and be harmful to those who have experienced violence or assault. This novel contains depictions of bondage, impact play, breath play, and sadistic topics. It is intended for mature audiences only.

The Assignment

Chapter One

"Hi, Bree. I know you're at lunch right now, but I need you to come see me as soon as you return to the office. I've got a new assignment for you. It's a good one."

I clear my throat and let out a long sigh, because every time Chase has told me my next assignment would be a good one, it was anything but. Last time, my "good assignment" had me on the front lines of a protest between union workers and their employer in Hunting Park. It took all of two minutes to realize this protest was going to get ugly, and I ended up in the hospital after being pepper sprayed and hit in the leg with an asp by riot police. As good of an editor-in-chief as Chase Murdock is, working for him as an investigative journalist feels a lot like jumping from an airplane without knowing if the bag attached to your back is a parachute or a tote bag.

"Okay, Chase," I answer reluctantly. "I'll be in your office the minute lunch is over."

"Great. See you soon."

The call with my boss ends and I set my phone down on the table next to my iced coffee and crispy grilled cheese on sourdough bread. As hard as it may be, I try not to think about the impending threat of my new assignment and return my attention to my two girlfriends who agreed to meet me at Starbucks for lunch this afternoon.

"So, how's your hot boss doing?" Teagan asks as she raises her perfectly manicured eyebrows. Her blue eyes reflect the light of the sun shining through the window and almost make her look like a beautiful White Walker from Game of Thrones.

"Chase is *not* hot," I reply with a frown.

"He kind of is," Melissa responds from my left, and my face reacts with a grimace all on its own. Melissa is a gorgeous blonde just like Teagan, and while both of them are stunning, apparently neither of them has good taste. Then again, out of the three of us, I'm the only one who's still single.

"You're both out of your minds," I say with a giggle. "Chase is, like, fifty."

"Yeah, but he's got that Brad Pitt, silver fox thing going on," Melissa says.

"Oh, I'm sure Andy would just love to hear that," I shoot back. "After six years of marriage, poor Andy finds out his wife, and mother of his two kids, has a silver fox kink."

Melissa gasps and jolts back like I just whacked her across the face. "Umm, no. It's not a *kink*, Bree."

"Eww," Teagan chimes in under her breath, but loud enough to be heard.

"Kinks are for skanks," Melissa adds with raised eyebrows, and I'm forced to silence because I can't figure out if she's joking. "I just happen to think older men are … attractive. That's why my Andy is so much older than me."

"He's thirty-seven. Seven years isn't that much," I say.

"But it's enough," Melissa replies.

"Yeah, it's enough," Teagan chirps, before adding, "Russell is only two years older than me, but since I'm still in my twenties, him being thirty sounds so old."

"Oh, I felt the same way before my thirtieth birthday," Melissa says. "For some reason, turning thirty terrified me. I felt like I could never call myself young again, and all I had to look forward to in life was the slow deterioration of my body."

"I'm convinced I'll be using a walker before I turn thirty-one," Teagan says, and Melissa giggles. I, on the other hand, am stone-faced.

"You guys know I turn thirty in six months," I say with a furrowed brow. My girlfriends both respond with giggles, and I almost feel forced to join in.

Melissa, Teagan, and I have been friends since we met at the University of Pennsylvania right after high school. The two of them were already friends when I came along, and there was something infectious about the way they interacted with each other. Melissa was always the ringleader, maybe because she's the oldest, and Teagan always acted like the little sister trying too hard to impress her older sibling. Hell, they even look similar, with their golden blonde hair and blue eyes. Admittedly, they're a bit pretentious, but I love them all the same, and while I look like the outsider with my dark brown hair, we're still like a tight-knit family. We talk to each other about everything, and no matter how stilted they can be sometimes, there are no two other people in the world I'd rather be friends with.

"Speaking of you turning thirty," Melissa begins again after a sip of her Frappuccino, "I'm dying to know where you are in the boyfriend department these days. You're not getting any younger, you know."

"Yeah, you're not getting any younger," Teagan repeats. "I remind Russell every day that my dirty thirties are looming, so if he doesn't propose soon, we're going to have problems."

"You tell him that?" I ask playfully, but Teagan doesn't

answer blithely. She raises her eyebrows and sits up straighter in her seat.

"Oh, absolutely. Every woman in my family was married before the age of thirty, and you guys know how traditional *my* family is. We believe in marrying, settling down, and having kids with the man of your dreams. So, Russell needs to know I expect his commitment to come in the form of an engagement ring sooner much rather than later. We have no time for games."

"Wow," I reply. "So, you think Russell really is the one? He's your forever?"

I expect Teagan to answer instantly and with enthusiasm, but she hesitates, looking down at her drink as if it will whisper the answer to her before looking at me again.

"Of course," she says, although her voice tells me otherwise. "The two years I've been with Russell have been the best of my life. I can't wait to experience marriage with him ... which is why I think you should let us sign you up for Tinder."

"What?" I blurt out. "That was quite the subject change. Why do I need to sign up for Tinder?"

"Because you need to meet somebody, Bree," Teagan says, and I can see Melissa nodding her approval out of the corner of my eye. "We know you're busy with your job most of the time, but we'd love to see you meet someone who can take care of you so you don't have to work so much."

"But I like my job ... most of the time."

"I know, but wouldn't life be better with someone to come home to?" Teagan continues with maximum confidence and minimum self-awareness. "Someone calm, reserved, and as conventional as we are. That way, we could triple date!"

I pinch my lips together as I struggle to wipe the expression of shock and annoyance off my face. I've always known that Melissa and Teagan were the traditional types that love the idea of getting married and becoming stay-at-home moms. Melissa quit her job in advertising as soon as she got married, because Andy was capable of taking care of her with his salary as COO of the company she used to work for. Teagan is still working as a bank teller, but she's itching to quit so that Russell's bank manager salary can keep her warm and cozy at home. My parents were the same way, but I'm not sure that a "traditional" lifestyle is what I want for myself. I certainly don't have anything against Russell and Andy, but I have met them both, and I want something … more.

"Well, as much as I'm enjoying this conversation," I say sarcastically as I look at the time on my phone. "I have to head back to work. Chase has a new assignment for me."

"Oh, okay," Teagan says, immediately standing up to hug me as I rise from my chair. I stand and loosely drape my arm around her while she pulls me into a tight bear hug, squeezing my waist. Once we separate, I turn to Melissa.

"Let us know what your next assignment is. I hope it's something you love," she says with a smile as we embrace.

"Thanks. I hope it's something I love, too. I'll text you later," I reply, before spinning around and heading toward the exit.

Chapter Two

I've worked at the Philadelphia Inquirer for the last seven years. My time here has been incredible from the very beginning, and I can't remember a single moment where I thought I'd rather be doing something else. Suffice it to say that I've never seen myself as a housewife standing in the kitchen, waiting for a man to come home to me, because I'd much rather be outside with my pen and pad or my recorder.

I've always loved the thrill of finding out what's really going on somewhere, and I've been driven by my interest in the facts, whether they fit my beliefs or not. I was raised in a conservative household where religion reigned supreme, but my interest in the who, what, when, where, and why of things has always pulled me out of any religious orbit I was close to, and thrusted me into the world of unabated curiosity. My mother wasn't a big fan of my inquisitiveness, but that never stopped me from pursuing the truth.

The building where I chase down facts is massive. It's a giant structure that towers into the sky of the city with a wide bottom and narrow top, making it look like a brick space shuttle ready for launch. At the very top sits a large, circular clock that shows its face on all sides of the building like a giant, all-seeing eyeball watching the city from every angle. This is my sanctuary, and when I step off the elevator, I smile at the hustle and bustle of my office bullpen. Computer screens shine brightly with images of crime scenes and sporting events from all over the city. Reporters and journalists speed-walk from office to office, some chasing down leads, others turning in assignments to their designated superiors. It's a world of controlled mayhem, and I step into it with a happy heart full of familiarity.

I weave my way through the crowded space with my sights set on the office of Chase Murdock, my editor-in-chief. As I approach, I can already see him seated behind his desk with his eyes glued to his laptop. Even at the age of fifty, the man still has a full head of hair, but the gray is taking over from the middle of his scalp. Regardless of the incoming gray, Chase keeps his hair combed and styled, and his gray beard is neatly trimmed around his mouth. The wrinkles around his eyes are more endearing than anything, and they multiply when he smiles at me as I reach his door.

"Hey, just the woman I wanted to see," he says, leaning back in his chair and rocking a bit. "Did you enjoy your lunch?"

"I did," I answer as I step inside and take a seat on the light gray couch taking up most of the space on the wall to Chase's left. He turns his chair to face me and leans forward, resting his forearms on his thighs.

"So, I'm sure you're wondering what I've got for you," he begins, wasting no time because he has none to waste. As editor-in-chief, Chase is a very busy man.

"Yeah, I thought about it the entire drive back," I answer honestly. "I'm both curious and concerned."

"Concerned? What do you mean?" he questions with a playful frown and shrug.

"You know exactly what I mean, Chase. My leg still hurts from that asp."

"Oh, it wasn't that bad."

I scrunch my forehead and glare at him.

"Don't stare at me with those big, piercing, blue eyes, Bree Barrett. It makes me nervous."

"Good," I snap back before grinning. "Now, tell me what you've got."

Chase smiles as he leans back again, and there's something mischievous in his eyes.

"So ..." he starts, pausing to increase the tension before adding, "Have you heard about the new nightclub in Center City?"

My eyes dance around the room as I try to figure out which club he's talking about. Center City is an ever-growing place, so new clubs aren't particularly uncommon, but I can tell from the way he said it that this one is something special.

"No, not off the top of my head," I answer.

"I'm sure you've heard of it," Chase says. "It's called The Black Collar."

My eyes stop dancing and widen to twice their usual size. "The Black Collar? *Of course* I've heard of it. I've heard plenty of stories about it, none of them good. Isn't it a brothel?"

Chase pinches his lips together and gently shakes his head. "I don't think it's a brothel, but I know the rumors are running rampant through this city like an airborne virus. With those rumors in mind, it's hard to ignore the interest the public has in this new club. Apparently, it's very exclusive and requires people to sign up and be accepted just to get in. From what I've gathered through my own genuine curiosity, it's a BDSM club."

"Like ... S&M?" I ask as my heart starts to race. I can't exactly tell the reason for my heart's quickened pace, but I'm pretty sure it's fear about where this is going.

"Well, yes. S&M is sort of in the original acronym," Chase says, mocking me with a chuckle.

I let out a long exhale as my head drops and I stare at the floor while gathering my thoughts. Chase is all about public interest. It's a part of his job description, and Chase is great at gauging public interest and letting it guide where we place our efforts. Rumors and people talking on social media about a singular topic is almost always the reason Chase sends the hounds sniffing in a particular place. As much as I don't want to be, I am today's hound.

"Chase, are you about to tell me that you want me to investigate a BDSM club?" I ask, choosing to skip over the rest of the formalities.

"Pretty much," he answers. "Obviously, we want to know everything about The Black Collar club, but since the access is so exclusive, we're going to have to go through the club's enigmatic owner."

"The club's *enigmatic owner*?" I ask with dread taking up all the space in my throat. "You want me to meet up with some weirdo who's into sadomasochism, who owns a club that may or may not be a brothel? Come on, Chase."

"What did I tell you about glaring at me with those eyes?" Chase jokes with a pointed finger. "You don't know if he's a weirdo or not, and just because he owns a BDSM club doesn't mean he's into sadomasochism ... whatever the hell that means."

"Chase," I start, but he cuts me off.

"I don't want to hear it, Bree," he scolds, although there is jest in his voice. "This is the assignment. The entire city wants to know what's really going on in that club, and I refuse to allow another publication to get ahold of this story and run it before us. I pulled every string I have in order to get us an interview with this guy, and we're not going to back out just because you have an aversion to weirdos and kinkiness."

"Kinks are for skanks," I reply, parroting Melissa's statement before internally scolding myself for sounding like Teagan.

"Maybe you're right," Chase agrees with a nod. "But we've got the inside scoop on this, and we're going to take it. You're my most diligent journalist, Bree, so I want you on this. I already spoke to the owner on the phone, and he's just waiting for a call from you to schedule a date and time. He's giving us exclusive access for as long as we want it."

I let out a loud, exaggerated sigh that Chase ignores, and my shoulders slump as I realize I'm not getting out of this. As curious as I am about the ways of the world, BDSM and everything related to provocativeness has just never been my thing. Blame my upbringing, I guess, but the moral implications of this type of story sit heavily in my gut like a stomach full of rocks.

"Okay, Chase," I say, accepting my fate. "What did he sound like when you talked to him? Did he sound like a deviant?"

Chase laughs before leaning forward and handing me a card with a phone number scrawled across it in Chase's nearly illegible handwriting.

"He sounded like a normal guy to me," he answers as I take the card. "Maybe a bit reluctant to talk, but still normal —deep voice full of confidence."

"Well, if he's so reluctant to talk, why is he giving us exclusive access for as long as we want it?"

"We're not the only ones who hear the rumors around here. He knows people are talking about the club, and he knows that if he doesn't set the record straight about what happens behind those closed doors, the authorities might take an interest in the place. That's the last thing a new club owner wants. So, he's ready to show and tell."

Ugh," I say, shaking my head. "Fine, I'll go call him now."

I exhale one more time before standing up and turning to walk out the door. As I reach the threshold, I look down at the card and see that there's no name on it, so I spin back around.

"Hold on, Chase," I say. "What's this guy's name? I'd at least like to know who the hell I'm talking to."

"Nolan," Chase replies. "His name is Nolan Carter."

Chapter Three

When I step out of Chase's office, the air in the bullpen feels less oxygenated. I try to take a deep breath, but it catches in my throat, and I feel woozy as I stumble my way toward my cubicle. Maybe I'm more "traditional" than I care to admit, because the very thought of interviewing some kinky freak with a million tattoos and body piercings makes me nauseous. Why did Chase have to give this assignment to me?

The short trip to my cubicle gives me enough time to gather my composure and catch my breath, but my anxiety is rising high enough to tear the roof off the building. When I get to my cubicle, I step inside and reach for my chair so I can sit down, but the second I grab it, I feel I hand on my shoulder and hear a very familiar voice let out a thunderous guffaw. When I spin around, I'm met by the beautiful, annoying face of Octavia Washington.

"Oh, my god!" she shrieks, smiling big and wide. "I know he must've told you, because the look on your face is priceless, Bree. Priceless!"

My stunned face morphs to one of confusion.

"What are you talking about?" I ask, frowning as I sit

down in my chair and look up at Octavia, dressed in a black hoodie and black leggings. Her gorgeous brown skin is vibrant beneath the office lights, and her hair is tied into four separate balls on her head, called bantu knots. Out of every woman who works in this area of the Philadelphia Inquirer, Octavia is the most stunning. What's even more beautiful about Octavia is her infectious personality.

"Don't play dumb with me," she says, still beaming. "Chase told me all about his assignment for you, and I knew that shit would have you reeling. So, I can tell from that sad puppy look on your face and the way you stumbled over here like Bambi that he just dropped that kinky little bomb on you."

I gawk at Octavia with wide eyes. "You knew about the assignment?" Octavia nods enthusiastically. "What the hell? Why didn't you warn me?"

"Girl, why would I warn you and ruin the opportunity to see you all out of sorts like this? I still love you, but this is pure entertainment."

"Oh, that's messed up."

"I know, right?" Octavia quips with a giggle that whips out of her mouth like a lasso and pulls me into giggling with her.

"Ugh, you're too much," I say, leaning back in my seat. Octavia rests against the wall of my cubicle and crosses her arms. "Anyway, now that we both know about my assignment, I have to start this insane process and call the club owner to schedule an interview."

"I'm dying to know what kind of questions you're going to ask during this interview," Octavia says.

"I don't even know. What do you ask a BDSM club owner?"

"Shit, I'd ask him what kind of kinky shit he's into to see if it's something I've tried," Octavia says with a laugh, and I nearly fall out of my chair.

"Really? You like all that ... kinky stuff?"

"Girl, why did you whisper the word kinky?" Octavia asks as her face shifts from smiling to frowning in a millisecond. "We're all grown around here, and the only person I know who isn't into *that kinky stuff*, is you. Me? I want *all* the kink. Well, as long as he looks good being kinky. I can't be out there being freaky with a man who looks like Quasimodo."

I giggle before saying, "First of all, Quasimodo was adorable. Secondly, I can't imagine being into anything related to S&M. It's all just so ... violent."

"Violent? Bree, what do you actually know about BDSM?"

"Look, I'm an adult, and while I haven't heard a lot about it because it wasn't a topic of discussion in my world growing up, I've heard enough to know that it's dark and abusive. There isn't much more I need to know besides that."

The look on Octavia's face makes me stop talking. She almost looks offended, and definitely looks surprised at my answer. I don't know what kind of stuff she's into in her marriage of four years to Mike, but Octavia suddenly looks defensive.

"Wow," she exclaims with raised brows. "Well then maybe this interview is exactly what you need. It seems some education may do you some good."

I press my lips together into a thin line as I swallow a swell of guilt and regret taking shape in my throat.

"Umm ... I ... maybe you're right," I admit after stammering. "I was just brought up a little stricter than most people, and even my best friend Melissa says kinks are for skanks. I guess it's just branded into my brain that stuff like that is taboo."

"Your friend said kinks are for skanks?" Octavia asks, and if she frowns any harder I think her face will crack.

"Yeah, followed by the usual co-sign from Teagan."

"Melissa and Teagan," Octavia says with a furrow in her brow. "Are those the two girls you brought to the Christmas party last year?" I nod, and Octavia scoffs. "Oh. Right. *Anyway*, so when are you going to call the club owner?"

"I don't know," I begin. "I guess I can call him now and get it over with. The longer I wait, the more anxious I'll become about it, and procrastinating will only piss off Chase."

Octavia lets out an excited squeal and moves from the wall of my cubicle to lean against my desk. She slides my desk phone over to me and smiles like the Cheshire Cat.

"Yes! Call him right now so I can hear it. This will be the second highlight of my day."

"What was the first?"

"The look on your face when you found out about this assignment. Like I said ... priceless. Now, call him before Chase chastises me about not working."

I breathe deeply to try to settle myself, but it does nothing to calm the explosion of butterflies in my stomach as I reach for the phone. I hold the card Chase gave me, staring at the numbers and wishing they would disappear before I have the chance to dial them, but they don't. Those stupid numbers just stare at me, waiting for me to put them to use. I've never felt so nervous about setting up an interview in my entire career, but now that the moment is here, I have to power through and get it over with. That goes for the entire process. I want it all done as quickly as possible so I can move on to the next assignment that doesn't involve whips and weirdos. So, I ignore the grin on Octavia's face and dial the numbers. The phone rings twice before someone answers, and the voice on the other end sends shockwaves rippling through my cubicle.

"Hello?" a man says, and he sounds nothing like a creepy weirdo who's into abusing women. His voice is deep, but not gravelly. It's as smooth as velvet and commands my attention. Even Octavia's eyes widen at the sound of it.

"Umm ... I ... this is ... uhh," I stutter like a total amateur until Octavia hits me on the arm, which seems to reset my system. "Hello, I'm looking for Nolan Carter. I hope I have the right number."

"You do. This is he," the voice responds, and I shiver from the sound. Octavia covers her mouth with her hand, making it harder to ignore her, but I have to.

"Hi, Mr. Carter," I say, more confidently this time. "This is Bree Barrett. I'm an investigative journalist with the Philadelphia Inquirer. My boss, Chase Murdock, informed me this afternoon that he spoke to you about setting up an interview. I just wanted to call and see when you're available to talk about yourself and your club."

There's silence for a moment. It doesn't last long, but it's enough time for my heart to start racing again. Maybe he changed his mind and will turn the interview down. Would that make me happy, or would I be disappointed that I didn't get to see the face connected to the voice?

"This time tomorrow," Nolan answers, his words sharp and to the point. I expect him to say more, but he doesn't, forcing me to fill the silence.

"Oh, umm, okay. Yes, one o'clock tomorrow afternoon sounds good," I say. "Is there any particular place you'd like to meet?"

"One o'clock tomorrow, here at the club. Just go to the entrance and you'll be let in. See you then."

"Perfect. Thank y—" I start, but the call ends. When I look at Octavia, she looks as stunned as I feel.

"Is it just me or did he sound fucking delicious?" she asks, before releasing a giddy laugh.

"It definitely wasn't just you," I admit. "It doesn't change my expectation for the kind of person he is, but I know a sultry, deep, sexy voice when I hear it."

"God, I wish I could be there for this interview," Octavia says. "What if he's not some ugly weirdo? How are you gonna feel then?"

"What do you mean?"

"You're expecting to meet some strange pervert, but what if he's hot? Would that change how you approach the interview, seeing as how you've been single for, like, six months?"

"Of course not," I say quickly so I don't have to answer differently. "If he was ... attractive, I'd still conduct the interview as professionally as I always do. My being single has nothing to do with any of it. You know I haven't had time for a boyfriend. I'm dating my career."

"Oh, is that right?" Octavia says, smiling. "Well, good luck getting your career to fuck you."

"Oh, god. I can't with you," I say as I stand up. "Look, his appearance is irrelevant. At the end of the day, he's still the owner of a freaking sex club. Not exactly my type. So, at one o'clock tomorrow, I will approach this interview like a true professional. I'll spend as much time as it takes to squeeze every last drop of information out of this guy, and I'll write an amazing story about it. It'll be business as usual."

Octavia smiles like a woman with a secret. "Okay."

"Don't say it like that," I snap. "Everything will be fine, Octavia. You'll see."

"I hear you. It'll just be business as usual."

"That's exactly right," I say with a nod. "Business as usual."

Meet the Sadist

Chapter Four

The building that houses The Black Collar isn't extravagant. It's quite the opposite, actually. As the name would suggest, the two-story club that is sandwiched between two larger buildings is completely black. From the outside, it resembles more of a warehouse than it does a nightclub, with small personnel doors on the front and side of the building, and a large black rollup door in the back, opening into the alley. The words The Black Collar are fastened to the front of the building, and while they're not illuminated now, they still stand out with their large, masculine font. If I could imagine what a BDSM club would look like from the outside, this is exactly it: large, but also moderate so as to not draw too much attention, discreet—for the same reason—dark, and ominous.

I park in a pay-by-the-hour lot across the street from the club, and try to swallow the lump of nerves clawing their way up my throat as I approach the building. With each step, my heart picks up its pace. By the time I reach the door, I feel lightheaded, so I take a second to gather my composure before I lift my hand to press the buzzer on the black door. I hear the faint sound of buzzing when I press it, and it only takes a few seconds before the door is unlocked.

When it opens, it's not the inside of the building that grabs my attention, it's the beautiful woman in front of me. Her porcelain skin glows, as does her curly blonde hair. It's as if she has harnessed the sun and is keeping it for herself. She has dark blue eyes, round cheeks, and the glare of a woman who has never taken an ounce of shit from anyone. Between her beauty and the ice in her demeanor, I'm not sure if I should greet her or run back to my car.

"Can I help you?" she asks in a husky voice that snaps me out of my trance. I blink out of my stupor and manage to formulate words.

"Oh, yes, I'm looking for Nolan Carter," I reply, and any hint of happiness in the blonde's face instantly melts away. She slowly looks me up and down, taking all of me in without any regard to how rude it may come off.

"What do you want with Nolan?" she asks when her eyes finally make their way up to mine again.

I swallow hard. "My name's Bree Barrett. I'm a journalist with the Philadelphia Inquirer—"

"Get the fuck outta here," the blonde snaps. Her face tightens into an even more intense scowl as she glares at me, preparing to slam the door in my face.

"I have an appointment with him," I blurt out with a raised hand, hoping it'll somehow help.

"What?" she says, stopping the door halfway and reopening it.

"I have an appointment," I repeat. "I spoke to Mr. Carter on the phone yesterday, and he told me to meet him here at this time to conduct an interview."

The aggressive blonde freezes, staring at me as she calculates my words in her head.

"Nolan agreed to an interview?" she asks.

"Yes."

The blonde shakes her head before opening the door all the way and stepping to the side. "Fine."

While the blonde closes and locks the door behind me, I do my best to take in the scene in front of me. Before arriving, I expected to see sex swings all over the place, and perhaps red couches for people to have sex on in front of tons of onlookers. I thought I'd see sex toys adorning all of the walls for random people to grab and use on each other. I imagined a lot, but to my surprise, I don't see any of that. Instead, there are only black curtains and walls dividing the entrance from the rest of the club. There's no music blaring either. It's obvious the club is closed right now, but I still expected more than this.

"Follow me," the blonde demands after locking the door, and I silently follow her lead.

We walk through a hallway that has closed doors on either side, and I'd be lying if I said I wasn't dying to know what's behind those doors, but we don't stop. I see a few curtained off sections as we make our way down the hall before it opens up into a much wider area where the bar is located to the left. In the center of the open space is some sort of large harness hanging from the ceiling and touching the floor. While this certainly isn't my world, I'm sure the harness is made to dangle someone from the ceiling in front of everyone in attendance. It's the first sign that this place is a BDSM club, but it's not the last.

In all four corners of what I now see is some sort of dance floor, are massive silver cages big enough to imprison human beings. The cages are empty, but again, I know better than to think those are just for decoration. I'd bet my paycheck that when The Black Collar is open, those cages become display cases housed by latex-covered deviants.

"You coming?" the blonde's voice snaps, catching me off

guard and forcing me out of a spell I didn't realize I was in as I stared at the cages.

"Oh, of course. Sorry," I say, hoping small talk will ease the tension and keep me focused. "I was just checking out the cages. Those are quite ... interesting."

The blonde's eyes cut over to me for a second, before going back to the path in front of us leading to a staircase at the back of the dance area. She doesn't respond as we reach the steps and start to ascend.

"So, what's it like working at a club like this?" I ask, but get no response as I follow her up the stairs. "Does it get pretty raucous in here on the weekend when it's packed? I imagine a place like this—"

We reach the top of the stairs and the blonde whirls around. "Stop it. Save your questions for Nolan, which he will answer ... apparently."

"You seem bothered by the fact that Nolan is willing to talk to me," I say, keenly aware of how close the stairs are behind me.

The blonde shakes her head, not in disagreement but in apparent disappointment.

"It doesn't matter what I'm bothered by, *Bree Barrett*," she says, spitting my own name at me like it tastes disgusting in her mouth. "Nolan's the boss, so if he thinks giving an interview to a journalist from the Philadelphia Inquirer is a good idea, then I'll escort you to his office. My agreement with it isn't necessary or required. Nolan leads, and I follow. Gladly. Now, stop trying to get quotes out of me and let's go."

Without another word, she spins around and starts walking, leaving me no chance to respond. I don't want to burn the interview by pushing Nolan Carter's employees, so I pinch my lips together and follow her again.

We walk past what looks like a VIP section and a second, smaller bar, before we reach another corridor with two doors on each side, and a final door in the center at the end. Although there isn't a nameplate, it's obvious from the setup that this is Nolan Carter's office. My nerves flare up again as we approach the door, and the mean blonde raps on it three times. Nolan's voice booms from the other side.

"Yes?"

"Nolan, there's a *journalist* here to see you," the blonde answers. "Do you want me to throw her out?"

My eyes widen and I frown in shock, wondering how Nolan will answer.

"No, Maddy," Nolan says with obvious annoyance staining his words. "Let her in."

The blonde, who I now know is Maddy, glares at me one final time before placing her hand on the black door knob and twisting it.

"Bree Barrett," she says, looking at me before raising a hand and turning to the man in front of her. "Nolan Carter."

Maddy steps to the side, and the moment I see him sitting there, my lungs ice over. The air leaves the room and I stand there gawking at the most gorgeous man I've ever seen. By the time I'm able to take in air again, I only manage to mutter two words to myself.

"Holy shit."

Chapter Five

"Good afternoon, Miss Barrett," Nolan says as he rises from his seat and starts on a direct path toward me. He steps around his desk, and I'm blessed with my first glimpse of his entire body from head to toe.

Based on my best estimate, Nolan is six-foot-one, maybe two hundred and ten pounds, with the smoothest caramel skin I've ever seen. His beard is trimmed short, so it's more scruff than beard, and it outlines his jaw and full, luscious lips. His hair is thick and curly on top while faded short on the sides, and the man has the audacity to be wearing a white button-up with the sleeves rolled to his elbows, and a navy-blue tie with a matching vest adorned with eight buttons to keep it fastened. He's a walking GQ model, and my eyes bulge at the sight of him approaching me with an extended hand.

I clear my throat to knock the ice off my vocal cords. "Hi, it's nice to meet you, and please call me Bree," I manage to say as I take Nolan's hand in mine and shiver as he squeezes it. It's not enough pressure to hurt me, but it lets me know there is power in those fingers.

"It's nice to meet you as well. Thanks for coming," he

says, before turning to Maddy, who's watching like she's studying us for an exam. "Thank you, Maddy."

"Is that all?" Maddy asks. It's a simple question, but there's something extra in her words. They weigh more than they should, but Nolan doesn't acknowledge the added pressure.

"Yes," Nolan says, somehow cutting the one syllable word short.

I look at Maddy and watch the life drain out of her face. She stares at Nolan, and I see something in her demeanor as the two of them lock eyes, but it fades quickly as Nolan turns his attention to me. Maddy slowly shifts her body toward the door and walks away, shutting it behind her and leaving me all alone with the owner of The Black Collar.

"Thanks for being on time," Nolan says to me.

"Oh, it's no problem," I answer.

"Cool. We can set up on the couch and get started if that's okay with you."

"Sounds good," I reply.

Nolan nods his approval and starts to turn away, and that's when I notice something that nearly makes me stumble. As he angles his body to lead me to the couch, the lights above us reflect the color in his eyes. Blue. He has *blue* eyes. In some sort of unfair, cruel joke from the heavens, Nolan Carter has flawless caramel-brown skin and gorgeous ocean-blue eyes. It's like he was made in a special laboratory designed to intoxicate and stupefy women, and what's worse is that he doesn't seem to notice how dazzling he is. He doesn't smolder when he looks at me, or squint, or lick his lips. He moves with no agenda at all, and his presence has its own gravitational pull.

"You good?" he asks, and I snap myself out of another trance as I realize Nolan has already walked to the black couch and is standing in front of it, waiting for me to catch up.

"Oh, yeah," I blurt out as I speed walk over to him. "Sorry about that."

We sit down and I do my best to get myself under control. I'm a goddamn professional, and I'm not going to allow myself to be distracted by any of this—not his looks, or his sexy cologne that keeps wafting its way up my nose, or his stupid blue eyes that I can't stop noticing now, or how perfectly he has set up this office.

I glance around the room and notice that everything in Nolan's office is impeccably placed. The tiled floor is dark gray, while every bit of furniture is either red or black. The picture frames are black, while the walls are dark gray to match the floor, and the images on the wall are all black and white with the tiniest hints of red in them. There's a large photo of a black wall with nothing on it except a red rope dangling from a silver hook. Another picture showcases a massive bed with white sheets, but the handcuffs dangling from the headboard are red. The entire space is beautiful and well thought out, matching everything about the way Nolan carries himself, including the tall, black cabinet in the corner. Its decorative doors are beautiful and elegant, but it's also mysterious, just like its owner.

"Bree," Nolan says, stealing my focus as the sound of his voice saying my name casts a spell on me. "Are you ready?"

"Yes," I reply before clearing my throat. I gently shake my head and sit up straight. "I was just admiring your office. Did you hire a decorator?"

The side of Nolan's mouth twitches, but he doesn't smile. "No."

"Oh, well it's very well put together," I compliment.

"Thank you."

"You're welcome." I take a small audio recorder from my purse and place it on the black and gray table in front of us. Nolan eyes it like he doesn't trust it, but chooses not to comment. His gaze finds me and watches as I pull out a notepad where I've written down every question I want to ask. Once I'm settled, I take a deep breath and begin. "So, Mr. Carter, I've broken this interview into two sections. The first is all about you, and the second is about your new and infamous nightclub, The Black Collar."

"Infamous," Nolan repeats.

"Well ... yes. Surely, you're aware of the reputation your club has garnered in the three months since its opening."

"A reputation given to us by uninformed people who've never stepped foot inside The Black Collar, but I digress. We can get back to that later. Please continue."

Nolan shifts in his seat, but if he's annoyed by my statement about the club's reputation, he doesn't show it. He's a pillar of control as he places an arm on the back of the couch and awaits my first question.

"So, I guess the first question I have is what made you decide to grant us an interview?" I ask. "I hate to mention the word reputation again, but if I'm not mistaken, The Black Collar doesn't allow just anyone in. There's a form to fill out that has to be approved by the staff here. It all feels very exclusive and private. So, why talk to us?"

Nolan doesn't move a muscle before answering. "Because rumors can cause problems when left unchecked for too long. At first the blather and ... *reputation* didn't bother me, but now that I've had time to process it all, I think I'd rather use my position to educate. People fear what they don't understand, and they hate what they fear. So, I want to educate people who talk about me or The Black Collar without knowing what or whom they're talking about. Most folks don't even know what BDSM really is."

"So, you're here to educate people like me," I say without thinking better of it. "I can agree that my lack of education about BDSM certainly makes it more intimidating."

"That's understandable," Nolan says. "I was afraid before I learned and got into the lifestyle."

"The lifestyle?"

"Yes. BDSM is more than just sex. It's a lifestyle," Nolan states matter-of-factly, gazing at me with those mesmerizing blue eyes.

"That's very interesting. What made you decide to educate yourself and get into the lifestyle of BDSM?"

Nolan tilts his head back as he thinks about the answer. His eyes drift away for a moment before returning to me. "Sometimes people just know they're missing something without actually knowing what it is they're missing. I was okay in the vanilla life, but I felt that I could be *more* than okay, and it took research and education to understand the feelings I was having."

"I see," I say. "That's very responsible of you to go out and do your own research. Do you mind if I ask what feelings you were having that made you look for such understanding?"

Nolan suddenly goes still. His blue eyes bore into me, pinning me to the couch while he sits with his muscles loose but unmoving beneath his tailored clothes. His eyes latch onto mine and I can feel them asking if I really want to know the answer to the question I just asked. He waits, giving me ample time to take it back, but I don't. I'm a journalist. Our readers deserve to know what made the owner of The Black Collar who he is. Plus, while I'm being driven by the interest of the Philadelphia Inquirer's readers, my own curiosity is in the passenger's seat, along for the ride.

The side of Nolan's mouth twitches upward, giving me the briefest, most subtle tease of a smile that nearly sends me reeling, but it's his words that complete the job.

"The feeling I had ... *have* ... is a desire," Nolan says, his eyes never leaving mine. "I did my own research because I needed to know why I had such a strong desire to cause pain."

My eyes bulge before I can stop them, and Nolan finally lets go when he sees me. He smiles from ear to ear, and it's breathtaking, sending a monsoon of pins and needles splashing up my entire body. It takes a full five seconds for me to clear the fog in my head, and Nolan watches in amusement the entire time.

"A desire to ... cause pain?" I ask, my voice sounding weak and wavy. "You enjoy hurting people?"

"Yes," he states, still grinning. "I find pleasure and sexual gratification in inflicting pain on others, Bree. I'm a sadist."

Chapter Six

I'm stunned into silence. Nolan looks at me with delight dancing in his eyes as my shocked expression cements itself on my face. I don't even know what to think, let alone say, so my recorder sits on the table in front of us picking up nothing but the sound of our breathing. I know I have questions written on the notepad in my hands, but the pen I wrote them with may as well have been filled with invisible ink, because the page is basically blank to me now. The questions no longer exist. The Inquirer's readers no longer matter. There's only my awe ... and curiosity.

"Bree," Nolan calls to me, tilting his head to the side. "Shall we continue?"

After exhaling, I suck in a deep breath to steady myself. I've never been so thrown off during an interview before, and it's frustrating that Nolan has had this effect on me. I'm the best interviewer at the Inquirer, but I can't seem to get myself back on track.

"I'm not sure I understand," I finally say. "You're a *sadist*?"

"Yes," Nolan answers without hesitation. He isn't even remotely ashamed of it.

"I just ... I don't understand."

"What do you not understand?"

"You like hurting people," I snap, caught off guard by my own emotion. "The way I was raised, people who like to inflict pain on others are sadistic, emotionless, sociopaths. That's *sociopathic* behavior, and I don't understand how you can admit it with such pride in your voice. I'm just shocked, that's all."

Nolan raises his eyebrows but doesn't lose his cool.

"I can see that," he says, and I'm instantly annoyed by the amusement in his voice. "Luckily, I'm very used to the incorrect assumptions made about me and the BDSM community in general, so I'm not offended."

"I am," I snip.

"I've offended you?"

"Well ... I don't know, but I feel some type of way about this," I say, blind to the fact that the interview is going completely off the rails, and we haven't even gotten to the meat and potatoes of it yet. "Hurting people is objectively wrong."

"No, hurting people is *subjectively* wrong," Nolan rebuts. "If I were to hurt you, or anybody else for that matter, without your consent, then that would be wrong. However—"

"Who in their right mind would ever *consent* to being hurt?" I bark, cutting him off. I expect Nolan's response to match my intensity, but he remains calm and collected with his arm resting on the back of the couch.

"Lots of people would consent to it," he says, before raising his arms and gesturing to the office in front of us. "In this community, in this world of ours, nothing is off limits as long as there's consent. If I have my partner's permission to hurt them, then I will gladly cause them a world of pain for their pleasure."

"I ... that doesn't make any sense."

"To *you*," Nolan says stiffly, finally expressing some emotion before reining it in. "This is precisely why I'm doing this interview, Miss Barrett. I want people like you to understand that it's okay for things to not make sense to you, as long as they make sense to the people enjoying their lives. Sadists and masochists aren't doing anything wrong. We're not hurting anyone by partaking in our own pleasures, behind closed doors, with the partners of our choosing. Between the two of us, *you're* the one who's in the wrong."

My brows shoot to the top of my head. "*Me*?"

"Yes, *you*," Nolan answers quickly. "I'm simply living my life and hurting no one—"

"How can you keep saying you're not hurting anyone when you're a *sadist*?"

"While *you*, Miss Barrett, are riding your imaginary high horse and judging me for doing things I have consent to do. It has nothing to do with you. Just because your mind is not open enough to understand it, doesn't change the fact that it's a pleasure to cause pain for some people, and it's a pleasure to receive it as well."

"I've never felt a pain that was pleasurable," I say, and Nolan raises an eyebrow.

"You've never been with someone who could show you what you're missing out on," he says, making my muscles instantly rigid. "Being closed-minded doesn't protect you the way you think it does, Bree. It merely prevents you from experiencing pleasures that require you to be outside of your comfort zone. There's an entire world of happiness and pleasure out there, but in order to reach it, you'll have to leave the safety of your closed mind. You don't even know how satisfied you could be."

The two of us stare at each other without blinking. Tension forms and builds in the space between us as thick as smog, and my thoughts continue to run away from me. While I want to stay offended and upset by a man admitting that he likes to hurt women, there's something beneath the surface of my ire that keeps poking its head up. I know it's wrong, and know for a fact that my friends would've walked out of this interview already, but my curiosity continues to make its presence known.

What pleasure could Nolan possibly be talking about? I'm not some prude who has never done anything before. I've masturbated. I've had plenty of sex, and I've had great orgasms. With all of that, how could I be missing something? Nolan said I don't even know how satisfied I could be. Is that really possible?

I've never been afraid to admit that my upbringing has made me a certain way, and I don't blame my parents for being conservative and shielding me from things they thought were dangerous. I'm not resentful for the teachings they gave me, but maybe Nolan is right about me being closed-minded. I've never experienced anything anywhere near the realm of BDSM. My brain just associates pain with something I *don't* want. Pain is pain, not pleasure. Anybody who wants to hurt me is a psychopath or sociopath. It has always been that simple for me, and yet I can't deny the fact that I've felt like I want something more. Is this it?

"Sometimes people just know they're missing something without actually knowing what it is they're missing."

After a moment of intense silence, I place my notepad on the table next to my recorder and let out a long exhale. When I sit back, I try to recenter myself and get back to my usual calm and careful diligence.

"I'm sorry," I say to Nolan, whose face never changes. "I'm not sure why I went so far off track. I've never done that during an interview before, and I apologize for being so unprofessional."

"No need for apologies," Nolan replies. "Like I said in the beginning, I'm doing this to educate people. So, as long as you're willing to chip away at some of the barriers you have up, I'd love to continue. So, what's next?"

"Thank you," I say. "I appreciate your patience. As far as what's next—that's a great question."

I try to force myself to pick up the notepad and get back to the questions I have written down. The questions are my guide, and I know it'd be a mistake to ignore them. However, I just can't shake the growing need to know about this— about him and his experiences. I want to understand and be shown something that could convince me that there is more out there than what I've experienced. Maybe I really don't know what I've been missing, and I want to find out.

After a final exhale that blows out the voice in my head telling me not to do this, I leave the notepad on the table and sit back.

"Okay, I have a favor to ask you," I begin, to which Nolan nods his silent agreement. "I want you to tell me about it."

"Tell you about it. Tell you about *what*?"

"Your sadism," I answer. "Can you give me an example of what the experience is like from your perspective?"

"You mean a BDSM experience? A sexual experience?"

I clear my throat. "Umm, yes."

Even though he's already leaning back on the couch, Nolan somehow manages to sit back further and relax even more. I can see the thoughts dancing around in his mind as he eyes me carefully, again waiting for me to take it back, but I won't. Once he sees that I'm not backing out, he smiles and sits up.

"It'd be my pleasure."

Chapter Seven

~ NOLAN ~

"It'd be my pleasure," I tell the judgy little journalist from the Philly Inquirer. Excitement creeps up my body, radiating through me with each pulse of my heart as I think about where all of this began for me. This interview is bringing it all back, and I relish the idea of talking about it, especially to Bree Barrett.

Considering she has no idea what the lifestyle is all about, there's something about Bree that intrigues me. It's not the way she attempts being combative about a topic of which she is completely uninformed, but it's the way she says what she says. Her words speak one thing, while her voice says something else. Maybe I'm reading it wrong, but as much as Bree tries to convince me she's appalled by the idea of sadism, I think she's more intrigued by it than she'd like me to know.

I've never been one to get caught up on what a woman looks like. No, I leave the shallow methods of finding a woman to lesser men. For me, the focus has always been some-

36

thing much more visceral and innate. I'm looking for something deeper, something that speaks to me much more than words can, something primal. It's difficult to fit this into a one-word definition, but regardless of how it's labeled, Bree Barrett possesses it. I saw it the very first moment our eyes met, and I felt it when we shook hands—imagine static electricity making the hair on your arms stand. Bree doesn't look at me like a woman wanting sex. She looks at me like a woman who wants to learn. Instead of being turned off by her fear and wanting to run from it, she's intrigued by it, and that fascination pours from her eyes and seeps into her body language. So, while I hear what she says, it's her body language I'm listening to.

On the other hand, I'd be lying if I said Bree isn't stunning. She looks positively delectable in her burgundy skirt and matching belt. Her long-sleeved plaid top is perfectly in sync with the bottom, with black, white, gray, and burgundy stripes crisscrossing all over it, and her dark brown hair is gorgeous, coming down in waves just past her shoulders. She's around five-foot-six, but carries herself like she's six-feet tall, and her roughly one-hundred-eighty pounds is perfectly placed on her frame, giving her all the curves lesser men are afraid to navigate. She's a beautiful woman with porcelain-pale skin, and round blue eyes that mesmerize me every time I look into them. She's angelic, and the longer I'm in her presence, the more I want to do devilish things to her ... but I digress.

"Where would you like me to begin, Miss Barrett?" I ask. I have my own ideas of where to start, but I want to know what interests Bree.

"Umm, I don't know," she says. "You choose. You said you were here to educate. Well, consider me here to learn. Start wherever you'd like, with whichever story you'd like. The floor is yours."

"Well," I say, fighting back a smile. "As I stated earlier, I've always known there was something different about me. My fascination with sex went beyond the usual in-and-out of it, and I found that the color red made my heart race more than anything else."

Bree frowns and tilts her head. "The color red?"

"Yes," I answer. "Particularly, the way a woman's skin turns red when you touch it in just the right way, and I don't mean flushing red out of embarrassment or because it's warm in the room. I'm referring to how the skin streaks after it's whipped or slapped." Bree flinches, pinching her lips together, which only motivates me to continue. "Watching a woman's skin react to my touch sends me into a frenzy. If you're looking for something more specific for your readers, I could add much more detail of what I experience when I'm in a scene."

Bree presses her lips together again before forcing them apart with her tongue as she licks her lips. What Bree doesn't know about me is that I'm very attentive. When I'm interested in someone, I pay attention to everything about them, so I notice every little move she makes that may come off as a tick or quirk she has, but there's more to it. I notice how often she licks her lips, and I see how she moves when I say particular things. Bree is supposed to be an emotionless journalist, showing no concern for me and focused solely on extracting information. She's not supposed to be so affected by what I say. Nonetheless she is hanging on my every word. I see it. I see her, and there's much more to her than meets the eye.

"A scene?" she asks with raised brows. "For our readers, what exactly is that?"

"A scene is the act of performing BDSM activities. Not all BDSM acts lead to sex, so in our community, we don't simply refer to it all as sex. There's more depth to it than that. For example, if my partner simply wants to submit to me, and have me carry out the act of flogging her, then that is all we would do. There would be no sex involved if that's not what she consents to."

"I don't understand ... again. Why would someone want that?"

"Because impact play can be very therapeutic, Miss Barrett," I say. "Pain releases all kinds of hormones in the body, and a submissive can feel like they're unwinding, like they're letting go of all the stresses in their life, even if it's only in that brief moment of submission. Now, I'm not a submissive, so you'd get the best information from someone who is. However, the point is still the same, BDSM doesn't have to always lead to sex, so we use the term scene."

"I see," she says, before clearing her throat. "I wasn't aware of that, so I'd say your teaching is off to a good start. Sorry for interrupting with that question. Please continue."

"No need to apologize," I reply. "It's hard to learn without asking questions, and your inquiries let me know you're really interested."

I pause for a moment, letting that statement hang in the air between us, and I see Bree's mouth twitch. Try as she might, she can't hide the fact that her interest isn't purely professional.

"So, you want to know what a scene would look like for me," I start again, leaning back against the couch and crossing one leg over the other. "Well, let's start right here in this office."

Bree's eyebrows quickly raise. "Here? You've had a sexual experience here?"

"Well, it is a BDSM club, Miss Barrett," I say, to which Bree scoots back and looks down at the couch.

"I'm aware, but ... you've had sex *right here*?" Bree motions toward the spot she's sitting in, and I fight back a chuckle.

"Don't worry, I'm an extremely obsessive person when it comes to cleanliness. I've had everything in here sanitized more times than I could count, so you're good." Bree frowns, looking back and forth between the couch and me. "I promise."

After a moment of hesitation, she says, "Okay," and I begin again.

"I have a distinct memory from a particular scene that took place right here in this office. It began over there at the entrance." Bree turns to look at the door, as if she's imagining it all playing out.

"When I walked in, she was already there, waiting for me on her knees like a good girl," I say, and Bree's eyes snap back to me, but I don't stop. "She'd been waiting there for a while, and I knew it because I saw her slip into my office from my seat in VIP, as it was facing the hall. We made eye contact as she opened my door, and I nodded my approval, but I wanted to test her patience. This particular partner of mine was someone I had been seeing for a while, so I knew all of her limits, both hard and soft, and I decided to see how long she'd been willing to wait for me."

"So, this partner wanted to engage in ... a *scene* with you," Bree interrupts. "But you chose to make her wait? Why would you do that?"

"Her waiting was a part of the scene," I explain. "Through vetting this particular partner, and both of us being in the lifestyle for a long time, the two of us are fully aware of what we're getting ourselves into. All of this is communicated and agreed to at the start of the relationship, so my making her wait wasn't a surprise to her. It was something she agreed to a long time before this particular moment. In this lifestyle, Miss Barrett, nothing happens without consent. Nothing. Not even waiting patiently."

INTERVIEW WITH A SADIST

Bree slowly nods, biting her bottom lip as she realizes what she thought about BDSM isn't the reality of it. "I see."

"She waited twenty minutes for me," I say. "Right there in front of that door, on her knees, she waited for me, and when I finally stepped into the room and saw her there, I knew I was going to reward her greatly for being such a good girl for me. I knew she didn't want to wait, but she did it anyway, and she deserved to be rewarded with the treatment she craved."

"You mean ... pain?"

"Yes," I answer. "She wanted pain, and I desperately wanted to give it to her, because I knew it would be the greatest pleasure to us both. She'd been patient for twenty minutes already, and I wasn't going to make her wait any longer."

Chapter Eight

~ NOLAN ~

I closed the door with my back facing her, because I didn't want her to see the moment I shut my eyes and fought back a grin. Passion infused with excitement filled me up like a cup under a faucet. It started in my feet and quickly traveled through my legs, my torso, and finally came to an explosive stop in my head. I felt giddy, thrilled by the idea of what I was about to do. I was teeming with anticipation, but when I turned around, my demeanor was completely composed. She was only allowed to see the calm version of me—the one that's always in control. I only allowed her to see her Dom.

Our eyes met when I faced her, and once they did, she locked in. With other submissives, I demanded that they didn't watch me as I moved around them. I'd made others keep their eyes fixed on a spot on the wall, or look down at their palms in their lap, but with this submissive, I wanted her eyes on me. I wanted her to watch as I took my time choosing the weapons of destruction that I would use on her flesh. I wanted her to fill with antic-

42

ipation the same way I did when I walked through the door. By the time I touched her, I wanted her heart racing and her pussy dripping puddles.

She sat on her knees with her hands on her thighs, palms up, just as she had been instructed to do. Such a good girl for me. I had half a mind to crouch down in front of her and wrap my fingers around her throat while I kissed her, but I fought the desire back, choosing instead to perform my inspection of her. With her eyes still trained on me, I slowly walked around her, taking in every inch of her skin, noticing a faded bruise on her back and a faint red line on her ass from the last time we'd played. I'd blemished her, marked her as mine, and seeing her unhealed skin was like looking at property I'd used and worn. It doesn't shine like new anymore because I love it so much that I can't help but use it often. But, I didn't see her skin as irreparable or used up. I saw it as a brand, a stamp, an autograph that told the world she was mine, even if only behind closed doors.

Once my first inspection was complete, I stopped in front of my gorgeous submissive and stood in front of her. She looked up at me, I looked down on her—the perfect dynamic between a Dominant and his submissive.

"You waited patiently, Little One. You make me so proud of you," I told her as I crouched down so that we were face to face. From there, I could see the blue in her eyes clearly. I could smell her perfume, and feel the heat rising from her skin as she became more excited with every passing minute. Just being that close made me want to lash out.

"Thank you, sir," she answered, and I heard the happiness in her voice as much as I saw it written in her eyes. She liked making me proud and loathed the idea of disappointing me. Making me proud came with all the kinky perks she lusted for.

"Was it difficult for you to see me out there? I saw you watching me all night," I said as I stood up and walked behind

her. I crouched again, and began putting her curly blonde hair into a ponytail.

"Yes, sir," she answered. "I've wanted to touch you all night. I wanted them all to see that I belong to you. I wanted you to claim me in front of everyone."

"It was difficult for me, too. You're so fucking beautiful, and I swear I can hear your skin calling to me, begging me to wreak havoc on it. I've fought my desire all night, but now that I have you all to myself, I won't fight it anymore. I'm going to unleash it on you. Are you ready, Little One?"

She exhaled and let her head fall back onto my chest. "Yes, sir."

"Good."

In a flash, I wrapped my fist around her new ponytail and used it to lift her onto her feet. She let out an excited gasp as I made her stand and forced her to walk over to my desk in the center of the room. The second we reached it, I forced her to bend over the top. I pressed her face against the wood with one hand, and used the other to bring her wrists together behind her back. Nothing I did was sensual or romantic. It was all aggressive and forceful. Just the way she liked it, which is why I loved it.

"Don't fucking move," I said, still pressing her head against the desk.

"Yes, sir," she replied in a lustful whisper.

Now that I had her in position, I bent down and yanked her black pants from around her waist. She fought back a squeal of delight as I pulled them all the way down to her ankles, exposing her voluptuous ass. It took all of my restraint not to spank it or plunge my face between her cheeks. I barely managed to stand up. Luckily, I wouldn't have to wait much longer.

"God, Little One, you're so perfect," I told her as I took a step back just to admire how amazing she looked bent over in front of me. She was incredible—blemishes, bruises and all. She was a sheet of paper waiting to be drawn on. Her skin yearned to be

turned into a new work of art, and I was meant to be her Rembrandt.

My Little One remained quiet as I left her bent over on the desk and made my way to the back corner of the office, where an elegant black cabinet awaited me. Its doors are beautifully decorative, with thin pieces of mitered trim running diagonally across them. It's an exquisite piece of furniture, but it's not what's on the outside that I love. It's what's inside.

After entering a three-digit combination on a small lock, I opened the doors to the cabinet to reveal an eclectic display of sex toys. Just looking at it put a smile on my face, and I took a second to breathe in the smell of expensive leather. Inside sat three rows of vibrators, three rows of butt plugs, three rows of dildos, and three rows of clit suckers, all on separate shelves. The bottom shelf showcased a display of bondage toys—ropes, handcuffs, zip ties, chains, and duct tape, but the doors held my pride and joy.

On each door hung all of my toys used for impact play. The left door was covered from top to bottom with floggers and whips, while the right held paddles, riding crops, and a few bamboo canes. These are the toys that bring me the most joy, because they're the ones that cause the most damage to the skin. They're my favorite, and with a selection this expansive, it's hard to choose just one. So, I didn't.

Instinctively, my hands moved with minds of their own, grabbing everything I wanted to use on my submissive's perfect body, and I carried them back over to the desk. I placed each item on the wood directly in front of her so she could see what I was about to use on her. First was the riding crop, then the paddle, followed by the bamboo cane. I watched as her eyes fixated on the toys and grew with lustful anticipation.

"You waited so patiently, Little One. Are you ready for your reward?" I asked, my voice rumbling in her ear as I leaned over her back and pushed my growing erection against her ass.

"Yes, sir," she answered.

"Do you want me to hurt you?" I asked.

"Yes, sir. Please."

"Why?"

"Because I love the pain you give me. It feels so good to hurt for you, sir."

My cock throbbed against my pants just listening to her. The amazing thing about my Little One was that she was a masochist. She enjoyed the pain. She wanted it. She craved it, and she knew that I would inflict it on her better than anybody else ever would. My sadism has no limits, and together, she and I created the most beautiful chaos.

"You're so perfect for me, Little One," I told her as I stood up straight and reached for the riding crop. "It's my pleasure to ruin you."

"Ruin me, sir. Fucking destroy me."

"Spread your legs," I commanded, and she immediately did as she was told, granting me unfettered access to her bare ass and pussy, and once I had her permission, I began.

With a quick snap of my wrist, I smacked the leather end of the riding crop directly against her pussy. She let out a surprised gasp, but didn't move. Goddamn it, I loved it. The clit is such a sensitive place, most women wouldn't dream of having it spanked with a piece of leather, but in this lifestyle, barriers of fear crumble beneath our feet. We discover advanced forms of pleasure that would boggle the mind of someone outside of this community, and we proudly swim in it, allowing new sensations of bliss and satisfaction to wash over us like waves. Here, pleasure has no limitations.

Over and over again, I spanked the end of the riding crop against her pussy until it was as red. Blood gathered in her clit, making it even more sensitive for my touch, but I wasn't satisfied. I dropped the crop on the floor behind me and reached for the paddle. She watched me pick it up, and her body writhed on the desk, searching for a release of the tension that was building up, but she'd find none. Her only release would be what I gave her with my cock soon, but she hadn't earned it yet.

"Stop fucking moving," I snipped, and she instantly went still. "Good girl. Now bring your legs together."

"Yes, sir," she replies, before placing her feet side by side and sticking her ass in the air. She knows what's coming, and there's no need to drag it out.

The sound of the paddle smacking against her bare ass cracked like a thunderclap. Unlike the crop on her clit, I didn't have to exercise restraint with this toy, because her ass could handle much more than her clit could. So, I didn't hold back when I paddled her. I hit her again, and my insides exploded with fulfillment as her skin turned bright red. It was fucking beautiful to watch her go from white to crimson, and my cock stiffened to the point of pain. It turned me on so much I could barely take it, but I kept going, and her breathing became labored as the pain intensified with each hit. By the time I was done, the cheeks of her ass were like two glowing roses.

"You're a fucking work of art," I said with bated breath.

"Thank you, sir."

"Don't thank me yet, Little One. It's time for our grand finale."

I dropped the paddle on the floor next to the riding crop and lifted the bamboo cane off the desk. I know what this toy does, and my cock reacted accordingly, pushing against my pants as it reached its limit. I was ready to explode right there and then, but not before I finished my artwork.

"Do not move, Little One. Do you understand?" I asked, and she nodded her head, never lifting it off the desk.

"Yes, sir."

"That's my girl," I said, just before I bent over and smacked her across both of her hamstrings with the cane.

Against her will, her body jolted as the skin on her legs

instantly reddened. The cane leaves little room for pleasure. If a submissive is not accustomed to pain, then I'd avoid the cane, because it is not to be taken lightly. The marks on her legs were accompanied by raised welts on her skin, and it made me so hard I had to unfasten my pants to relieve the pressure.

I moved down two inches from the last place I smacked her, and did it again, harder this time. She let out another squeal, and I reveled in the sound of her pleasure mixed with her pain. I did it over and over again until I reached her knees, and the back of her legs were covered in stripes.

"Fuck," I growled, taking a step back to enjoy the view. "You're my perfect little candy cane. I can't fucking stand it anymore."

I dropped the cane next to the other toys and pushed my pants down until I could step out of them. Then, I positioned myself behind her and used my hand as cuffs around both of her wrists behind her back. I pushed my cock inside her pussy, and was stunned by how wet she was. Her wetness washed over me and spilled out in long, sticky drips that formed a tiny puddle on the floor beneath us. After waiting so long for this moment, both of us were already on the verge of eruption as soon as I filled her up.

My Little One sent her sensual moans of agony into the wood beneath her as I fucked her relentlessly. I used every one of my eight inches to pound into her with long, forceful strokes that rocked the entire desk forward. I fucked her like I couldn't stand the sight of her. I fucked her like she was my worst enemy. I fucked her like I absolutely hated her, so she'd know how much I loved being with her. I fucked her nonstop, until I felt the familiar sensation of an eruption taking shape in my balls. It came on fast, and I didn't slow down. I welcomed it and gave myself over when it arrived.

"Fuck, I'm about to explode inside you," I yelled, still thrusting with the intention of causing maximum damage.

INTERVIEW WITH A SADIST

"Yes, sir. Please come inside me," she screamed in response, and this time, it was me who did as I was told.

"Goddamn!" I growled as my hands tightened on her waist, and I unleashed back-breaking strokes into her. My vision blurred and I could hardly breathe as I came, and my Little One took it perfectly.

"Oh, god," she bellowed. "Yes, keep going. I'm going to ... oh god!"

She let out a guttural scream from the back of her throat as she came all over my cock. Refusing to stop until she was finished, I kept pounding into her. I stroked in and out until my own cum began to leak out of her already dripping pussy, and mixed with her wetness on the floor. We became a drenched mess of bodily fluids and heavy breathing as the bliss of our orgasms finally receded and we separated.

My Little One slid off the desk and layed on the floor right next to our puddle, while I walked with weak knees over to the chair behind my desk and flopped down into it, still naked from the waist down. We remained that way—her, lifeless on the floor, me, exhausted in my chair—until we finally regained our strength sometime later. Eventually, we pulled ourselves together and left the room, eagerly awaiting the next time we could come together and destroy ourselves with pleasure again.

Chapter Nine

By the time Nolan is done telling his story, I can barely breathe. Have I moved a single muscle since he started? Have I blinked? Has my brain even been capable of having a thought? I'm not so sure. I was mesmerized the entire time he spoke, and in moments where I thought I'd be disgusted, I was captivated and stuck in a trance. There wasn't a moment where I wanted Nolan to stop talking about it, and now that he has, I'm wondering what the hell is wrong with me. Not only that, I'm wondering why I'm wet.

Nolan sits in front of me with one leg crossed over the other, his fancy navy blue vest still wrinkle-free, and his gaze locked onto me. His face is neutral, but there's a glimmer in his eyes. I see something lurking beneath the surface of his expression, and while I can't put my thumb on it, I see it. It's there, smiling at me behind his eyes.

"Miss Barrett?" he says, raising one eyebrow, his voice like the low rumble of rolling thunder. "Are you okay?"

I swallow hard as I wiggle my fingers to reignite the blood flow in my hands. The tingle in my fingertips fades away and I feel present again.

INTERVIEW WITH A SADIST

"Yes, of course," I lie. I'm not okay. I'm not even close to okay after that, but I can't let him know, so I have to play it off. "That was a fascinating story. One that I know our readers will simply devour."

"Your *readers*?" Nolan asks with raised brows.

"Absolutely. The interest in The Black Collar is rising all across the city, with tons of people becoming more and more interested in what kinds of activities go on here. So, I appreciate your candor and openness."

Nolan tilts his head to the side and lets out a barely audible scoff. "Yeah, no problem. I definitely want to keep *the readers* interested."

I have to swallow again, because it's clear he's not talking about our readers. I clear my throat and check the recorder to make sure it's still on. I'd just die if he told me that story on the record and I didn't actually record it, but if I'm being honest, I could probably recite the entire thing from memory.

"So," I start again, trying to keep my mind on the story and not the man. "Now that we've learned a little more about you, let's move on to The Black Collar for a bit." Nolan shifts in his seat, but doesn't object, so I continue while I can still focus. "The club has a bit of an interview process for new patrons. Rumor has it, some people have been denied entrance to The Black Collar, and some have even felt discriminated against. Can you explain the way your staff is directed to carry out admissions?"

Nolan's blue eyes peer into me, pushing me back against the couch like he has mind control, and for a moment, I think he might shut the interview down. His face sinks into a bit of a scowl, and I see the slightest hint of a furrow in his brow, but he doesn't let it overtake his face. Whatever is brewing in his mind, he doesn't let it out.

"First, let me be clear," he begins, although the reluctance in his voice is palpable. "No one has ever been discriminated against at The Black Collar, especially in the context in which it has been insinuated. While my mother is white, my father is Black, so I take the word discrimination very seriously. What may feel like discrimination to some, is actually us vetting our patrons. In the spirit of keeping The Black Collar inclusive to all genders, sexualities, and kinks, we ask our patrons to fill out a questionnaire online to make sure they're not closed-minded bigots trying to ruin fun. We prefer our patrons to either be in the lifestyle, or be escorted by someone who is. We want people who know what this is before they step inside. I'm not interested in dealing with the issue of someone thinking our club is just like any other, just to lose their shit when they find out it's a kink and BDSM spot. So, we vet to protect ourselves and our clientele."

"Wow, that actually makes sense," I reply. "So, your goal is to make sure the experience here is, shall I say, kink-friendly?"

"Of course. There's a lot that goes on here, and we don't intend to water it down for the sake of people who aren't in the lifestyle. Here, we embrace who we are, and we embrace our kinks."

I nod along as I write the phrase *Embrace your kinks* onto my notepad and underline it three times.

"I think your regular patrons would certainly appreciate that," I say, but my eyes linger on the underlined phrase. Something about it threatens to lock me in and I have to shake my head to push it away. "Umm, so tell me more about the club. We've sort of danced around the topic of what goes on here when the club is open, which is what our readers *really* want to know. So, what exactly does The Black Collar have to offer to those who get past the questionnaire?"

Nolan leans forward for the first time in a while and flashes a brief, mischievous smile.

"Well, when it comes to what goes on behind our closed

doors, it'd be much easier to show you than it would be to tell you, Miss Barrett."

My eyes bulge. "What is that supposed to mean?"

"It means we're done for today," Nolan says. He looks down at the blue-faced watch on his wrist and frowns at the time. "I have another meeting I have to get to, so let's continue this conversation tomorrow night when you come back."

"Excuse me?" I snip, as Nolan stands like he's already prepared to escort me out. "Wait, you think I'm coming back tomorrow?"

"Of course you are," he answers quickly. "How else could we continue the interview?"

"I ... Mr. Carter," I stammer as I stand up with a racing heart. "Will the club be open tomorrow night?"

"Of course," he says. "You didn't expect to get a great interview for your readers without experiencing The Black Collar scene for yourself, did you? Besides, the best way to learn about the lifestyle after you've heard about it, is to see it for yourself. So, come back tomorrow night, and I'll show you everything. By the time we're done, Miss Barrett, you'll have an experience like no other—a story about the club and the lifestyle that only *you* could tell from your experience. I'm going to give you, and *only you*, exclusive access to both me and The Black Collar. Don't let your fear of stepping outside your comfort zone convince you to throw the opportunity away."

Worry takes over my face as I think about walking into this club while it's full of party-goers. What will I see? How will I be treated? Will it be too intense for me, and most importantly, will I like it?

"Umm, I don't know what to say," I state as I stand in front of Nolan and lift the recorder off the table. I press stop and shove it back into my clutch. "I guess I just thought we could do it all in one sitting. Even if we had to do multiple sessions, I thought we would do it while the club was closed."

"Nah, that would only be scratching the surface," Nolan says. "What I have to offer is much deeper than that, and if you're willing to follow me, I'll lead you into a sea of passion and excitement you never knew existed. You simply have to be unafraid of the dark. So, will you follow me, Bree?"

The sound of my first name floating off of his tongue continues to make me feel like I'm swimming through thin air, and it coaxes me. Nolan has a sense of gravity about him, and it pulls me to a place I'm not sure I want to be. He scares me and excites me simultaneously, and no matter how afraid I am, the urge to say yes to him is a riptide pulling me out to sea.

I should say no. Regardless of how gorgeous the owner is, The Black Collar isn't my type of scene. I'm used to tea and iced coffee with Melissa and Teagan, not leather-clad masochists wearing blindfolds. But, I know Chase would lose his mind if backed out of this interview just because I don't agree with the lifestyle Nolan proudly flaunts. Hell, I'm not sure Chase wouldn't fire me for dropping this story without a reasonable cause. So, I don't really have a choice.

"Okay," I answer, looking Nolan in his eyes and finding comfort there. "Yes, I'll follow you."

Denial

Chapter Ten

"You're kidding. Please tell me you're kidding."

"Nope, I'm not," I say, lifting my freshly poured glass of red wine to my lips. "It was ... absolutely insane. I ... he ... I'm not even sure how to describe it."

"How about *bonkers*?" Teagen chimes in, giggling to herself. Maybe it's the effects of the wine, but probably not.

"Umm, sure," I say, trying to hide my frown behind my wine glass. "I guess that works."

"Bree, you're telling us you had an interview with the owner of that depraved, sketchy sex club?" Melissa asks. "I never would've thought in a million years that anyone I know would ever step foot in that place. I can't believe Chase gave you that assignment."

I don't know why I told them about the interview. I guess Melissa, Teagan, and I have been friends for so long now that talking to them about what I have going on in my life is just second nature. Teagan and I were there when Melissa talked about Andy getting a little too friendly with someone at his job. Melissa and I were there when Teagan slept with her college professor before meeting Russell. This is what friends are for, and we've always done it. So why does it feel like I may have made a mistake this time?

The three of us are at Melissa's dinner table, an open bottle of wine sitting in the middle like a centerpiece. We're dressed comfortably tonight, all of us wearing sweatpants and baggy T-shirts for a girl's night in, even though Melissa's husband, Andy, is in the back of the house somewhere trying to stay out of sight. After such an eventful day at work, I needed to meet up with my friends and have a drink, although I can't pinpoint exactly why I feel the need to unwind after leaving The Black Collar. Usually I reserve these girl's nights for stressful days, but stress isn't the word I'd use to describe how I felt as I walked out of Nolan Carter's office. Since speaking to him and hearing the story about the sadistic sex he had on his desk, I've just felt tense.

Luckily, Melissa's house is the perfect setting to relax. Whoever Andy hired as their decorator was obsessed with eggshell. The walls and couches are all eggshell, while the countertops in the kitchen are light gray. Melissa chose curtains to match the counters and cabinets, and while the entire place looks sterile, it's still beautiful with plush couches and gorgeous art on every wall, which is a good distraction from the table when I start to feel flustered by Teagan parroting Melissa.

"Yeah, it's crazy that Chase gave you that assignment," Teagan says, right on cue.

"It's not that crazy," I answer, trying to keep annoyance out of my voice. "It's part of my job to investigate stuff like this. I just wasn't expecting it."

"But what was he like?" Melissa asks, sipping her Merlot. "I can only imagine he was just insufferably aggressive."

"I hope you didn't drink anything. He probably tried to slip you something," Teagan says, and I flinch.

"Wow. No, it wasn't anything like that at all." I place my

wine glass on the table and cross my arms. "He was ... quite normal, actually. He didn't do or say anything that made me feel uncomfortable. To be honest, he was just interested in educating people about what goes on at the club, and what kind of person he is. He thinks BDSM gets a bad rap."

Melissa laughs. "Seriously? BDSM gets a bad rap? It's freaking *BDSM* for crying out loud! How could you get a *good* rap when you go around slapping and whipping each other?"

"Yeah," Teagan says. "And now they have a club in the heart of Philly dedicated to slapping and whipping each other. It's obscene and gross. I bet there's all kinds of STDs just floating in the air at that so-called club."

Melissa laughs and looks at me, making me feel the need to at least giggle with her. "Can you imagine if you had gone at night?" she asks. "Who knows what those people would've subjected you to. I bet there's people having sex right out in the open while a group of weirdos watch and stroke their dicks."

Teagan bursts into laughter that nearly makes her double over. "That's so gross, Melissa."

"What? It's true. And I bet the owner is floating above them all like the god of depravity, with his big ole johnson out, watching it all take place while he laughs like the devil himself. Just a disgusting group of people."

The two of them laugh together, but I can't find the strength to join in. While I don't necessarily have the highest opinion of people who are into that kind of stuff, I'm not interested in ridiculing an entire group of people I've never met and know nothing about. Just because we're different doesn't mean they're *the devil*.

"If I'm being honest, Nolan really wasn't that bad," I inform them as the laughter finally starts to simmer down.

"Oh, the criminal has a name?" Teagan asks sarcastically.

"Criminal?" I repeat, frowning hard.

"Uhh, *yeah*! Anyone who gets off on assaulting people is definitely a criminal," Teagan explains with more confidence than she should have.

"I mean, it's not really assault if they have consent," I answer, and the air in the room is sucked out immediately.

"Seriously, Bree?" Teagan says. "Are you condoning that kind of behavior now?"

"Uh-oh," Melissa says. "It looks like Bree may have spent a little *too* much time talking to that club owner. Are you interested in BDSM now, Bree?"

"Yeah, are you ready to take a walk on the wild side?" Teagan asks.

I throw my hands up. "God, no. All I'm saying is that it's not really assault if the person *wants* to be assaulted. I still think it's ... you know ... disgusting and all of that. I'm not defending it, I'm just stating the facts."

The two blondes stare at me like they're suspicious that I might be a serial killer.

"Well, facts or not, those people are sick," Melissa states matter-of-factly.

"Maybe so," I reply. "But, I have to keep an open mind because the interview isn't complete. Nolan invited me to the club tomorrow night. He wants me to see the place when it's open."

"Oh, my god. Are you actually going to go?" Teagan asks.

"Of course, I am," I nearly shout. "It's my job."

"That's insane, Bree," Melissa says. "Surely, Chase can't force you to go to a BDSM club to witness that immorality up close. That's the same as forcing you to watch porn against your will."

"I don't think it's the same. This is my job," I try to

explain, just as Andy comes waltzing into the room with an empty can of Bud Lite. He crushes the can and tosses it into a recycle bin in the pantry before walking over to the table and standing behind his wife.

"Babe," Melissa says, looking up at her husband. "What do you think about Bree's job forcing her to go to a sex club against her will under the guise of journalism?"

I lift my hand to object, but Andy plows over it like it was never there.

"Against your will? Oh, they can't do that. If you threaten to sue, they'll back off," Andy says.

Melissa hops on his back and follows his lead. "Yeah, tell them if they don't get someone else to do it, you'll sue for sexual harassment. Andy knows a good lawyer," she says.

If I frown any harder, there's no doubt my face will get stuck forever.

"You guys really think it's that big of a deal?" I ask, shocked by how seriously they're taking this.

"Absolutely," Melissa says, with Andy nodding right behind her.

"That is, unless you're *okay* with going to a place like that," Teagan adds, and all three of them stop to stare at me, awaiting my response.

There's a part of me that wants to explain that I actually do have a tiny interest in this, but it's for the story. I want to write a great article and inform people of what really goes on at The Black Collar. However, there's an even bigger part of me that agrees with my friends and wants them to know I'm still on their side. Call it peer pressure, but these are my friends, and I don't want them to think I've changed.

"No, of course not," I say, looking at all three of them. "You guys are right. I'm sure Chase can find someone else to finish the story, because of course I'm not interested in anything like that. I can just pass over my notes to whoever he gives the assignment to." Suddenly, all of their faces unclench, and I feel like I've made the right choice. "Yeah, I'll just talk to Chase first thing in the morning so I don't have to go to the club. I'm sure he'll be okay with it."

Chapter Eleven

"Of course I'm not okay with it. What are you, out of your mind?"

Chase sits behind his desk with a scowl on his face that nearly makes me tremble. For reasons beyond me, I walked into his office this morning convinced that he'd be okay with me dropping the Black Collar story. I should've known better, but I let Melissa, Teagan, and Andy convince me that I should threaten to sue if I didn't get my way. What the hell was I thinking? Well, now I'm in a hole I have to try to find my way out of.

"Did he do something inappropriate?" Chase asks, sitting back in his seat. He's giving an interview today for a local news station, so he's wearing a suit and tie, but it makes him look uncomfortable and stiff, adding to his already-intimidating look.

"No, he was actually really nice," I admit, but I wince, because I know it doesn't help my case.

"Okay, so then what's the problem?"

How do I say that I let my friends talk me into this without saying it?

"It's just ... it's a sex club, Chase," I try to explain. Sweat beads on my forehead and my heart rate starts to climb from the nerves, but Chase is as steady as a rock.

"No, it's a BDSM club, where sometimes people have sex. I think we've established that it's not a brothel. You're an investigative journalist, Bree—a good one at that. I've sent you into the goddamn trenches on previous assignments, chasing leads for stories that we didn't even run. So, what's so different about this one that you want to drop a story for the first time in your career?"

I let out a deep breath and look up at the ceiling, wondering why the answers to all of my questions aren't up there. I know Chase has a point, and between listening to my friends and assessing the way talking to Nolan made me feel, I don't even know what to say anymore. I've been all over the place since I walked out of the Black Collar, and there doesn't seem to be any stable footing for me to walk on anywhere.

"What was wrong with him?" Chase asks again.

"Nothing."

"Then talk to me. You've gotta give me something if you want me to consider this." When I can't put a sentence together that makes sense, Chase extends his hand over his desk. "Let me hear the audio."

After a sigh, I pull out the recorder I used for the interview with Nolan and hand it to Chase, who places it on his desk and immediately presses play. We spend the next thirty minutes listening to the audio of my interview, and I'm catapulted back into his world of sex and kink by his baritone voice. Chase and I listen to Nolan's story about the sex on his desk, and the two of us are enthralled for completely different reasons. Chase is stunned and entertained, while I'm ... what am I? Disgusted? Entranced? Excited? I listen as Nolan talks in detail about using a riding crop to spank a nameless woman's clit, and I find myself biting my lip. Does it gross me out? Do I think he's a demented psycho I need to stay far away from? Or is this what it feels like to be turned on by something you don't understand?

"Bree, you okay?" Chase asks, slicing through my thoughts and pulling me back into reality.

"Huh? Oh, yeah, I'm fine."

"Good, because there's no way we're dropping this story, and I'm not assigning it to anyone else."

"What? Why not?" I snip.

Chase chuckles. "Did you hear this?" he asks, holding up my recorder as evidence. "While we obviously have to edit it way down because we don't publish X-rated stories, everything he said was phenomenal. I was on the edge of my seat listening to that, and he has barely scratched the surface. Bree, this has the potential to be an amazing story. This could be humongous, and I'm not taking you off for obvious reasons."

"What obvious reasons?" I blare, glaring at my boss.

"What, you can't see it?"

"See what, Chase?"

"The man obviously wants to talk to you, Bree. This Nolan Carter guy does not like giving interviews, which is why this is his first one. Hell, I thought for sure he was gonna kill the whole thing before you ever even showed up, but instead of killing it, he wants to open up to you. He has gotten extremely personal, and even invited you to come back because he wants to talk to you. You're chosen, and there's no chance I'm going to send somebody else in there when Nolan obviously wants it to be *you*."

I pause, wondering if what Chase just uttered could possibly be true. Why on Earth would Nolan want to talk to me? I didn't have anything nice to say about him, his club, or BDSM in general. So, why choose me to give this story to?

When I look up at Chase, he's grinning as he holds the recorder out for me to take. "Have fun at the club tonight,

Bree. Keep me updated." Without another word, I take the recorder and walk out.

The second I'm out of Chase's office, I'm startled by Octavia bumping into my shoulder, making me stumble.

"Girl, are you a crazy person?" she asks, smiling from ear to ear. "Did you just try to get out of your story?"

"Ugh, not now," I whimper as I walk to my desk and drop into my chair, tossing the recorder next to my keyboard. Octavia follows and leans against my cubicle.

"I heard the recording," she says with raised eyebrows and a look of pure joy on her face. "What on Earth made you want to drop it?"

"I don't know," I admit, shaking my head. "I was out last night with my friends, and they were talking to me about how horrible all of this is. I guess they just got in my head."

"You mean Melissa and Teagan?" Octavia groans, and I don't have to look at her to know she's frowning. When I don't respond, she catches on. "Bree, no disrespect to your girls, but why are you listening to them, especially when it comes to your job?"

"They're my friends, Octavia."

"I know they are, but—no offense—they're very judgmental."

"They are not," I start, but I stop myself. "Okay, maybe they're a little judgmental. *Maybe.*"

"Sure, *maybe*. Again, I mean no offense, but they don't strike me as the kind of girls who like anything that's different from them."

"They're not like that, and if I'm being honest, I'm just like them."

"No, Bree, you're not," Octavia says, her face and voice serious for the first time. "Anyway, so you really don't want to do this story, huh? Was it really that bad?"

After another long exhale, I rub my hand down my face. "No ... I don't know."

"What was the owner like?"

"He was nice."

Octavia lowers her head and cuts her eyes up to me. "Come on, Bree. You know what I mean."

We stare at each other for a moment before I finally relent and say, "He was gorgeous. He was probably the sexiest man I've ever met in real life, and he carried himself with a poise and control that nearly made my head spin. Is that what you wanted?"

"Exactly that."

"He has blue eyes, Octavia. Caramel brown skin and *blue* eyes."

"Lord, have mercy."

"Exactly. He's beautiful, and he told that story without a lick of shame or apprehension, meaning he's completely self-aware and confident in who he is."

"Then why the hell are you trying to drop the story?" Octavia inquires, throwing her hands up.

I bulge my eyes at her. "I don't know. Okay?"

"I know you don't! But you better get your shit together soon, because I heard you were going to the club tonight. I've never been to a BDSM club, but I imagine it takes an open mind to walk in there."

"Yeah, I know," I say, sighing.

"If you don't have a real reason to drop the story, then stop bullshitting and do what you really wanna do, girl. Feel how *you* feel. Don't listen to Melissa and Teagan. You have to do the story, you have no real reason to drop it, and the owner is both nice *and* gorgeous, so you may as well embrace it and have some fun."

I pinch my lips together as I think about it, and I know Octavia is right about everything, but I'm just not conditioned to operate within this world. It's like it's ingrained in me to think negatively about this. There's something in me that wants to force me to hate it, even when the truth is that I'm interested.

"Embrace it and have some fun," I say, repeating Octavia. "I'm not even sure I know how to do that."

"Well," Octavia says, smiling as she places a hand on my shoulder. "I think it's about time you learned. Starting tonight."

Chapter Twelve

What the hell are you supposed to wear to a BDSM club?

I stand in my closet with my hands on my hips, staring at my clothes as if I'm seeing them for the very first time. This is Philly, and I've been to plenty of nightclubs, but this isn't a nightclub. It's a club for BDSM and kinkiness, and with that in mind, I can't imagine what the dress code will be. Formal? No fucking way. Informal? Hell, even that doesn't feel right. Will everyone be dressed in leather? Will people be walking around with ball gags in their mouths? Would I be turned away if I showed up naked? I have no idea how to proceed, so I decide to stick with professionalism. After all, I'm not going to party. This is for work, so I will dress accordingly.

I end up donning a long black skirt that stops at my knees, with a tucked in white button-up that's not too loose, but also not tight and sexy. To keep things light, I choose black heels with white straps. These are heels I would actually wear to a nightclub, while my clothes are what I would wear to the office—a good mixture of both that I think will work tonight. After a final review in the mirror, I tie my hair back and give myself a nod of approval.

68

"Good," I whisper as I spin halfway around to check how my ass looks in this dress. "Keep it professional, Bree. This is business, not pleasure. Get in, get the info from Nolan, and get out. Just business. This is your job, now go knock it out of the park."

My apartment is nearly half an hour from The Black Collar club, which is much too short of a drive when you're trying to mentally prepare yourself for what's to come. The entire ride over, I keep reminding myself that this will be quick and easy. I'm not participating in anything, there will be no drinking, and I'm not looking to have fun. It may seem like it, but this isn't a night out. It's work, and as conflicted as I feel about all of it, I will keep my head on straight and come out of this the exact same way I went in. I'm a conservative girl with morals, and being exposed to a lifestyle such as this will not change that.

By the time I'm parked and ready to exit my vehicle, I feel confident that I'll be able to walk in, observe enough of the club to write about it, talk to Nolan briefly, and leave. I'll plan a final interview between him and I at a later date so that we don't have to struggle to communicate in a loud, packed space, and this whole thing will be over. When I close my door and lock it behind me, I'm full of confidence. I've got this.

I walk across the street with my clutch tucked under my arm and see a small line of people standing out front, with a very large Black man in a black tuxedo at the front of the line. The large man has long braids and his back to the door, making it obvious he's the bouncer. When I approach, I don't go to the back of the line, choosing instead to walk straight to the front. He sees me coming and glares at me.

"I don't think I should have to explain that there's no skipping to the front of the line," he says in a high-pitched voice that surprises me because it doesn't fit his muscular body.

"Good evening," I begin, maintaining my professionalism without letting him know I'm press. "My name's Bree Barrett. I'm here to see Mr. Carter. I don't know if there's a list, but if there is, I'm sure I'm on it."

The man eyes me for a moment before turning around and whispering something into the radio on his shoulder. After a minute or two, the door to the club opens, and I'm greeted by blaring music and the irritated face of the blonde who escorted me to Nolan's office last time. Her name was Maddy, if I'm not mistaken, and she scowls like she's trying to murder me with her blue eyes. She stares for a second before bouncing her eyes over to the man in black.

"Thanks, Kendrick," she says with a nod, before refocusing on me. "So, this is still happening. Great. Okay, let's go."

My smile doesn't reach my eyes as I nod and follow Maddy over the threshold. Inside, I'm confronted by a sea of people moving from place to place, and sexy R&B music. I expected house music, but this is much better suited for the club's vibe. The lights are very low, with a few strobes flashing on and off over the dance floor, but the rooms in the first hall are lit with colored bulbs, so when Maddy guides me past them, I can see exactly what's going on inside, and it takes my breath away. Now that the club is open, there are no curtains or closed doors to hide the truth, and I realize there was no way I was ever going to get the dress code right tonight.

In the room on my right, there are probably twenty people standing in a half-circle. Some of them are shirtless, some only wearing undergarments, and some really are stuffed inside thick, leather outfits that cover them from head to toe. It's absolutely unreal. I can see them all watching something taking place along the far wall, but I can't make it out from here, so I pause at the door to try to catch a glimpse of what's drawing so much attention.

"Don't be scared. Go in and see," Maddy says from behind me. I turn to her and see her grinning as she watches me. There's a look of superiority on her face that I don't like. It's like she knows I'm new to this and finds it amusing that I'm awestruck. She looks at me like I'm afraid, and I refuse to let her think that of me. So, just to prove I'm not some scared little girl in a new world, I walk inside.

After pushing my way past a few people, I find that the furthest wall from the door is lined with bondage devices, and each of them is holding someone captive. There's a set of chains attached to metal rings protruding from the wall with a man and woman bound to each. There are three pillories, each of which houses a woman with her head and hands secured through the holes in the wood. Lastly, there are three beds with short posts on all four corners, where thick ropes are tied on one end while the other end is wrapped around the ankles and wrists of the women who've volunteered to lay down. My heart revs just seeing it all, but I'm thrown off by the fact that every bound person looks like they're enjoying themselves. They all want to be here, even with all of these people watching them be humiliated. What kind of place is this, and what kind of people are these?

"Confused?" Maddy's husky voice slithers into my ear, and I whirl around to find her standing directly behind me, still grinning.

I clear my throat and turn back to the wall of bondage, watching in horror as people begin to step forward and touch the bound individuals.

"I just don't understand," I admit sheepishly. "They're all bound and being touched by strangers. Who in their right mind would want that?"

"What makes you think the people touching them are strangers?" Maddy asks.

"Are they not?"

"Of course not," she answers, frowning as if she's offended by the question. "Every person who is bound is there by choice, and the people touching them are the ones who have their consent to touch them. Everybody else in the room is simply a spectator, and if any of them put their hands on someone without consent, not only would their partners and the bouncers handle it, Nolan would break their fucking fingers before tossing them out of here bloody and beaten. I know you're just a reporter who has no idea what this lifestyle is about, but if there's one thing you need to understand, it's that nothing in here happens without consent, and that rule is never broken. Ever. So, you better make sure that's written in bold in your little article."

Maddy and I eye each other before I end the staring contest and look at the wall again. I try to focus on the fingers of the people who are participating in this little show, and I see that most of them are wearing wedding bands, so the people who are bound are only engaging with their husbands or wives. The realization shocks me, because I never knew such a marriage could exist. It never dawned on me that married people could dive into this lifestyle *together,* and find happiness and satisfaction through a mutual interest in bondage and voyeurism. It's like my eyes are being opened to an entirely new way of thinking that my upbringing kept me from, and I'm not sure how I feel about that.

"Come on. Let's go," Maddy says, practically pulling me out of the bondage room and back into the hall.

On our way toward the dance floor, we walk past another room with onlookers huddling in the middle to watch. While Maddy keeps walking, I take a second to lean into the room and see that the entire perimeter of the space is lined with small cages only big enough for people to either kneel or lay in. Half of the cages contain naked women, while the others contain nude men. Just like before, each cage has a partner interacting with the person inside, while everyone else in the room keeps their distance. Who would've thought that a place like this would operate with law, order, and respect, while also being a forest of kink and debauchery.

I step out of the cage room and continue to make my way down the hall toward the dance floor that I'll have to cross in order to get to Nolan's office. I'm not in a rush to ride the sea of people dancing their problems away, so I slow down and take my time, stopping to look into another room in the hall. Like every other room, the colored lights are bright enough to see everything taking place, but it's not what I see that draws me in, it's what I hear.

The thunderous sound of leather smacking against bare skin grabs me by the ears as I step to the threshold. Peering inside, I'm once again greeted by a room full of people in the center, and walls covered with large Xs, where people are strapped by their hands and feet. The Xs look like literal torture devices, and the men and women doing the torturing are holding everything from paddles, to floggers, to whips, and canes.

Unlike the other rooms, there's no easing into it, because every person bound to an X is being hit by the person they're with. The crack of whips and the smack of paddles erupt all at once, followed by the pleasure-filled cries of their partners. I'm jolted each time someone is hit, and heat rises inside me. My body becomes a tea kettle as I watch from the door, wondering what it must feel like to be hit with a flogger, and I grow hotter the more I see. One bound woman is facing the X, so the man she's with is flogging her backside, and I gasp with each swing of the toy and the moans it pulls from the woman's throat. She doesn't sound in pain. Somehow, the impact of the flogger brings her pleasure, and I've never been more curious in my life.

"Someone looks intrigued," Maddy says from behind me. I don't even bother to turn around this time.

"There's just something about it," I say, still watching the woman with deep red streaks across her ass and back. "I've experienced pleasure, but what must it feel like to have pleasure *and* pain?"

"It's indescribable," Maddy replies.

"And to experience in front of all these people," I go on, fully immersed in the scene in front of me. "It must be such a rush. How do you bring yourself to do it?"

Maddy sighs. "I wouldn't know. I've never done it before."

I turn to her with a furrowed brow. "You've never been flogged before?"

"Of course I have," she says. "I've never been on display like this."

"Not your cup of tea, huh?"

"No, it is. I've just never been in a relationship that serious. You have to understand what it is you're seeing here. These people are committed to each other on a level most couples won't reach. It's not that one of them is into voyeurism—*both of them* want to display their lifestyle *together*. It's an agreement and union that's much deeper than it looks, and while I've wanted to be put on display, no one has ever wanted to claim and display me."

I look at Maddy and find that she's suddenly looking very vulnerable, which really stands out in the environment we're in. She looks timid as whatever she is thinking about plays in her mind like an emotional movie that only she can see. We don't know each other, but I suddenly feel for her. I get the sense that a BDSM relationship has the power to become much deeper than a regular one, and Maddy has seen something I couldn't even dream of.

"Are you okay?" I ask as Maddy's eyes begin to mist, but

she quickly shakes her head and erases all traces of emotion just as fast as they came.

"I'm fine," she snips without looking at me. "Let's go, and stop pausing to look in every room."

Maddy spins around, determined to leave behind her emotions, and I follow her lead. The two of us quickly walk out of the impact room and turn the corner, and the second we return to the hall, we nearly slam into an intimidating figure standing in front of us like a silent sentry.

"Nolan," Maddy says, startled by his sudden presence.

Nolan, wearing black pants with a form-fitting black button-up, glances at her for a moment, before looking directly at me, his blue eyes glowing under the strobe lights.

"Good evening, Miss Barrett," he says with a wicked grin. "Welcome to The Black Collar. I'm so glad you could make it."

Chapter Thirteen

"I was just on my way to bring her to you," Maddy says before I can speak. Nolan's eyes flash over to her, but I don't see the same spark in them that he had when he looked at me.

"It's all good, Maddy," he says, extending his hand for me to take. "I appreciate you. We're okay from here. Head back upstairs."

I can feel Maddy's eyes burning a hole in the side of my face as I reach out and take Nolan's hand. She doesn't say anything else, but I know she's watching as Nolan guides me away from the first hall of the club, leaving Maddy standing there by herself.

Nolan, with my hand firmly in his, walks us through the packed club. Strobe lights dance on the walls and floor, shining brightly on the many club-goers who are engaging in all types of fun. I try to focus on exactly what's taking place behind me, but with my hand being held by Nolan, it's hard to care about anything else.

As he walks, the sea of people parts for us, forming a narrow path for us to take without many obstacles in the way. It's as if everyone in the club knows who Nolan is, because

INTERVIEW WITH A SADIST

they're all staring at him like he's a mythical creature walking amongst men. The women clearly gawk at him before frowning at me for holding his hand, and the men stare with admiration and reverence pouring from their eyes. I'm clearly walking with the most revered man in the building, and it gives me a rush I didn't expect.

When we reach the bar, every seat is full. We approach from the front, giving me a clear view of the massive display of alcohol on the back wall, and the bald Black man behind the counter. His face is completely devoid of hair, and he smiles a brilliant white smile when he sees us coming toward him. Just as we reach the counter, he leans forward and whispers into the ear of a man sitting at the bar. The man spins around, makes eye contact with Nolan, and immediately stands up to offer his seat.

"Nice to see you again, Nolan," the man says, holding his beer bottle. "Here you go."

The man presents his seat like a new car, and Nolan guides me toward it.

"Thank you. If you don't mind, I'll have Miss Barrett take this one," Nolan says.

"Of course," the man says, just before the woman next to him stands up, leaving her seat for Nolan to take. When we sit, both of them scurry away, looking over their shoulder with smiling faces as if they just saw a celebrity they've loved for years.

"Wow," I exclaim. "You have quite the effect on people here."

"I suppose so," Nolan says.

"Man, you better stop acting modest," the bartender says, still shining his radiant smile. He steps closer to us wearing a tight black T-shirt with a literal leather black collar around his neck. "Don't believe him when he acts like that. He knows they love him, and he knows why."

77

"Is that so?" I say, turning to Nolan completely intrigued. "Well, do tell, Mr. Carter."

"I don't think there's anything to tell, but I'm sure Ethan will have something to say," Nolan replies, and the bartender doesn't miss a beat.

"Oh, absolutely I do," he chirps. "When Nolan first opened this kinky little haven for us, he made a point of demonstrating the proper way to use every room in the club. He asked for volunteers from the staff or the crowd to step inside the cages or to be bound to a Saint Andrew's Cross, but everyone involved had to give their explicit consent and be prepared to use their safe word. In those early days, people got to see him really be in his element, and when you witness Nolan Carter in his true comfort zone, it's a sight to behold."

Nolan glares at Ethan, shaking his head. "You're doing too much. It's not that serious."

"Whatever bro, I was there," Ethan fires back. "And I'm telling you now, if I wasn't married and you were gay, I would've been all over you, too. That shit was like watching a god descend from the heavens to put on a show of true Dominance. We've known each other for years, and even I was shook."

My eyebrows nearly rise to my hairline. "Wow. That's quite the reputation."

"What Ethan isn't telling you, is that he and I have been best friends for a long time," Nolan says. "I was his best man when he married Jackson, and I refused to open the club if he wasn't my partner. So, he's obligated to think highly of me."

"Bitch, please," Ethan replies behind a scoff, and the two of them chuckle together before Ethan adds, "So, are you the new lady in his life?"

Nolan glares at Ethan again, but quickly says, "No. This is Bree Barrett. She's a journalist from the Philly Inquirer. They're running a story about me and the club, and I figured I better give them an interview so they don't crucify me in the story. So, she's here to learn."

Nolan looks at me, and I see Ethan staring at him with a combination of a smirk and frown on his face at the same time. Ethan's eyes narrow as he tilts his head to the side, seeing something in Nolan only a best friend would notice.

"Is that right, Nolan?" Ethan asks, and Nolan cuts his eyes over to him.

"Of course," he answers, and maybe I'm distracted by the colorful lights and loud music, but his words don't carry any weight. He barely even sounds serious, and the smile on Ethan's face doesn't help.

"Okay," Ethan replies, before erasing all traces of incredulousness from his face. "So, can I get you two something to drink?"

"Yeah, the usual for me, E," Nolan says, gaining a nod from Ethan.

"What's the usual?" I ask.

"Cristal," Nolan answers. "Do you drink Cristal?"

"I've never had it before."

"Hmm. Perfect night to try something new," Nolan says, and the look in his eyes pins me to the seat. Is he talking about the drink?

Ethan pours two glasses of the expensive champagne, sliding them over to us before setting the rest of the bottle in an ice bucket. Nolan grabs his glass and holds it in front of me, waiting for me to lift mine.

"Oh, are we toasting?" I ask, picking my glass up.

"We have to," Nolan answers. "To new friendships and experiences."

We lock eyes as we clink our glasses together, and they remain locked as we sip at the same time. Nolan's eyes simply call out to me and I have such a hard time ignoring them. Coupled with his natural charisma and the reverence he carries in this club, he's the sun, forcing me into his orbit.

I shouldn't be drinking. This goes against the mantra I kept chanting in my head before I left my apartment, yet here I am with a full glass and a strong desire to do whatever Nolan asks. Even though I know I should stop, I don't. I keep looking at him, wondering what lies beneath the surface of this gorgeous human being, and my mind quickly veers off course, forgetting all about the story I'm supposed to be interviewing him for.

"So, Miss Barrett," Nolan starts, and I cut him off, shaking my head.

"You have to stop calling me that," I joke, before sipping the delicious champagne again.

"You don't like being called Miss Barrett?"

"My name is Bree. Seriously, just call me Bree. I know this is supposed to be business and all, but my first name will do just fine."

"Understood," Nolan says, and I nod my approval. "So, Bree, what all did Maddy show you before I found you?"

My mind quickly replays images of the rooms in the first hall, and I can feel the warmth in my cheeks making my blush.

"Oh, there was, umm ... a few rooms by the entrance," I start, trying not to give away the thoughts and emotions caused by seeing it all, but Nolan notices my hesitance and pounces.

"Did you look inside?" he asks.

"Umm, yeah. Sure," I say, giving it everything I've got to sound aloof.

"What did you see?"

I release a loud exhale. "You don't know what's in your own club, Nolan?"

"Of course I do, but I want to know what *you* saw."

"Just ... you know," I say, shrugging while I shake my

head. "Bondage, cages, and a room where people were being flogged and spanked."

"Ah, impact play," Nolan says with a smirk, obviously thinking about the specifics.

"Yes."

"How did seeing it make you feel?"

"It doesn't matter."

"Oh?" Nolan shoots back, his champagne glass on the tip of his lip. "*What* doesn't matter?"

"How it made me feel, because I'm here for *business*. Nothing else is supposed to matter besides the interview. I'm only supposed to be here for the story."

Nolan takes a big swig of his champagne and places the glass on the bar.

"I hear you, and I can respect that," he says. "But saying it doesn't matter how it made you feel is an admission that you did feel *something*. Not to mention you keep saying you're supposed to be here for the story. *Supposed to be*. It's like you're trying to remind yourself so you don't forget. But why would you? What is it about being here that could make you forget why you came in the first place?"

I move my mouth to respond, but words don't come out. Instead, I freeze with my mouth open long enough to let bugs in, before realizing I have nothing to say. I pinch my lips together, looking down at the bar for some semblance of control over myself. My thoughts begin to swirl and I feel the arrival of an angel on my shoulder telling me that this isn't how this is supposed to go—that I don't belong in a disgusting place like this. I hear the words playing in my head on a loop, and it's as if they were placed there a long time ago to protect me from the outside world—the world of stepping out of line and breaking away from my upbringing. The words are bars keeping me trapped, and I suddenly hate them. I hate being caged against my will, because even in this foreign

81

world of kink, I'm supposed to give my consent to being trapped. In my life, I was trapped before I ever knew what was happening.

Just as my world begins to feel even more unsteady, Nolan's eyes find mine. I look up at him and see him smiling, ready to protect me from my own thoughts.

"Come with me," he says. "Let's get you out of your head. Let me show you what else this world has to offer."

I swallow hard, knowing this is the moment I can choose to stay within the cage I was raised in, or break out of it, opening myself up to all the dangers of an unknown universe. This is my chance to be free, but freedom can seem terrifying when you've been told your whole life that emancipation will result in peril. Freedom will require stepping off a ledge without knowing what's beneath me. Who will catch me if I fall? That's when I look down and see Nolan's hand waiting to help me off the barstool. I take it, and allow myself to freefall into a new world.

Chapter Fourteen

This is the second time Nolan has held my hand and guided me through the crowd, and my heart races the same as the first. Music blares with heavy thuds of bass pumping through the speakers above us, and the lights seem to be shining even brighter when the strobes flash on, painting everyone bright white every few seconds. The music has switched and become more uptempo, and everyone inside The Black Collar has responded with high energy dancing all around us. The dance floor is so packed, I wouldn't be surprised if it collapsed. No one would ever know it from the outside, but The Black Collar has a strong electric current running through it, and the people inside know how to have a magnificent time. I feel the energy coursing through me, mixing with the Cristal I drank and making my knees feel weak, and it's Nolan who holds me steady on my feet.

He guides me around the bar, where there's a hidden backside of the club that I didn't know existed. I can tell from the obvious secrecy that this section will probably be more explicit. As we approach, I can see there are three rooms, all of which have black curtains blocking their entrance and a muscular man guarding the door. When we reach the first room, the doorman nods to Nolan.

"Good evening, Mr. Carter," he says.

Nolan nods in return before turning to me. "All right, Bree" he starts, looking directly into my eyes and suddenly becoming serious. "You wanted to see what The Black Collar is really about. Well, this is it. Unlike the rooms at the front of the club, these rooms allow nudity. They also allow sex."

I hold back my gasp and swallow it before Nolan has a chance to notice.

"Umm, okay," I say, trying to sound calm. "You allow sex in here?"

"Protected sex that everyone in the room must consent to," Nolan explains. "The security at the door asks everyone who enters if they know what they're getting themselves into, and if they consent to seeing what's behind the curtain. No one who comes to The Black Collar has to participate or even see what's happening back here. There are no prostitutes or escorts in my club. Sex is not sold here, so please don't mistake what you're about to see for what you might expect at a brothel. Everyone here is a volunteer, and everyone abides by my very strict rules of consent and composure, which is what BDSM is really all about. Anyone acting out of line will be dealt with accordingly and banned from ever returning. If you're still thinking about your story at all, please be sure to include everything I just told you. If you're not thinking about the story, which is what I hope, please consider it all before answering my next question. Now, Bree, would you like to enter this first room? Do I have your consent to guide you inside?"

My heart suddenly goes into overdrive, pumping hard and fast as the question shoots into my veins and fills me with

INTERVIEW WITH A SADIST

anxiety. There's something powerful and *terrifying* about being asked directly for your consent. I wouldn't have fought him if he just dragged me into the room, but the fact that he stopped outside, explained what we might see, and then asked for my consent has me sweating bullets.

"Are the rooms different kinks, like the main hall?" I ask, trying to calm myself with more information.

"Yes," Nolan answers.

"What's this first room for?"

"This room is for sensation play."

I clear my throat, wondering exactly what sensation play might mean. I could ask Nolan to explain, but I want to see it for myself.

"Okay. Yes, you have my consent to guide me, but if I ask to leave, you'll let me without hesitating or trying to convince me to stay."

Nolan smirks. "Of course."

He takes me by the hand and turns to the man by the curtain, who pulls it out of the way so we can step through. The second we're inside, I understand why Nolan gave me a warning. As expected, there are both men and women in the room, but what I didn't expect is for virtually everyone to be naked. There are loveseats and tables scattered about the large space, and all of the naked people are seated at the tables using toys on each other, but these toys aren't the same as the ones in the main hall. One couple has feathers and blindfolds, another is using ice, while a woman is pouring candle wax on her man at another couch. There's even a couple using some sort of electrostimulation on each other. It's all a sight to see, and while it's a little jarring to see naked strangers all around you, I still find myself curious about what all of this must feel like. There must be a driving force behind why someone would want to do this, and I'm dying to know what it is.

"What do you think?" Nolan asks, and I suddenly feel the sting of his eyes staring at the side of my face.

"It's mesmerizing," I admit. "I've never seen anything like this. I didn't even know BDSM had a soft side like this. What's that over there?"

I point to an interracial couple at the far end of the room, and Nolan gently pulls my hand down.

"Try not to point," he says with a light chuckle, before adding, "They're using a Wartenberg wheel, also known as a pinwheel. It's a metal disc covered in sharp spikes. It's meant to be used gently, although some people like it a bit rougher."

"Meaning *you* like to use it rougher, Mr. Sadist," I say, and Nolan smiles from ear to ear.

"You're catching on."

"I guess I am," I reply, grinning at the smile still on his lips. "Now, take me to the next room, please."

"Absolutely. Follow me."

Once again, Nolan takes me by the hand and acts as my guide as we exit the sensation room, bypass another guard in front of a black curtain, and step into a room filled with the erotic moans of men and women.

"Oh, my god," I whisper to myself as I take in the scene. "What room is this?"

"This is the edging room," Nolan answers. "All of the toys you see being used have condoms on them, and they'll be sanitized after each use. Here, everyone is allowed to utilize the toys, but no one is allowed to orgasm. If you orgasm in this room, you'll be kicked out. Penetration with the toys is allowed, but again, it's about control and composure. Everyone must always abide by the rules."

"Wow," I say, for what feels like the thousandth time this evening.

I look across the room and see multiple women using rose vibrators on other women, and men having Fleshlight mastur-

INTERVIEW WITH A SADIST

bators stroked up and down their erect penises. My eyes bulge at the depravity of it all, but I'm stunned into silence. Directly in front of me, a woman pinches her lips together and grasps at the cloth covering her couch, before her partner pulls the vibrator away, granting her temporary relief from the tension before starting over again. I can just tell from looking at them that they are going to tear each other apart when they get home. Hell, I'd be surprised if they made it out of the parking lot.

"Did you think of all of this yourself?" I ask, still staring at the beautiful women in front of me.

"Yes," Nolan answers. "There are a lot of kinks out there, and I wanted to capture my favorites."

"You definitely captured them," I say, surprising both of us.

"Which is your favorite?" Nolan inquires, and I look at him without knowing what to say. Clearly I've been paying attention to the things taking place in each room, but I can't pick a favorite. At least, not based on observation.

"It's hard to say," I reply. "Watching and experiencing are very different things."

"Have you experienced any of them?"

No, but I'm starting to really think I'd like to. However, all I manage to say is, "No."

After watching me momentarily, Nolan says, "There's one more room I'd like to show you. Are you ready?"

"Yes," I respond, and Nolan takes me by the hand and whisks me away again.

The final room on this tour of deviancy looks more like an auditorium. There are rows of seats starting just behind the curtain, leading to an elevated platform at the front that looks a lot like a stage. The chairs are filled with quiet onlookers, while the stage is occupied by three people—a man and two women—engaging in a threesome. My eyes bulge as I witness the man pounding into a blonde from behind, while she buries her face between the legs of a redhead, all three of them sending their moans out into the crowd. I take a look around, and while some couples are kissing or inconspicuously caressing each other, no one is masturbating or having sex in the seats. Every person has their eyes glued to the stage, and you can feel the sexual tension in the room growing thicker with each gasp of pleasure coming from the front.

"This is voyeurism," Nolan informs me in a whisper. "No penetration of any kind is allowed in this room unless you're on the stage, and the stage itself is reserved for VIP members only."

"What makes someone VIP?" I ask, my eyes never leaving the show on the stage. The man spanks the ass of the blonde, and I bite my lip as if he just hit me.

"They have to have been in the lifestyle for over five years," Nolan explains. "They pay a monthly fee, and they pass an in-person interview with me. This particular group is a throuple, and they're all in a committed relationship with each other. We call this the main stage, and it's reserved for members who want to put their dynamic on display for the world to see, as an example of how incredible a BDSM relationship can be. As outlandish as it may seem in a place like this, if you're not in love with your partner, you will not grace the main stage. I want my patrons to witness BDSM being fulfilled properly, where it reaches greater heights than just kinkiness. Love does exist in this lifestyle, and I want to make sure it is witnessed."

Once again, I find myself mouthing the word, "Wow," just as the two women on stage kiss each other passionately. One of them whispers the words *I love you* into the ear of the other, and they embrace as the man backs away and watches them with pure adoration in his gaze. You can practically see the love wafting off the three of them, and I shake my head as

I realize Nolan is right. Even to a perfect stranger, I can tell these three people are in love with each other.

We step out of the main stage room and come to a stop just outside the curtain, where Nolan turns to face me.

"So, you've seen everything on the first floor. All that's left now is the VIP section upstairs," he tells me, and I glance up to find Maddy standing at the top of the stairs watching us. As soon as we make eye contact, she turns on her heel and quickly walks away, so I don't mention it to Nolan, who is solely focused on me.

"All of it is incredible," I tell him instead. "I'm not sure what I expected before I showed up tonight, but it wasn't this. You've done a great job with this place, Nolan. I'm impressed. I think our readers will be, too."

Suddenly, Nolan's demeanor hardens. He tilts his head to the side and frowns.

"You know, Bree, I admire your determination," he says.

"My determination? What do you mean?"

"It's impressive just how much effort you're putting into convincing yourself that your only interest is the story for your paper."

Now it's my turn to frown, because although I've been affected by every single thing I've seen tonight, I've done a great job keeping those feelings off my face. I thought I was putting on quite the performance, but Nolan continues to see right through me. Nonetheless, I try my best to keep the mask in its place.

"Nolan, my only interest *is* the story," I say, but it doesn't even sound convincing to me. "There is nothing personal about this. It doesn't matter how I feel or where my interest lies. I'm here for the story. Can't you understand that?"

"Then why did watching it all make you so hot?" he asks, and my entire body stiffens. "You liked everything you saw tonight, and I don't need your words to tell me that you're interested in more than just documenting this lifestyle. I can see it in your eyes that you want to know how it feels. You want to know what draws all of these people to a life like this. You want to know how it feels to be as free as the people you watched today. Now, tell me it's not true."

I stare into Nolan's gorgeous blue eyes and try to find a way to lie to him. This is the part where I'm supposed to revert back to everything I've always known. I'm supposed to say that I don't do stuff like this and have no interest in it whatsoever, and even become offended at the accusation. I know what I'm supposed to do, but I can't bring myself to do it, so I just stand there.

"You don't have to say anything, Bree," Nolan continues. "I see it in you. I recognize it. I know it's there, but you don't have to worry. I'm not going to do anything until you ask me to."

I scowl so hard it hurts.

"Ask you to? I'm not going to ... I'm not going to ask you to do anything," I stammer.

"You will," Nolan responds, full of self-assurance. "And when you do, I'll gladly show you whatever you ask. I'll show you there's nothing to be afraid of."

I lick my lips at the thought of Nolan showing me any of the things I've been curious about tonight, but I force the thoughts away.

"I'm not afraid of anything, and the only thing I'll ask you will be questions for the story when we meet for the final part of our interview," I snip, feeling frustrated at how he reads me so easily. "Other than that, I won't ask anything of you. So, thanks for the tour of the club, and I will call you later to schedule what will be our last meeting."

Nolan looks down at the floor, his thoughts making their presence known through the expression on his face, but as usual, he keeps his wits about him, burying it all before he looks up at me.

"Okay," he says.

"Okay," I reply. "Then I'll be in touch. Have a good rest of your night, Nolan."

"Goodnight, Bree," Nolan says, just before I spin around and walk out.

A Breaking Dam

Chapter Fifteen

My shower was cold this morning. I needed it as a distraction from the thoughts that seem to have taken over my mind ever since I left The Black Collar last night—thoughts that weave in and out like a snake in the grass, consuming me, holding me hostage. Everything I've done since leaving the club has been bogged down by the memory of everything I saw, and the conversation I had with Nolan—the one where he said he'd be ready and willing to teach me about anything I was curious about. How could I possibly get him out of my head after that?

I'm walking a tightrope now, trying to keep my balance so I don't fall to my doom, and in my head, collapsing into a world of kink and sexual freedom is the same as being doomed. It doesn't really matter how much time has gone by or how old I am, the way I was brought up still has me in a chokehold, and I can't see BDSM as anything other than taboo. My parents and friends would certainly call me a whore for being with someone like Nolan, and it feels nearly impossible to break free of the chains. I'm locked down, and I don't even know what freedom looks like.

I realize the drive went by quickly as I'm pulling into the parking lot of The Inquirer. My mind was on autopilot the entire commute as I thought about the scene in the impact room of The Black Collar over and over again. The roads and bridges in Philly were replaced by naked bodies strung up on massive Saint Andrew's Crosses with their limbs spread over the X. The sound of car engines and tires were drowned out by floggers and whips cracking over flesh and sensual moans. As I climb out of my car, I think I might need another cold shower before I begin my workday.

I make my way inside, stepping onto the elevator with the same wild thoughts in the back of my head. I have to try to keep them at bay, or I feel like I might go insane. But how do I do that when I have a meeting with Nolan this afternoon? I don't know the answer, but if I take some time to not think about the interview, maybe I'll feel composed enough to prepare later.

"So, tell me all about it," Octavia blurts the second the elevator doors open.

Damn. So much for that plan.

She stands in front of me with a warm smile and a face that's eager for adventure, but I ignore it as I walk past her without saying a word, heading for my desk.

"Bitch, I know you're not ignoring me," she snips, the front of her feet nipping at my heels. I reach my cubicle and sit down with my back to her, but she spins my chair around and stares at me with bulging eyes. "You better stop playing with me."

"Octavia, no," I whine, dragging the words out like a bratty child.

"What is the matter with you?" she asks, scowling. "You go to a freakin' BDSM club, getting exclusive access, and you don't want to come in here screaming about it through a megaphone? You're ridiculous, Bree Barrett. *Ridiculous*."

"Ugh," I groan, throwing my head back against the head-rest. "Can't I have one second of peace from this world? One second!"

"No. How dare you," Octavia says flatly. "Bree, you're taking this situation for granted. You have the best assignment in the building right now and you're acting like you hate it, which I know is bullshit because *nobody* would hate this assignment. Even if you're not into BDSM, the details of it all are still interesting, so all this agonizing you're doing is really suspicious, and I don't buy it. So, maybe you should stop fronting and tell me what's really going on."

Octavia spins around and grabs a chair from the empty cubicle across from mine and slides it over, sitting down so close to me that I have to back up to avoid feeling awkward.

I debate it in my head before I speak, because I know once the words leave my mouth, I won't be able to bring them back. There's no putting the toothpaste back into the tube once it's out, but there's so much pressure building up inside me that the tube will explode if I don't release some. Even when I pinch my lips together, the urge to speak is a crowbar prying my mouth open.

"Oh, shit," Octavia suddenly whispers, drawing my attention. "You're into him, aren't you?"

I pop forward, sitting up straight with my face only inches from Octavia's.

"What?" I say in nothing more than a whisper.

"You're into him," Octavia repeats, making my nerves constrict.

"I ... no," I say weakly, and Octavia's mouth drops open.

"You just lied to me," she says. "Oh, shit. You're into him, you're into BDSM, you're into *all of it*, aren't you?"

I try to keep it at bay. My eyebrows draw in and I clamp my mouth shut, even pressing my hand over my lips and making a complete ass of myself just to hold it back, but I

INTERVIEW WITH A SADIST

can't do it anymore. I've seen and heard too much, and my curiosity has grown into a dragon that can no longer be chained up inside a cave. It has to fly now, and God only knows what kind of damage it will do. All I know is that if I try to keep it locked away any longer, I'll be the one it hurts.

"Fuck," I whisper through my fingers. Octavia's ears perk up, anticipating what I'll say next as I drop my hand. "Yes."

Octavia gasps, leaning in even closer. "What? *Yes*?"

"Yes," I say again, louder this time as I fall back into my chair. "I don't know where it all came from. Maybe it was the story he told about using the toys on someone in his office—the same office we were sitting in at the time. Maybe it put my imagination to work a little *too* much. Maybe it was everything I saw last night while he gave me the tour—and there was *so much* to see. There was a room dedicated to each of his favorite kinks, but then there were all of these rules in place to keep people from doing too much. He was held in such high regard by everybody in the building. Not just the people who work for him either. Even the patrons looked at him like he was some sort of god. They parted like the fucking Red Sea when he approached, and came back together behind us once we passed. All of it was absolutely surreal, and I was mesmerized. Everybody was happy and in a good mood. His bartender was super cool. The place was controlled and packed with a type of fun I didn't think people could have without acting like total deviants and psychos. I just never knew that type of lifestyle existed, and now that I've seen it, it feels like it has cleared my vision. Now, I can see I've been missing something. I prejudged the lifestyle, and now that I've seen it for real, I ... I think I'm interested in it. Fuck. What the hell is wrong with me?"

Silence hangs in the air a moment before Octavia smiles wide and pulls me into a tight hug.

"Aww, I'm so proud of you," she says, sounding like a

pleased mother before she backs away and looks me in the eye, still beaming. "I'm glad to hear you finally admit it, because it has been written all over your face since the moment you met the guy. Oh, and *nothing* is wrong with you. If anything, being closed-minded was wrong, but admitting you're interested in something isn't wrong at all."

"Then why do I feel like I need to ask my parents and friends for forgiveness?" I say, pouting.

"Because—no offense—they're closed minded like you were. Where do you think you got it from?" she replies. "But you're finally in a place where you're starting to become comfortable with the idea of trying new things. This is a good thing, Bree."

"But isn't it wrong to be interested in this kind of stuff?"

"Why? Because your parents said it was when you were little? Because your friends shut it down without knowing anything about it at all? Hating something without even knowing why is not a good thing. Your mind is opening because you saw it in person and realized that it's nothing like you thought it'd be, and now that you know, you have an interest that you *absolutely* should explore."

"What? I should?"

"Of course you should!" Octavia barks before correcting herself and whispering again. "Of course you should. You're a twenty-nine-year-old single woman, Bree. You should be out there exploring the shit out of your sexual fantasies until you find a man—or woman—that can satisfy them all. Luckily for you, you may have already found him."

I bulge my eyes. "Excuse me?"

"Oh, please," she says, scoffing. "You can save that act for when you talk to Chase about the story, but I know a crush when I see one."

"I do *not* have a crush on him. I'm too old for crushes."

"Yeah? Well, call it what you want, but you like him. You

like the power he holds, and I don't blame you. That story about the office was like a fucking inferno it was so hot—and what's not to like about a man that people move out of the way for? He sounds like a badass, and if he's interested in you too, then you should go for it."

"I can't do that," I say, suddenly feeling terrified of the idea of even seeing Nolan after this admission.

"Why?" Octavia asks with an exaggerated shrug.

"Because ... he's a *sadist*!" I snap, trying to stay quiet and failing.

"And let me guess, you've been taught that sadism is bad?" Octavia says, and I suddenly feel dumb. "You keep trying to judge all of this based on what you've been taught and other people's opinions, but you need to go and learn about it on your own. Sure, he's a sadist, and maybe that does sound scary to people who don't know what it really means. It sounds scary to people who don't get it—to people who aren't into that kind of thing, but maybe that doesn't apply to you."

"What? Why wouldn't it apply to *me*?"

"Because you're interested in it." I freeze, watching and listening to Octavia as if she's the only person in the world. "Maybe you feel something about everything you've seen because you *really are into it*. Maybe you're enticed by his sadism because you're curious about being a masochist."

I shake my head as fear grips me. "That can't be true."

"Why not?"

"Because it's ... *pain*! I'm not interested in being hurt. That's ridiculous."

"But, is it, though? You're acting like the pain he'd give you is the same as being tortured to death. This isn't having your arm chopped off or being waterboarded. It's not bamboo under your fingernails. My husband and I have done plenty of experimenting, and trust me, girl, some pain is worth it."

" I ... What ... I know, but ..."

"Stop fighting it, Bree," Octavia says, finally leaning back in her seat but still eyeing me closely. "Stop thinking about what your friends might say, too. True friends will love you no matter what you're into, as long as what you're into isn't hurting anybody. I think it's time you started thinking about yourself. You keep going back and forth with this, and there's no reason for that. Just do what the fuck you want to do. The only person you really have to answer to is yourself."

I don't know what to say. I'm not even sure I'm capable of disregarding what my friends and family think of me, because it has always been in the back of my mind with every decision I've ever made. Now, I'm being flooded with an entirely new way of thinking, and it's all so overwhelming.

Nobody wants to be judged for being who they are, and nobody should have to keep themselves hidden either, but I'm not one hundred percent sure about anything right now, and that needs to change.

I feel what can only be described as terror as I try to focus on myself for the first time in my life. I've been battling internally since the moment I met Nolan, denying myself every thought that would be out of place in my perfect little world where everything different from me is bad. I've been immature. I've been scared to live. I've been too hard on myself, and I've done everything except what I want to do.

I take all of those thoughts and swallow them down. I choke on it at first, but eventually I get it down and refuse to let it come back up, heartburn be damned.

Octavia is right. The only person I have to answer to is myself, and I've never given myself the proper care and attention. Well, it's time for a much needed change. A permanent one.

Chapter Sixteen

I've never given much thought to impulses. Even at the age of twenty-nine, I've never thought about whether or not I had them, and if I felt anything sexually impulsive, I discarded the idea. Like too many people, I was taught that being sexual in any way was wrong, and that it would lead to horrible things happening to me. Obviously, the best way to avoid the damage being "promiscuous" would cause was to avoid unclean or impure thoughts. It became a habit that I continued subconsciously my entire life, and now that I'm breaking out of my cell, the hardest part of being free is discontinuing the habits that kept me caged. With my mind more open, I'm feeling things that are brand new to me. New, terrifying, and exhilarating.

Just seeing The Black Collar from the outside has my stomach in knots. I know what takes place behind those doors. I know what magic lies within each room—and that's what it is—*magic*. The ability to turn pain into pleasure is as close to real magic as my world will ever know. My memories excite my entire body, filling me up from my feet to my head.

My heart races and I feel the need to swallow more than I normally do. My breathing shudders and my skin flushes. All of this just from looking at the building with a new set of eyes.

I step out of my car and walk on wobbly legs across the street, adjusting my plaid, ruffle trim, pinafore dress as I go. Maybe I took some extra time to pick out a dress that leaned more toward the sexy side than it did the business side. Maybe I didn't. The world will never know. All that matters now is that I'm here, feeling as confident as my mind will allow, and ready to see where my life will go after the final part of this interview concludes today. When we're finished this afternoon, I'll ask Nolan if he'd like to spend some extra time together. Maybe dinner. Maybe ... whatever the hell he wants to do with me. He won't know just how open I am to things, but he will know I'm interested in him and what he calls the lifestyle. Before the day finishes, my life will be on a new path. A path my friends will judge and critique endlessly.

I let out a long exhale as I knock on the door, hoping to set free any more thoughts about my friends that could distract me today. Octavia was right—I can't allow other people to dictate how I live my life, and by the time Maddy opens the door, I'm no longer picturing the judgmental, unobjective faces of Melissa and Teagan. I'm in the moment and ready to embrace it.

"You're back ... again," Maddy says, swinging the door open. Her curly hair isn't as well put together as it usually is, and her blue eyes have bags under them. She must have just woken up from a difficult night, because it's written in the pores on her face.

"Yes, I am," I begin, stepping inside. "Today should be the last part of our interview."

"So, this will be the last day we see each other?" Maddy asks, closing the door.

"Well ... who knows," I answer, feeling sheepish and protective about what I'm thinking. "Maybe we'll see each other around."

Maddy cuts her eyes over to me and scoffs. "I doubt that. I don't usually hang out in many vanilla spaces, and we both know I won't see you here. So, this *will* be our last time seeing each other."

Instead of arguing with her about it, I simply nod and follow Maddy down the hall. As we pass the rooms on both sides of us, I picture what's behind each of the black curtains hanging in the doorways now. I imagine the chains on the walls, the beds, the cages, and the crosses—so many devices used to bind and hurt people.

Damn. I have to get out of thinking about all of this in such a negative way. The people who participated in what I saw here weren't just being hurt. They were being satisfied after having given their consent. They wanted what they got, and they loved it. No negative connotations are necessary. This is a house of pleasure, even if it's painful.

Maddy leads me down the hall and into the big open space that is the bar and dancefloor of the club. The bright overhead lights are on and the place is completely devoid of people, with the exception of two men at the bar. As we approach, I recognize Ethan, the bald man behind the counter from the other night, but the new man with the shaggy, curly hair is someone I've never seen before. His skin is caramel like Nolan's, and the hair around his mouth is neatly trimmed and connected to a perfectly manicured beard, while his almond eyes seem to look into the depths of my soul as Maddy and I reach them.

"You're the girl from the other night, right? The journalist?" Ethan says as he cleans out glass cups with a white towel.

"Yeah, that's right," I answer. "And you're Ethan."

"Just call me E," he replies. "This handsome man sitting next to you is my husband, Jackson. Jackson, this is Bree."

"Oh, it's nice to meet you," I say, extending my hand, which Jackson immediately shakes.

"It's nice to meet you, too," he says. "You're a journalist? Shit, I'm surprised Nolan even let you in here."

"Me too," I answer with a giggle.

"Good, you all know each other," Maddy cuts in, practically rolling her eyes. "So, you'll be comfortable waiting here for Nolan to finish getting cleaned up. He just came back from a run and is in the shower. He'll come get you when he's ready. For now, hang out with these two idiots."

My eyes widen as I look at Jackson, whose eyebrows raise in a flash.

"Bitch, please," Jackson snips, joking with a smile. "Who are you calling idiots? Get your miserable little ass back up those stairs. Always trying to rain on somebody's parade lookin' ass."

"Big head ass trying to call *us* idiots?" Ethan jumps in, shaking his head as Maddy turns on her heel to walk away.

"Praying mantis head ass," snaps Jackson, making Ethan chuckle before he piles on another insult.

"Praying mantis?" says E, fighting back a laugh. "You're so right. Bitch got a triangle head."

Now it's Jackson's turn to snort. "Ole isosceles head ass girl."

"Not the isosceles!" E blurts, and the two of them fall into uncontrollable laughter. They howl like teenagers, and the sight of the two of them engaged in this jovial behavior puts a smile on my face. I end up laughing with them, but when I look at the top of the stairs, my snickering stops. Maddy glares at me over the railing, and she most definitely *isn't* laughing. She doesn't linger long, but when she walks away, I can still feel the cold from her gaze as I pull my attention back to Jackson and Ethan.

"Don't worry about Maddy," Ethan says, finally calming himself down.

"Yeah, she's always in a shitty mood," Jackson adds.

"Seriously," Ethan says. "Especially since—"

"Ah, there's no need to get into all of that," Jackson interjects quickly, stopping Ethan in his tracks. "So, what made you decide to do a story on this place, Bree?"

I pause, frowning at their weird exchange, before answering, "My boss. He said interest in the club was crazy, and people had their suspicions about what goes on here, and who runs the place. So, he reached out to Nolan and he agreed to an interview."

"Wow," Jackson says, nodding in silent agreement with Nolan's decision. "Well, good on Nolan."

"I'm both surprised and not surprised at all," Ethan says, looking at his husband. "You know how Nolan is. He doesn't want people thinking the worst of him, and he's big on showing people things they never knew about so they won't judge without knowing the facts."

"He's the perfect loving Dominant," Jackson says, smiling.

Ethan grins. "Right? He wants to smack the shit out of you with a flogger, then go volunteer somewhere and donate to charity."

"He donates to charity?" I inquire, pulling out my notepad to jot this down.

"At least twice a year," Ethan answers. "Nolan is not your typical Dominant. He's a control freak by nature, but also selfless, and he specializes in empathy. He feels deeply, and when he cares about something, he cares with every ounce of him. With Nolan, you either get all or nothing."

"Some people can't take Nolan because he can be so intense, and he doesn't mince words," Jackson continues. "He can be a lot to get used to at first, because he's completely unashamed of who he is, and that includes living the lifestyle. Hell, it's because of him that we've grown to be so comfortable about who we are."

I stop writing and look at the two of them. "Really?"

"Oh, for sure," says Jackson. "I know it's 2023, but being gay in America is still terrifying, and there's a million reasons to keep it to yourself. But with Nolan around, you get a sense of pride that's completely contagious. He exudes confidence and if you can't accept who he is, he doesn't want you around. He's such a pure person that most people end up wanting *his* acceptance, not the other way around."

"Facts," Ethan chimes in for added measure.

"Wow," I say, which seems to have become my motto these days. "Sounds impressive."

"He is. Nolan is the best friend either of us has ever had," Ethan says.

"Well, besides each other," Jackson cuts in.

"How does someone like that end up single?" Ethan asks his husband.

Jackson scoffs. "You know why."

"Wait, can I know why?" I jump in with a raised finger.

The two of them glance at each other, silent words being exchanged back and forth. It's Jackson who answers after their muted conversation.

"Like I said before, Nolan can be a lot to take. He's honest about who he is, and if he gets the sense that you're not, then getting his approval can be difficult. For some people, gaining his approval is all that matters, and that can be a problem, because if he doesn't trust your motives, you'll never get it."

Intrigue comes to life in my heart and spreads to the rest of my body through my veins. You can never judge a book by its cover, but I never would've guessed that Nolan had so many layers. He's a walking enigma, and the more I learn about him, the more drawn to him I feel. I want to learn more and more as fast as I can, because the way his friends describe him makes him sound truly special.

They also seem to know his secrets, and I want those too. Especially when I look up and find Maddy watching us again. She stands at the top of the stairs with hatred and heartache in her eyes, and when we make eye contact this time, she doesn't look away until the sound of Nolan's office door steals her attention. She spins around, her entire demeanor softening as Nolan strides past the VIP section and starts down the stairs without ever acknowledging Maddy. He's wearing a black button-up with white pants, all of it tailored to his perfect physique, and as he approaches, he looks me up and down with curiosity in his gaze. He looks just as interested in me as I am in him, and I couldn't fight off my smile if I tried.

"I hope these two aren't bothering you too much," he says, smiling at his two friends.

"No, not at all," I reply. "I actually learned quite a lot about you."

"Accusations," Nolan says, jokingly pointing his finger at E and Jackson. "*False* accusations."

"We didn't accuse you of anything except being awesome," Ethan jokes, and the three of them laugh together. With these three, their love for each other is on full display. Whereas with my friends, I wonder if people can tell if we even like each other when they see us together.

"Anyway," Nolan says, holding out his hand to help me off the barstool "If you're ready, we can head upstairs and begin."

With a smile and a nod, I clasp my hand in his. "Absolutely."

Ethan and Jackson smile suspiciously as we turn to walk away, but Nolan doesn't acknowledge them. He guides me up the stairs, never letting go of my hand, even as we pass a glaring Maddy who watches us until we enter his office. Her eyes stay fixated on us until the moment Nolan escorts me inside and slowly closes the door behind us. Even through the wooden door, I can feel her still watching.

Chapter Seventeen

My nerves vibrate beneath my skin, because I'm more anxious now than I've ever been. Nolan sits across from me with that same sultry, seductive, awe-inspiring look on his face, and it melts my insides. He's so gorgeous—so poised and sure of himself that it makes me feel like I have no control over myself. If he is what self-control looks like, then I certainly don't have any, because Nolan is the essence of calm. I want to rile him up just to see what he's like when he's not so collected, but he looks at me with unmoving eyes, completely unfazed. Knowing I can't break him makes me wonder what it would feel like to be broken *by* him.

Shit. There go those impulsive thoughts again. I've been occupied by them all day, and now that I'm sitting in front of the man who helped me open the portal to them, it's only getting worse. When he looks at me, I can envision myself strapped to one of the Xs in the impact room, waiting as he stalks behind me with something dangerous in his hand. I don't even know what he's holding, and my every breath is laced with fear, but my blood flows faster than ever. I crave it.

I lust after learning the unknown—what will the pain be like? How can it feel so good?

"You seem distracted," Nolan says, his words like a knife through the soft butter he turns my thoughts into.

I clear my throat and try to refocus, but allowing myself to be more open has altered my mind and body. Sitting in front of Nolan now isn't the same as when I was fighting how I felt before. Now, there's a constant current flowing through me. I'm more tense and on edge.

"I'm okay," I lie.

"Good. So, how do we begin? If I'm not mistaken, this is supposed to be our final interview, is it not?"

I clear my throat again to settle myself, because the thought of walking away from all of this makes my stomach hurt. I haven't experienced enough yet. So, this may be the final portion of the interview, but it's *not* our last interaction. There *has* to be more.

"Yes. After the depth of our first interview, and the amazing things you showed me last night, this *should* be the end. I expect to have enough to write a thorough, detailed story about you and The Black Collar, and I imagine it will set our readers' worlds ablaze. I'd expect a spike in sales after this is published."

Nolan chuckles, raising his eyebrows. "Wow. You must have some pretty nice things to say about me then. I can't imagine people flocking to a BDSM club because of a story in The Inquirer. No matter what you write, people will still find a reason to hate a lifestyle they don't live themselves. It's just the way things work in the world we live in."

"Maybe that's true," I reply, setting my recorder on the table. "But I'm following your lead, Nolan. If we flood them with the correct information and they still hate it, it's on *them*, but at least they'll be educated about it. I want to enlighten the world about what I've experienced here, because it has been truly eye-opening."

"I'm glad to hear you say that, Bree," Nolan responds with a smile. "As much as you've seen, there's so much more to it than that."

"I know," I say, maybe a little too quickly. "I ... umm. I'm intrigued by all of it, actually."

He goes still, his eyes fixated on me while the gears in his head go to work like they always do, leaving me to wonder what he's thinking. Most people would just come out with it, but he is nothing like most people. He is a vault with a code that only he knows. He may open it enough to give you bits and pieces of the contents inside, but you'll never step in and see it for yourself.

"Anyway," I say, trying to move past the fact that he is still staring at me. "Shall we begin?"

Nolan finally blinks. "Absolutely."

I press the button for the recorder to start and sit back on the couch. His blue eyes peer into me, snatching my attention. God, he's so good-looking.

Fuck, I have to get it together. The interview isn't done.

"So, Mr. Carter," I start. I shake my head to scatter distracting thoughts. "After everything I've learned here at The Black Collar, what has struck me most about communicating with you is how much you value BDSM as a lifestyle. The final room you showed me in the club was the main stage, where only VIP guests of the club are allowed to get on and perform for the viewers. To some, it may only be seen as voyeurism, but to those in the room who were blessed to witness it, it was love. Why is it so important to you that people understand that love exists in BDSM?"

Nolan raises an eyebrow and nods his approval. "Great question. The common misconceptions about BDSM are that our lifestyle is violent, hypersexual, criminal, deviant, and lust-driven. People on the outside have no idea that those who choose to engage in BDSM are just as normal as anybody else walking down the street. The same way that anybody else would want love, members of the lifestyle want it as well, and when we manage to find it, it's more glorious than anything I've ever seen.

"Our connections are deep, and our bond is strong within the dynamics we choose to make us happy. People need to see that this is more than just lust-filled nights with random strangers we don't care about. They need to know that this isn't the exploitation of rape culture or assault. BDSM is a lot of things, but our core value is consent, and that alone makes us better than what our detractors think of us. We are worthy of love, and we certainly are capable of it. They don't believe us when we tell them, so I like to use the main stage to show them."

I find myself staring at Nolan and losing track of the seconds that tick by. As much as I'd like to deny it—because I don't *really* know much about him—he mesmerizes me. With every conversation, I learn something new about him that makes him that much more astonishing. When he speaks, he becomes mystical to me—a god-like creature with an aura that brightens every time he opens his mouth. Stunned, I shake my head and try to continue.

"And what about you, Mr. Carter?" I ask, to which Nolan raises a brow.

"What about me?"

"You're a strong advocate for showing love in the lifestyle, but what about you? Have you ever been in love?"

His mouth flinches like it's ready to smile, but it slips away. "No, unfortunately I haven't."

"So, you're passionate about love in BDSM, but you've never experienced it? You've never had your own love on display on the main stage?"

"No, I haven't found the right person yet—the person that I'd want to put on display so that the world knows she's mine, but I have high hopes that one day I will."

I literally bite my tongue with my front teeth to keep from saying what I'm thinking. I don't want to ask if he's interested enough to test the waters with me, but it certainly crosses my mind. Instead of being too forward and embarrassing myself, I ask another question that I hope doesn't give me away.

"So, you're currently single?"

Nolan nods. "Yes."

"Are you looking?"

"I wouldn't say I'm looking or I'm not. I'm just living, and I'll be open to whatever comes along."

"What kind of qualities do you prefer in a girlfriend?"

Nolan tilts his head a bit, eyeing me carefully. Maybe my questions were enough to give me away after all.

"Interesting question," he begins, charging the air around me with his gaze. "While I'd obviously prefer a submissive in the lifestyle, the most important thing is that I end up with someone who knows themselves well. I want a person who isn't afraid to be open about who they are, or to explore new ways for us to express our feelings for each other. I want a connection that's deeper than what's on the surface. I want to earn my partner's trust and submission through actions that prove I'm worthy of that trust. So, I don't care if I have to take baby steps with someone when it comes to sadism and masochism. I'll gladly take it slow for the right person, because in the end, what we learn *together* is what will make us unbreakable."

When he looks at me, I can feel desire through his eyes. They seem to be an even brighter blue now, as if he's hypnotizing me, and I absolutely feel like I'm being put under his spell. Either I'm overthinking, or Nolan knows I'm interested in him. He can sense that I want to explore the lifestyle he cherishes. I want him to be my teacher, and he must be able to sense it in the air.

Feeling invigorated and emboldened by his eyes on me and the words he just spoke, I feel myself lose control. My ability to keep the interview centered around what the readers want to know slips through my fingers, replaced only by what I want. Fuck the readers. I want Nolan all to myself now.

"You're different today," he says. I blink my shock away with fluttering eyes, but I don't try to rein in how I feel now. I embrace it, swallowing it and letting the energy consume me. I don't know what it is, and it scares me ... which is why I *have* to explore it.

"Can I ask you to do me a favor?" I question. My voice shakes with nervousness, but I exhale and steady myself. I'm doing it. I'm going for it right now.

"Of course," Nolan replies. He leans forward and places his elbows on his knees, his black shirt straining to contain the muscles in his arms and shoulders.

"Tell me a story," I say.

He nods. "Another story? About what?"

"Before, you stated that your favorite toys were the ones that cause the most damage to the skin. Well, there are a lot of toys that could do that. I was wondering if you had a favorite."

"A favorite impact toy?"

"Yes."

Nolan smiles devilishly, sending heat radiating between my legs. I shift in my seat and cross one leg over the other.

"Flogger," he growls, his voice shifting to something low and animalistic. "The flogger is my favorite toy."

"Tell me about it," I say without holding back. "Tell me your favorite story."

"I'm not sure I understand."

"Surely you have a memory of a scene you conducted

using a flogger. I want to know your most cherished memory using your favorite toy."

Nolan licks his lips, and I can already tell that his mind is scrolling through his extensive catalog of BDSM scenes he has participated in, searching for the one he cherishes most. His eyes flicker and dart around the room, focusing on nothing at all until the moment he finds it. He lowers his head and looks up at me, and there might as well be devil horns sprouting from his head. The sadist in him has emerged.

"Are you sure you want to hear about it?" he asks, requesting my consent before giving me the dark details.

"Yes," I say, swallowing hard. "I'm sure."

Nolan's smile reaches his eyes as he leans back, settling in.

"Good," he says. "Then let's begin."

Chapter Eighteen

~ NOLAN ~

I was never a fan of having my Little One at my place, but on this day, I was teeming with anticipation. I could feel the blood squeezing through my veins as I rushed home, my cock already hard from just thinking about what I was going to do to her. A difficult week was coming to an end, and I needed this release. The fact that she had been the cause of most of my annoyance for the week was not lost on me. In fact, it was at the very forefront of my mind the entire drive, and it buttressed the sadistic fantasies I carried with me as I parked in the driveway and walked inside the house.

Her naked body greeted me the second I stepped through the door. She kneeled in my living room, completely nude, and the absolute embodiment of submissiveness. This was her greatest gift. The fact that my Little One could completely and fully submit to me is what kept me coming back to her. She was just as dark as me, and while other people clung to the light at the end of hard times, I needed the darkness. I needed to tighten my grip around the handle of a toy that could bruise and rip flesh, and let my arms work out my stress. When the world closed in on me, it was my darkness that kept me comfortable. It was my need to strike that kept me straight, and the Little One on her knees in front of me was always willing to give herself over to the darkness for me. I didn't love her, but I loved what she let me do to her.

"You ignored me today," I said as I sauntered into the house, unbuttoning my black blazer as I walked. Little One didn't speak. She kept her hands on her thighs and her eyes on me, clinging to my every word with pure obedience in her gaze. No matter what else happened during the day, she was mine now.

I tossed my blazer onto the couch next to her and sat down beside it. My Little One was kneeling in front of me, still facing the door as I leaned forward and untied my shoes. I took my time with each string, watching her the entire time. If she moved as much as an inch, I was ready to lash out. There were no toys in the living room, but I was ready to grab whatever was closest and brutalize her if she didn't obey the rules of our dynamic now.

"I texted you," I said as I slipped off each shoe and neatly placed them beside the couch. Pulling out my tucked shirt, I stood up in front of Little One and began to unfasten my belt only inches from her face. "I texted you four times, and you ignored each one. You were a brat, and you know what happens to brats, don't you?"

My Little One swallowed hard, drinking down fear and excitement. "Yes, Sir."

"Yeah? What happens to brats who ignore their Dominants?"

"They're punished."

"Yes," I say, just as I finish with my belt buckle and let my pants fall to the floor, exposing my aroused cock in all its glory. My thickness pulsated in front of her mouth, and her eyes flickered down to it for a brief, lustful second, before climbing up to meet my gaze. "Punishment is what happens to brats who annoy normal Doms, but I am not a normal Dom. Am I?"

"No, Sir."

"So, we both know you won't be punished, Little One. You are going to be brutalized. You will be abused and dehumanized. By the time I'm done, you will know who you belong to, and you'll never ignore me again. I don't give a fuck how busy you are. When I text or call, you answer because you belong to me. I own you. If you don't want to be owned by me, then say it now. This is your one chance to get it out."

I crouched down until we were eye to eye, a predator inches away from butchering its prey. "Say it, Little One. Don't hesitate."

"You own me, Sir," she responded in a whisper. "You still own me, and you always will."

"Always?" I asked, tilting my head.

"Always. I'm yours."

"Then why didn't you respond to me?"

"I was just upset," she said, and it annoyed me more than anything else. I knew what she was referring to, and it set my need to hurt her ablaze.

"Upset," I repeated as I stood up. "Fine. Ignoring me is how you responded to being upset. Let me show you what happens when I'm upset."

Before she could even think to prepare, my hand was already around her throat. I could hear her struggling to breathe beneath my grip as I squeezed while pushing my growing erection into her mouth with my other hand.

The second I was in her mouth, I began fucking it. This

wasn't making love. This was not sensual. It was brutal, bordering on painful even for me, but I didn't care. I needed everything to be hard on this day. I was pure aggression, and I plowed into her mouth relentlessly, relishing the sound of her gagging on my length. She was struggling to survive, and her hands quickly went up to my thighs to hold me. The very sight of her trying to control my movement sent fire rushing up my limbs. Little One knew the rules. If what I was doing was too much, she was to use her safe word. Her hands on my thighs was not the safe word, and I refused to respond to anything else. Then again, she did have my cock down her throat, but fuck it.

"Don't you dare fucking try to stop me," I screamed, yanking my dick out of her mouth and crouching down in front of her. "Put your motherfucking hands back where they belong, you fucking little slut. Now!"

"Yes, Sir. I'm sorry," she squeaked as I stood up again.

"Prove it. Open that fucking mouth."

My Little One did as she was told, and I didn't wait to start again. I slid my cock in and went back to work, using her mouth as my personal fuck toy until I felt the urge to come beginning to work itself up my legs. It was only then that I stopped and backed away, both of us panting.

"Don't fucking move," I commanded as I walked away with slobber and precum dripping from my cock.

From my bedroom, I could still hear her gasping for air, and I smiled because I knew it would only get worse for her. She had put me in this mood. She was the cause of it. She was my undoing, so I would be hers.

After ripping off my button-up, I went into my closet and opened the black locker in the corner. Bypassing the plethora of toys at the front of the locker, I grabbed a leash and collar, plus a wand vibrator and my favorite toy—a black-on-black flogger with leather rope tresses roughly two feet long, and thick leather strips on the end of each one. It's called the Cat O Nine Tails, and it's my absolute favorite toy to wield.

Completely naked, I stalked back into the living room holding all of my prized possessions, fighting back a grin as Little One's face melted into anxiety. She enjoyed me fucking her mouth before, and I knew it didn't matter how rough I was. Little One could take just about anything, but I'd never used the Cat O Nine Tails on her before. She eyed it closely as I placed the collar, leash, and vibrator on the couch next to her, but held onto the Nine Tails. Just for show, I let the tails dangle in front of her face like a pendulum. I let it hypnotize her, forcing her to wonder what they would feel like once they were whipped across her skin. I wanted her fear and she gave it to me. Usually, I would give her a small sample of what the material of a new toy would feel like so that she wouldn't be afraid, but not today. Today a brat was being broken by her Dominant, and she deserved to be afraid.

Once I was satisfied by the look of angst on Little One's face, I set the Nine Tails down and picked up the collar. I fastened it around her neck as tight as I could before it became too much and she passed out. I wanted her awake for the journey we were about to go on, but I cinched it tight enough so it took effort when she swallowed. I secured the leash to the ring on the collar and stood up, fully erect in front of Little One's face. I knew she wanted my cock, but she didn't deserve it, so I kept it just out of reach.

"You want it?" I asked, teasing my play thing.

"Yes, Sir," she said, panting.

I scoffed. "Do you deserve it?"

"No, Sir," she answered, but I was unmoved by her truthfulness. It was too late for that. Only savagery would make up for ignoring me.

"You're a fucking whore. Do you know that?" I asked as I tugged on the leash until it was taut.

"Yes, Sir."

"*Luckily for you, you're* my *whore,*" I said, before turning around and walking, pulling the leash with me. "*Now crawl, slut. Crawl, and show me that you remember who owns you.*"

I yanked the chain forward and my Little One followed me on her hands and knees like a good little whore. I walked my naked, slutty, little dog around the living room with nowhere to go, forcing her to obey me over and over again every time I stopped and started. I walked her into the kitchen and made her lick water out of a bowl, and made her sit beside me like a good girl, waiting for her owner to give her permission to move again. Time after time, I humiliated my Little One to reinforce my Dominance, and time after time, she obeyed.

"Good girl," I said once we returned to the living room.

"Thank you, Sir," she said, pressing her lips together.

"Are you happy?" I asked.

"Yes, Sir. Happy that I made you proud of me."

"Hmm," I scoffed. "Do you think you deserve pleasure now?"

"I deserve whatever you think I deserve, Sir."

I grinned. "Good answer. You're exactly right, and I think you deserve pleasure, but your pleasure will be laced with pain."

I left Little One on her knees while I plugged in the wand, then handed it to her.

"You have one rule now," I said, looking her directly in the eye. "No matter what happens, do not take this wand off of your clit. Keep it pressed there until I'm done using you. If you feel yourself about to come, you know what to do."

"Ask your permission, Sir."

"Exactly. Good girl. Now, turn it on and do as you were told."

She turned on the wand and immediately pressed it against her clit, letting out a soft moan before sealing her mouth shut and eyeing me again, awaiting my next instruction.

"How does it feel?" I asked, knowing what she would say.

"It feels so good, Sir."

"I'm glad. Hold on to that feeling once we begin. Now, crawl over to the couch and lay your torso on it, keeping the wand in place."

Without another word, Little One did exactly as she was told, crawling over to the couch while still holding the wand against her, and leaned over until her entire torso was on the couch, her ass up in the air for me to use however I wanted. In this position, I had total access to her backside. Her flesh was completely exposed for me to decorate, but these decorations would be additions to the bruises that I'd already left there from a previous scene. Tonight, however, would be worse.

Little One let out another moan. I could tell she didn't mean to, because she turned her head and shoved her face into the couch cushion, but I wasn't mad at the sound. I was glad the wand felt good to her, because when I lifted the Cat O Nine Tails, I knew I was going to unleash hell.

The weight of the flogger in my hand gave me a sense of power I couldn't describe. I felt superhuman—like a god ready to show the strength of his almighty hand. I squeezed my fingers around the shaft, savoring the sensation of the leather against my palm. Just holding it immediately put me in Dom Space—a euphoric mindset and world where I was consumed by the control until I felt like I had ingested ecstasy. I was ready. The sight of her beautiful skin, and the heaviness of the Nine Tails pushed me to the edge, and I jumped.

I raised the two-foot long tails over my head with a wrist-flick, and whipped the flogger back down across Little One's back. All nine of the tresses struck her and she jolted.

"What did I say?" I asked, my demeanor as serious as a death in the family.

"Hold the wand against my clit, Sir," she answered, breathing hard.

"That's right. Don't disappoint me by breaking the rule."

INTERVIEW WITH A SADIST

"I won't, Sir."

"Time will tell, Little One." I flicked my wrist again, harder this time, and the tails left multiple individual streaks across Little One's back. The squeal that escaped her mouth was almost unnoticeable, but I caught it. It was fine, as long as she didn't take the wand off her clit. I knew I was going to abuse her, and I wanted to make sure she felt some semblance of pleasure within all of the pain I was going to inflict.

I whipped her again, whirling the flogger in an arc that splashed leather across her ass. When she squealed this time, I could hear the pleasure in it and it made me rock hard.

There's a difference when someone squeals from pleasure and pain. It's deeper than when it's from satisfaction alone, because pain takes pleasure to an entirely new level. It spikes the endorphins for a millisecond, overwhelming the senses in a way that can only be understood by being felt. It's a level of sensation that can't be explained without knowing it for yourself.

I started a vicious rhythm with the Nine Tails, sending them crashing against Little One's backside over and over while she held the wand against her clit. After a few minutes, I noticed changes in her body. Her back became red and inflamed, while her pussy began to literally drip. The visual was almost too much to take, and I could barely contain myself. I was almost ready to fuck her senseless, but not yet, so I kept hitting her. After another minute, Little One's legs tightened and she arched her back, nearly caving in on herself.

"Sir," she called to me, and I could hear the question in her voice before she spoke. *"Can I please come?"*

I thought to deny her, but watching her come had always been my achilles heel. I couldn't get enough of seeing her body writhe and tremble beneath me. So, I allowed her to come, even if it was only for my own pleasure.

"Yes," I barked before whipping her again. *"Come for me, baby. Right fucking now."*

My Little One went into a series of convulsions that shook her entire being, and it was my distinct pleasure to bear witness to it. She shrieked like a fucking banshee into the couch, never dropping the vibrator.

Such a fucking good little slut.

My cock was so hard from watching her that it dripped precum without ever being touched. I was already tightroping an orgasm I hadn't even worked up to yet, and I couldn't wait any longer. I rubbed two fingers across Little One's soaking pussy, wetting my fingers with her juices before slithering it over the tip of my cock. Then, I positioned myself behind her and impaled my whore. She moaned as her body quivered again, and I waited, letting my cock slowly stretch her pussy out. I needed her ready, because once I started, I wasn't going to stop until I filled her with my cum.

"Don't move the wand, baby. No matter what," I reminded her, just before I began fucking her harder than I ever had.

I absolutely plowed into Little One's pussy with strokes that bordered on rage. I fucked her angrily, releasing all of my tension into each thrust so hard that our bodies slamming together quickly grew painful, but I didn't care. I grunted with each stroke, then lifted the Nine Tails and brought them raining down on her. They cracked onto her flesh, sending a dark streak of gorgeous red color scattering across her back. Little One wailed, but still managed to obey me.

She pressed the vibrator against her clit, using it to distract from the pain as I flogged her mercilessly. I gripped her body with my left hand, and swung the flogger with my right, the tails whooshing in the air like the crack of lightning in the sky before striking an innocent victim on the ground. Little One screamed for me, and I soaked it in, watching as her back reddened more and more, and her pussy splashed from the pounding of my cock.

INTERVIEW WITH A SADIST

"Fuck yes!" I roared to the heavens as I kept my eyes on Little One's damaged skin.

"Oh, god. How? ... I'm ... Sir, can I please come?" she yelled with an urgency that told me it was already too late for her to turn back now.

"Yes! Fucking come all over me. Soak the fucking floor with it, baby. I want it everywhere." I yelled as I swung the Nine Tails again.

Little One absolutely exploded. The scream she released rose from her gut and came out like she was being gripped by death itself. She quaked uncontrollably until her legs gave out and I had to hold her up, my muscles burning from the beautiful work being put in. This was worth the price of exhaustion. I even managed to swing the Nine Tails again, and it landed on her ass so hard that her skin opened.

I paused, eyeing the damage I had done. All nine tails of the flogger had landed on her ass, but three of them left behind open wounds—three streaks of blood spread across her right ass cheek. The sight of it sent me into a spiral, and I felt woozy from the rush of adrenaline. My cock stiffened and I was taken over by the sudden urge to go all out. I dropped the flogger on the floor and placed my right hand on her ass—right where the gashes were. Her blood smeared across my fingers as I began fucking her again, and it was only ten thunderous strokes before I was undone.

"Shit. I'm going to fucking come inside you." I bellowed, and like a fucking goddess, Little One managed to throw it back, stroking my cock with her pussy as I unloaded my entire soul into her. Now I was the one screaming like I was being tortured, and when I finished, both of us collapsed onto the floor.

Surely, there was sweat, cum, and blood soaking into the couch and hardwood, but I didn't care an ounce. There wasn't a single bone in my body or hair on my head that would've *changed what we'd done, even though I knew Little One would be in pain for days after.*

I was glad, actually. It was good that she'd be sore. It was perfect that she wouldn't be able to sit down without flinching. Now, she wouldn't forget who she belonged to. No matter what would end up happening to us, she wouldn't forget me for as long as she fucking lived.

Chapter Nineteen

The sound of blood rushing in my ears is so loud I can't hear anything else. Luckily, Nolan isn't speaking anymore anyway, his story having come to a seductive end that has me sitting on pins and needles. My heart races, my thoughts scatter, and any semblance of control I had when I woke up this morning has disintegrated into nothingness. All hope is lost, and I feel nothing more than desire. Desire to learn. Desire to explore. Desire to know what pain feels like.

The sound of my labored breathing fills the space between us as our eyes meet. Nolan smirks as he watches me, and I'm sure I see entertainment dancing in his eyes. He's so fucking unreadable it terrifies me.

I clear my throat, hoping it will force me back into the middle of my lane, but it's no use. I'm still veering off the road, and Nolan will be who I crash into.

"Is that a true story?" I ask, leaning forward and turning off the recorder on the table. "Or, are you just messing with me?"

"Messing with you? Why would I do that?" Nolan questions, somehow managing to sound playful and serious at the same time.

"You know why," I blurt out, shocking myself. My stomach churns from the internal battle raging within me, making me feel sick. It's like watching a movie where the side I'm rooting for is slowly being killed, and I know they won't make it to the end. The wound is too deep. The damage has been done, and it's only a matter of time before it's all over.

"I really don't," Nolan says with raised eyebrows and a shrug. "But I do know you seem flustered. Are you okay, Miss Barrett?"

"I told you not to call me that," I fire back.

My skin sparks with pinpricks. I sit up in my seat and start to move around nervously, fidgeting like an anxious child and fumbling my hands around, reaching for support that isn't there. Every time I look at Nolan's face, I lose more and more of myself. I want and need more of him. I need to know what it's like. I'm being changed from within and I can't stop it. I wasn't raised to feel desire like this, and I've been taught to hate myself for letting it win, but I don't hate anything right now. How can I hate something that consumes me in the best way imaginable?

"Bree," Nolan calls to me, but his voice sounds distant. "Seriously, are you okay?"

"No," I snap. "You know what the fuck you're doing."

Nolan's eyes double in size. "Wow. I didn't know you had that in you."

"What? You didn't know I had *what* in me?"

Now he smirks as he looks me up and down. "Fire."

His words are gasoline to the fire he speaks of. He pours it on and forces me into an uncontrollable blaze.

"Goddamn it. I don't get it. I don't understand this," I bark, standing up. I begin to pace around the room with my hands on my hips, furious that I can't douse the heat he has worked me into. Nolan, on the other hand, stays seated.

"You don't understand *what*?" he asks calmly, which only makes me want it more.

"What is wrong with you?" I bellow. I feel myself trip and fall over the edge of my sanity, and I'm plummeting now. There's no climbing back up.

"Me?" Nolan says. "With all due respect, Miss Barrett, I'm not the one pacing around the office with flushed skin."

"My name is Bree, and I don't understand how you can sit there all calm and collected after telling me a story that ... *bothered* me so much. It's not possible to be the apotheosis of control, and also flog a woman so much and so hard that she bleeds. You can't sit here looking like that and also get off on someone's blood being smeared across your fingers. You can't. You just *can't*! I don't get how any of what you just said could possibly feel good to anyone. She came? Are you fucking kidding me? What is this—spicy romance written by a man? This woman was just so turned on by your ridiculous good looks and rock-hard man-pecks that she had a fucking orgasm from you beating her? No way. I don't buy it, and I'm not going to publish it. I ... you ... stop smiling!"

At some point during my ranting, Nolan has turned his body toward me and is smiling in amusement. Is he doing this on purpose to get a rise out of me? There are too many unanswered questions, and I can't fucking stand it.

He makes me feel like I'm somebody else. I'm a stranger to myself when I'm in this man's presence, but there's a strange part of me that likes all of the new things he makes me feel. I'm excited, flustered, nervous, and so completely turned on by him. When I leave, it all goes away, only to return the second we're face to face again. Nolan thrills me. He makes me feel alive, but the person I've always been can't survive this.

With every passing second, the woman I used to be

before I met Nolan sinks further beneath the waves. If I let her go completely, she'll never come back from the dark abyss, and that scares me because she is all I've ever known. But I can't help what Nolan has shown me. He helped to open my eyes, and now I don't want to close them. I want to see more, and if that means the old me must drown, then so be it.

I stand in the middle of the large office with my head down, looking at my feet so I don't have to see Nolan's unfair, beautiful face. I try to corral my thoughts and focus, needing to feel like I'm standing on solid ground instead of the quicksand I've been trying to escape all this time. I think about Melissa and Teagan. I think about my upbringing. I even think about Chase and Octavia. My daily life consists of being pulled in different directions all the time, and trying to please all sides. It's no wonder I've been confused and stressed for so long. This isn't living life for myself. I've been living it for them, and I want it to stop. I *need* it to stop for my own good. So, instead of searching for solid ground, I stop pacing and let the quicksand pull me under.

"Show me," I say. The room becomes so silent that I'm sure Nolan is holding his breath, but I continue. "Show me how it's possible for pain to become pleasure. Show me how you could make a woman come while you hurt her. Show me how you degrade someone by walking them around on a leash, and still manage to make them love you so much that they'd allow you to flay their backside. Show me what this world is, Nolan.

"I don't mean to be so forward, and I apologize for being unprofessional. I was supposed to be here for the story, but you've opened my eyes and mind in a way I never knew anyone ever could, and I can't go back—back to sitting at a table with my friends from college making fun of anything different from our personal experiences—back to being fearful of anything new. I won't go back, so show me, Nolan. Please."

He looks at me with awe in his face at first, but then he sinks into something different. He's still calm and restrained, but I see something else in his eyes now. Excitement.

"Bree, do you know what you're saying right now?" he asks.

I nod. "Yes."

"It's my strong belief that once you step over this threshold, it's nearly impossible to cross back over. Do you understand that?"

"Yes."

Nolan nods as if he can't believe this is real, before asking, "What exactly are you asking me to do right now? Be specific."

My heart pumps hard and fast, making me lightheaded. My breathing becomes erratic, and I'm gripped by fear. This is it. This is where I let the old me sink into permanent darkness, never to be seen or heard from again. This is where the new me takes over. I swallow hard as I realize how deep this is, and I suddenly feel emotional. It's the bitter-sweet sadness I feel, like watching a friend slip away but believing they're going to a better place.

Goodbye, Old Bree. I've got it from here.

"I want you to flog me," I say. My voice sounds foreign, and the power I feel is brand new.

Nolan raises an eyebrow, watching me closely.

"You want me to *flog you*?" he asks.

I don't hesitate. I no longer will. "Yes."

"Here?"

"Yes."

"Now?"

"Yes."

He lets my words wash over him, taking a moment to

analyze everything, and I wait patiently. When he stands up, I swallow my fear and keep my feet planted. I will not run back to who I was.

Nolan walks over to me, keeping his eyes locked onto mine until he's only inches away. We make an unspoken agreement with just a look, and I see the moment he accepts that a new Bree has just come to life. He tilts his head downward, cutting his eyes up to me, and that's when I see it. The Dominant emerges. The sadist steps forward, pushing the professional Nolan aside.

"Okay," he growls, his voice a low rumble. "It'd be my pleasure."

Swept Out To Sea

Chapter Twenty

When he steps closer to me, the old Bree screams from the depths of my stomach that I should step back. I can hear her voice like a faint whisper in the wind, but I ignore her. She's merely a memory now, and after this moment, she'll be completely gone.

I don't step back when Nolan approaches me. I hold my ground and meet his gaze, which has turned dark and hot. I feel an urge to do whatever he says—go where he tells me to go. He's a black hole—massive and pulling me in, sucking up all of the light I thought I had before I stepped across the threshold of The Black Collar. Once we're face to face, there is no office. There are no people downstairs at the bar. There is no world outside the five-foot space the two of us occupy. There is only here and now.

"Are you afraid?" he asks, and something about the way he says it tells me he hopes the answer is yes.

"No ... not really," I stammer. *No* is too definitive, so *not really* is more accurate.

"We hardly know each other, Bree," Nolan says as his eyes

begin to drift down the length of my body, starting at my neck and sliding down slowly, inch by inch. "You're investing a lot of trust in someone you don't know well—someone who will gladly hurt you if only to see your flawless skin marred by my touch. You're prey standing before a famished lion, and while it's true that I would tear you limb from limb, I need you to understand that I would never do it out of rage, anger, or spite. More importantly, I would never do anything without your consent. Ever. It doesn't matter how much I've fantasized about caressing you before slapping you. The fact that I've dreamed of bruising and breaking your flesh means nothing. Without your explicit consent, my desires don't exist. They have no strength. I have no power without your permission. Do you understand that? I need you to comprehend it fully."

My heart revs at his words, because that was the most terrifying and romantic thing I've ever heard. I stare at him in awe for longer than I should, only because I don't understand how he could be so sweet at the exact moment of being sadistic and brutal. Even crazier is the fact that I've never been more turned on in my life. How? Fucking *how* is that possible? How is *he* possible?

"You've given me permission to flog you," he goes on, his confidence growing with each completed sentence. "You've asked me to show you how to extract pleasure from pain, and how someone can come while being hurt. That's exactly what I'm going to do. Today, we will not move to the right or left of your specific request, and after we're finished, you're free to continue talking to me or not. The decision will be up to you. As for me, I simply appreciate the honor of you allowing me to be the one to destroy you."

I suck in an astonished breath as Nolan closes the gap between us and places a hand on my hip, squeezing it gently.

"You want me to flog you," he says. "Why? Do you desire pain?"

"Yes," I answer, my breath shuddering. "I want to learn about it. I want to understand it."

"You want me to be the one to inflict it on you?"

"Yes ... please," I reply, my voice reduced to a quivering whisper.

Nolan raises an eyebrow as he reaches up and pulls down the straps to my dress, leaving them dangling at my sides while the rest of the material clings to my torso, holding on for dear life. The white turtleneck beneath my pinafore dress still covers my entire upper half, but I don't want it to. I want him to have access to all of me.

"Say that again," Nolan commands as he begins pulling the rest of my dress down my waist, crouching until his face is at my crotch and sending waves of heat scattering throughout my body.

With my head aimed up at the ceiling, I repeat, "Please."

"Yes," he whispers, just as the rest of my dress falls to the floor, leaving me in nothing but my turtleneck, black panties, and heels. I lift one leg at a time to step out of the dress, and when I raise each foot, Nolan removes my heels. Just as I think he's about to take off everything else and expose me completely, he stands up. "Don't move."

"Okay," I answer, and Nolan's eyes flash red hot as he glares at me, but he doesn't say anything. It's as if he is unhappy with my response, but instead of reacting, he walks over to the fancy cabinet in the corner of the room and opens the doors.

I watch as he reaches inside and carefully extracts a flogger with a black handle and red tails. From here, I can see that the many tails on the flogger are fairly short, maybe eighteen inches at most, and they look soft, but I know that can't be

INTERVIEW WITH A SADIST

right. I eye the toy closely as Nolan also pulls out a black wand vibrator and walks back to me.

"Come with me," he says, holding out a hand. I wrap my fingers around his palm and allow the most gorgeous man I've ever met to escort me back over to the couch, where he lays the flogger and vibrator on the table next to my recorder.

"Kneel on the couch," he says, his voice commanding and lustful.

"But ... my underwear. Should I take them off?" I ask, and he steals the rest of the air in my lungs with a stone-cold look. He doesn't like being questioned or disobeyed—not when the Dominant sadist is in control. He doesn't have to say another word. I move forward and kneel on the couch.

"Lean forward ... and hold this," he commands before handing me the black wand vibrator. He plugs it into an outlet next to the couch and comes back to me just as my nerves reach the peak of their excitement and anxiety. "The rules are simple, Bree. You will hold this vibrator against your clit while I flog you. I'm going to talk you through it, but if at any point you want to stop, you simply have to say it."

"You mean, like, a safe word?" I ask.

"Yes. Do you have one you'd like to use?"

"Umm ... no, I can't come up with one. You choose."

"Okay. Your ... *our* safe word will be ... goddess. Saying the safe word is like invoking your powers as the submissive. You're in control—not me. When you say the word goddess, even in a whisper, everything stops. No guilt. No shame. Just support. Do you understand?"

Once again in awe of Nolan, I whisper, "Yes."

"Good. Your only job now is to breathe," Nolan says. He moves closer to me and places a hand on my cheek, caressing it gently like a husband supporting his wife through labor. "You're extremely nervous right now, so your entire body is going to be more sensitive to pain. It's your fear, and you have to breathe and relax your way through it. I know we don't know each other well, but you have to trust me. This is what I do, and I've got you. You're safe with me, Bree. We won't begin until you say so."

As I look at Nolan sitting next to me with such patience, I wonder if my astonishment is showing on my face. My mind baffles with wild thoughts that bounce around in my skull at random, trying to calculate how a man could possibly be this way. He's gorgeous, sincere, sweet, and caring, with the added bonus of being able to empathize with me. At the same time, he's a fucking Dominant who wants to manhandle me. He wants to show me pleasure like I've never seen it before. How is it possible for all of this to be rolled up into one man?

Nolan watches me closely, without an ounce of agitation or impatience in his face. He waits for me while I take deep breaths to try to calm my nerves. He raises an eyebrow and smirks after I briefly close my eyes and open them again. His calm, controlled demeanor helps me rein in my fears, and before I know it, I'm prepared to start.

"Okay," I say. "I'm ready."

Nolan licks his lips. "Okay. Take a deep breath."

I suck in a breath as he reaches over and grabs the cord to the wand, and just as I release it, He flicks the switch, sending powerful vibrations through the machine. It rattles my hand, buzzing quietly in my grasp, and he places his hand on the wand and guides it up for me, pressing it directly on my panties, where it vibrates my clit perfectly.

"Oh, god," I whisper, my eyes closing on their own.

Too focused on my own pleasure, I don't hear the moment he gets up from the couch. All I hear is the low hum of the wand and my own ecstasy-laced thoughts about how good it feels. When I finally open my eyes and realize he's gone, I expect to feel the sudden sting of the flogger tails crashing against my ass. Instead, what I feel is the soft, gentle caress of the tails being rubbed across my butt from top to bottom.

"This is what they feel like," Nolan says from behind me. Admittedly, it's hard to listen with the wand still massaging my clit, but I manage. "The tails on this particular flogger are made of suede. I hope you imagined they'd feel hard and rough, so that you can learn not to listen to your fear when it is created by the unknown. Just because you've never felt it before doesn't mean you need to be afraid of it. Close your eyes and focus on both sensations—the wand on your clit, and the tails on your perfect, flawless ass."

Nolan pauses a moment, continuing to rub the tails of the flogger across my skin while I masturbate with the wand. The combination of the suede and wand feels incredible already, and I immediately have no regrets about taking this leap.

"Now take another deep breath," Nolan commands.

I suck in air, and as I'm releasing it, I'm jolted by the sudden slap of the flogger. Now it's my turn to pause. I freeze to let my thoughts collect, and I realize ... it didn't hurt. At least not that particular slap. It stung a bit, but it didn't *hurt*. I ... think it felt ... *good*.

Nolan whips the flogger again, harder this time, and the sting makes the muscles in my legs tighten. I end up squeezing the wand between my thighs, sending ripples throughout my entire lower body, and out of nowhere, I moan.

What the fuck? I can't believe the words whirring around in my head. When I'm finally able to grab and focus on a phrase, I'm stunned by it. It does feel good, and I fucking like it.

Nolan uses the flogger on me again, even harder, and it all happens again. My muscles tighten, my clit throbs, a moan escapes my mouth, and my brain goes into a frenzy. I *love* the sting. I love the way my body reacts to it before my mind does. I love it. I crave it. I want more of it.

"Tell me how it feels," Nolan demands, his voice tighter than ever before. I can hear his breathing picking up as he lets his sadistic side run free.

"It's so good," I answer.

"Does it hurt?"

"Yes, but also no. I can't explain it."

"You don't have to, Princess. I already know."

Did he just call me his princess?

Nolan effortlessly flicks his wrist again, but this time he does it twice, sending the tails of the flogger whipping against me two times in succession. I moan louder than I expected and start to wonder if Ethan or Jackson can hear me from the bar downstairs. What if Maddy is listening with her ear against the door? I'm terrified by the thought of us being heard, but also a little turned on by it, and the last thing I need is to be any more turned on.

My blood courses through my veins like a violent river as Nolan flogs me again. After a moment, the pain of the sting begins to increase from being hit so many times, but it only sends me closer to the edge of bliss. I jolt with each strike—my legs flinching, my stomach tightening, my pussy throbbing every time he hits me, and I feel the oncoming orgasm growing in my stomach more and more.

"Do you like it?" he asks rhetorically.

"I love it," I answer, just before another smack pushes me further to the edge.

"You want it again?"

"Yes, please."

He hits me again, and I jerk forward. "Yes!" I scream.

Fuck, I'm losing control. They're all going to hear.

Another whack of the flogger shocks my muscles, and I moan like a fucking porn star.

Fuck it. Let them hear.

I suck in a deep breath as pin pricks and needles spread across every inch of my flesh. My eyes squeeze shut, shooting white specks across the dark tunnel of my vision.

Another splash of the suede flogger tails punches me, and I fall over the cliff.

"Oh god!" I yell.

"Yes! Come for me," Nolan growls from behind. He flicks his wrist once, twice, three fucking times before stepping forward and smacking my ass with the palm of his hand so hard I nearly fall over.

"Goddamn it ... I'm ... coming!" I blare as my entire world erupts into fireworks.

White light explodes in my vision, illuminating the darkness behind my eyes until I see a galaxy of bright stars. I lose all control of my muscles, and my legs quiver so hard I can't hold myself up. I drop the wand onto the couch as my knees knock together and I convulse. My entire consciousness spins until I can barely tell up from down or left from right. I'm rocked like I've never felt before, and I crash onto the couch facedown when it's all over.

Tears fill my eyes even though they're closed, and I hear Nolan moving around in front of me. I'm almost too embarrassed to look at him, because I've never had an orgasm do that to me, but when I open my eyes, he's kneeling in front of me with sweat on his brow.

"Are you okay?" he asks, which only makes me feel even more embarrassed.

Panting, I answer, "Yeah."

"Good," Nolan says. "You were incredible."

I swallow hard as I realize my panties are soaking wet. Fuck, I knew I should've taken them off.

"That was ... I don't even know," I say through ragged breathing. "It was *unreal*."

"*You* were unreal," Nolan says. "You're a natural."

"A natural?"

"Oh, yes," he says. "You took it so well, it's no wonder you've been interested in the lifestyle. You're a masochist, Bree."

Hearing the word is like finally being diagnosed. It's an answer to the questions I've been wondering about myself for so long, and I've never felt more relieved.

I could try to argue and deny it, but it'd be a lie. I've pondered and speculated about this a long time, and after experiencing it, I know for sure now. Nolan is right. I enjoy pain, and I know without the slightest doubt that it takes pleasure to heights that can't be reached with normal sex. Nolan has helped me to step over the boundary and into a new life. He has cemented New Bree's place, and everything I was before is gone. It's behind me now. There's no going back, and there is no part of me that wants to.

Nolan runs his fingers through my hair as I lay my head on the cushion, still undressed from the waist down and exhausted from the workout.

"Talk to me," he says. "Tell me what you're thinking."

"Thank you," I reply, because besides a brand new sense of satisfaction, gratitude is all I feel.

"For what?"

"For showing me the truth," I say. "For showing me who I've always been. For guiding me. For accepting me."

Nolan grins. "You don't have to thank me for that. Like I said—it's an honor."

Even through building up the strength to pull myself together and get dressed, I know something. A fact plays on repeat in my head as I slip my dress back on, and Nolan cleans off the wand I just soaked. Through fixing my hair and makeup, and letting enough time pass that the redness in my skin dissipates, and we prepare to walk out of the office, I know everything just changed. I'll never look at sex the same way again. I'll never have a negative thing to say about things I don't understand. I've become a different person, and no matter what happens, I know there is no going back.

Thanks to Nolan Carter, my life will never be the same, and this is only the beginning.

Chapter Twenty-One

I'm sore as I walk into Starbucks on my lunch break. Each step I take sends a dull pain through my ass cheeks, reminding me of what Nolan and I did yesterday in his office. The pain keeps the memory at the forefront of my mind, and I continue seeing the images of us together behind my eyes every time I blink. Nolan holds the red-tailed flogger while I'm on my knees on the couch, my top half bent over while I'm holding a black wand between my legs.

I can still feel the sting of the tails. I can hear the crack of the wind as Nolan flicks his wrist and sends the tresses whirling around in an arc of electricity that shocks my entire body, tightening my muscles and shooting scorching hot pleasure through my veins. I can still feel the ripple effect of the orgasm that nearly sent me into another dimension. It's all right there on the surface, poking and prodding me with every step as I walk into the small restaurant toward the table where Melissa and Teagan await, already eating together.

The two of them resemble angels with their golden blonde hair and statuesque skin. Melissa is in a white cardigan, while Teagan is rocking a teal blouse with matching earrings.

When I sit down, they smile simultaneously and sip their iced coffee in sync like twins. Once again, I look like the odd woman out with my dark hair, and green, geo print blouse.

"Hey, sorry I'm late," I say. "It has been a struggle at work lately, to say the least. Chase is already looking for my next story and I'm not even finished with this one."

They think I don't see when they glance at each other, but I do. The two of them exchange a silent look, and I get the feeling they've communicated about something before I arrived.

"So, how has that been going, by the way?" Melissa asks. Her eyes latch onto me like a mother inspecting her child's face for signs of fibbing.

I'm not sure how to respond. I flip through images in my mind of everything I've seen and heard at The Black Collar, and each picture comes with the feelings it birthed in the moment: meeting Nolan for the first time, strolling through the club and seeing the joy and respect everyone had for one another, seeing the love on the main stage as spectators gathered to view what true BDSM is supposed to look like, and embracing the lash of the flogger as it tortured me with the most intoxicating pleasure.

This is a situation where Old Bree would respond with words of vitriol. I would lash out at people I don't know and call their lifestyle by horrible names, invoking laughter from my friends, who would agree without evidence that anything I've said is actually true. This is what we do. This is what our friend group has always done, so stepping outside of those lines would be driving a bulldozer through the house we've all shared since we met. There's only one problem—Old Bree is gone.

"It's umm ... it has actually been going really well," I reply, and you would think those words were a giant vacuum sucking the air out of the establishment. Clocks stop ticking, people stop moving, the fucking air conditioner shuts off, leaving nothing behind but silence and fiery glares.

"Wow," Melissa says with raised brows. "That's great. So, you're enjoying it then?"

"Yes," I respond quickly. Heat prickles up my neck, but I don't shy away from the feeling. I embrace it. "I've loved every second of it, actually. Nolan has been beyond anything I ever could've imagined, and the club is incredible."

They look at each other again, sending a sick feeling straight to my gut. I feel Old Bree flinch down there, but I ignore her. She has no power here, so seeing them exchange eye contact annoys me.

"What?" I ask, furrowing my brows..

"The club is *incredible*?" Melissa says. "You're talking about the BDSM club with the tight leather outfits, and the sadistic weirdos who like to cut people open and use their blood for lube? That club?"

My face morphs into an expression of disbelief and annoyance.

"Where did you get the idea that they all wear tight, leather outfits and get off on blood play? It's not like that," I say, my eyes glued to Melissa.

"Oh, you know the terminology now?" Melissa questions in the world's most mocking tone. "Blood play?"

"It's not *knowing the terminology*, genius. It's common sense."

"Well, maybe you should explain it to us since you know so much, because all I see is pervs and psychos who like to hurt people."

"That's just an uneducated way of thinking about it," I say, trying my best to explain without going off. "It's really about love, commitment, and trust. It takes a lot for a person to trust someone enough to let them have full control over their body. It's all about consent."

"Really?" Teagan blurts out.

I glower at her. "Yes, Teagan, really," I state, my head snapping over.

"What's with all this attitude, Bree?" Melissa says, followed by her sidekick, Teagan.

"Yeah, why are you so defensive?" she squeaks like an annoying little mouse.

"I'm not being defensive," I start to explain. "I just think it's weird that you have such a strong opinion about something you know nothing about."

"Oh, now you're a BDSM expert because you did an interview with a club owner?" Melissa snips. "I know just as much as you do."

"No, Melissa, you *don't*," I fire back. My words hold a little too much aggression and truth, because Melissa's jaw tightens as she tilts her head to the side the way she does when she has figured something out.

"Wow," she exclaims, looking back and forth between Teagan and me. "I think *somebody* may have gotten a little *too* close to their subject, Teagan."

"That's what it looks like to me," Teagan cosigns.

"Ever since you started this interview you've been acting different," Melissa goes on. "I was curious, but now I *know* you've changed. You've turned into one of them."

"Them? Who the fuck is *them*?" I ask with a snarl.

Both blonde girls flinch, but it's Melissa who speaks while Teagan just shakes her head.

"You don't even talk the same," she says. "So, you don't have a problem with those perverts? It's a sex club, Bree. You're cool with that now?"

"I'm cool with having the correct information before I judge people, Melissa, that's all. And yes, Nolan has taught me a thing or two about the lifestyle that I certainly didn't know before, and knowing what I do now, I don't look at all of it the same as I did. I understand it now more than you will ever know. So, if you're looking for someone to sit here and talk shit about people for no reason, I guess you have Teagan for that."

"Hey," Teagan says sharply—but who gives a fuck? I lift myself up from my seat and glare at them both.

"Wow, Bree. I'm shocked that you've allowed yourself to become one of those freaks," Teagan says, tossing her words at me like grenades.

"You're going to regret it," Melissa adds. "Mark my words, there will be a day that you regret falling into the life of sex and drugs. Wait and see."

I know I have plenty of reasons to get mad, but sometimes all you can do is shake your head at people's audacity, because that's all they deserve.

"God, you're stupid," I say with a humorless laugh. "I never saw it before, but I was different then."

"You got that right," Melissa says. "The Bree I went to college with would never sink this low—affiliating herself with lowlifes, and throwing away her friendships in the process. I don't even know who you are anymore."

I smile as I turn on my heel, aiming my body toward the door.

"Well, you're right about one thing, Melissa," I say as I start to walk away, still looking over my shoulder. "You don't know who I am anymore. The old Bree is gone, and the new Bree doesn't need anymore of your bullshit. Goodbye."

I walk out of Starbucks and let the door to the restaurant slam shut behind me—the perfect metaphor for what just happened to that chapter of my life.

Chapter Twenty-Two

I sit at my desk with my face resting on my hand. To say I'm stressed would be an understatement, and my mind is a swirling vortex of confusion as I stare at a blank Google Doc on my computer screen. I guess that's the thing about pushing the old, dated version of yourself to the wayside—the new you is like a baby just coming into consciousness. Your new eyes see everything as bright and shiny, but it is also brand new to you. Your sense of direction is thrown off because you're navigating the world for the first time, and you're unsure of how to operate. This is my life right now, and it's beautiful and brutal. I approach everything I see with new vision and open-mindedness, but I have no sense of familiarity, no sense of comfort, no sense of home.

Old Bree was a great journalist who knew how to approach her career. New Bree keeps thinking about how good it felt to embrace pain and succumb to her impulses and desires. New Bree craves the thing that brought her to life, and that is her masochism. New Bree doesn't know how to pick up the story that Old Bree started, because the thought process is completely different now. Unlike Old Bree, I've experienced the sensation of being flogged and made to orgasm. I've witnessed the beauty behind the curtain of BDSM. I'm not some naive girl approaching the story with an uneducated pessimism. I'm wide awake with lessons I'll never forget, and I can't write this story the way Old Bree planned to before Nolan and The Black Collar came into the picture. I have to start anew. Unfortunately, I don't know what the fuck that means.

As I stare at the screen in front of me, I'm bombarded by memories from Old Bree's life with Melissa and Teagan. There were some really good times back in college, and it saddens me now that everything has shifted so quickly. None of this was on purpose, so to approach the table today with a mindset that I never saw coming was as much of a shock for me as I'm sure it was for them. Before Nolan, I could never relate to anyone living a lifestyle I'd never encountered, but seeing things in person forces one's perspective to shift.

When Chase handed me this assignment, it was never my intention to discredit The Black Collar. As closed-minded as I was, I went into the story as receptive as I could possibly be, intent on gathering the information and seeing it all for myself. Obviously, I didn't think seeing it would result in experiencing it, but now that we're here, I think a shift is required.

"Girl, you look like you're in here stressed to the max," Octavia's voice booms into the cubicle from behind me. When I spin around to look at her, all the stress I'm feeling must be written across my face in bold letters, because she flinches when she sees me. "Damn, Bree. You okay?"

"Hi. Yeah, I'm fine. Just a frustrating lunch," I admit, but saying it out loud somehow makes me feel worse. It's okay to think it, but saying it out loud makes it real.

"Oh?" Octavia says as she pulls the chair from across the aisle to sit down. "What'd you do, work through lunch?"

I scoff. "I wish. That would've been better than spending the hour arguing with Melissa and Teagan about how much *I've changed* since I started The Black Collar story. After today, I'm not even sure if the three of us are still friends. Well, there's no separating those two, so I guess I'm the odd one out."

Octavia huffs and leans back in her chair, arms crossed. When I look at her face, I can see she's thinking hard about something. Her eyes bounce back and forth between me and whatever far-away thought she's envisioning, and I'm sure she's struggling with what to say about my so-called friends. Octavia has always been nice to me, but I'm not dumb—I know she has never liked Melissa and Teagan. However, out of respect for me, she has kept those feelings to herself. While I've always appreciated it, I'm ready to hear how she really feels.

"It's okay," I tell her. "I know you've never liked them. It's cool if you're honest about it. Your perspective might've kept me from a lot of heartache in the past."

Octavia exhales, still looking at me suspiciously, before chuckling. "Well, if you *insist*. You're right, I've never liked those bitches! Girl, they're so bougie. I don't know how you stand it, because I've never thought you were anything like them. Ever since they looked at me funny at that damn Christmas party, I've felt some type of way about them. They don't deserve you, Bree, but I understand they're your college girlies. Sorry, let me dial it down. I know they're your friends. But, I mean, you did *insist*."

Both of us laugh at the expense of my friends ... *ex*-friends, which is exactly what I needed. This day has been annoying enough, so it's good to smile at the ridiculousness of it all.

"I know they're a mess," I say, still smiling. "But I've known them a long time, and we sort of grew up in the same way, so we had that in common. Their problem is that they never learned another way to think. They're stuck seeing the world the same way they did when they first went off to college. But, things change—at least they're supposed to. At some point, we have to learn how to break away from only considering the things we were taught, because what I've come to realize is that a lot of the stuff I was told as a kid was actually bullshit. I had to evaluate things with my own eyes to see them as they truly are. Melissa and Teagan just aren't capable of that, and it sucks that I can't tell the women I've known for so long that I'm going through something drastic. At the time I need to talk to them most, they don't have my back. It just sucks."

Octavia places a hand on my knee, and I'm suddenly surprised at how serious she becomes. Not that I expect her to always be in a joyous, playful mood, but she usually is. I'm not sure Octavia realizes how much she brightens up our entire office, so to see her suddenly switch gears catches me off guard.

"I know you haven't known me since college," she begins. "But if you're going through something, you can always talk to me, Bree. So, let's forget all about the office right now. Fuck Chase. Fuck the stories. Fuck these ugly ass people who keep walking past us looking in the cubicle being nosy. Fuck everything else. Let's just talk. Tell me what's up."

I smile, because all this time I've been stuck on Melissa and Teagan, when Octavia has been the best friend in my life since I started working here. I just didn't realize it until now.

"You're awesome, you know that?" I say, beaming.

"Oh, I know," Octavia quips. "Now, for real, what's up?"

"Okay. So, you know I've been working on finishing up the story on The Black Collar."

"Of course."

"Well, things have sort of shifted between the owner and me."

Octavia's eyes bulge. "Shifted how?"

"Like ... we've done a little more than talk about the club and his lifestyle. He has *shown* me a couple of things."

Octavia pinches her lips together as she stands up and walks into the aisle with her hands on her hips. I fight back a laugh as she walks into the cubicle next to mine, sits down, exhales, stands up, and comes back to my cubicle, reclaiming her seat.

"What was that? You okay?" I ask.

"Oh, I'm fine," she replies. "I just needed to keep myself from screaming, and that was the only way I could think to use up the energy. I'm good now. So, you hooked up with the club owner?"

I lean in to whisper. "Well, not exactly. Over time, I've just become more and more fascinated by everything he has shown me and talked about. I started to feel like I was going to implode if I didn't experience some of it for myself. I was intrigued beyond measure, and I needed to know. So, I asked him to show me about the thing I was interested in."

"Don't you dare hold out on me," Octavia whisper-screams. "What was the thing you were interested in?"

I hesitate momentarily, knowing she might lose it, but I've come this far. "I wanted to experience some pain, so I asked Nolan to flog me."

"Girl," Octavia says, before stopping herself and getting up again. She walks out of the cubicle and down the hall, before reaching the end and doing a U-turn to come back. Once she's seated again, she continues. "Cool. Cool. So, then what happened?"

Giggling, I go on. "Well, he agreed, and said we wouldn't do anything other than what I asked for. I was totally fine with that, so he asked me to bend over on his couch. Then, he flogged me ... while forcing me to hold a vibrator on my clit ... until I came ... really fucking hard."

Octavia nearly falls out of her chair.

"Bree!" she squeals, struggling mightily to keep her voice to a strained whisper. "You fucking did *what*? God, that's so incredible."

I smile, absolutely loving the fact that she's not chastising me for giving in to my impulses.

"You don't think I went too far?" I ask, wondering if the other shoe is about to drop.

"Did you fuck him?" Octavia asks.

"No."

"Then you didn't go far enough," she says, laughing hard. "Wow! I'm so proud of you, girl. I know it must've been hard for you to ask him to do that, because if he would've said no that would've been *embarrassing*. The fact that he was down to do that for you makes him *so much* hotter. Good lord, that's better than every erotic book I've ever read. My jealousy is real, Bree. It's *so* real."

"I know, it was *incredible*," I say, trembling with excitement. "But now I don't know what to do. I'm still on this assignment, but now everything has changed. I'm not just writing about it. I'm living it, and I have no idea how to write the story. I'm not allowed to tell the world that he made me come."

"Why not?" Octavia inquires, and we both laugh again.

"The Inquirer isn't that kind of magazine, Octavia," I answer. "So, I'm not sure what to do. I don't know what Nolan will be okay with me publishing about him, especially now that it has gotten a little personal."

"Are you guys officially seeing each other?"

"No. Well, I don't think so. We haven't really talked about that."

INTERVIEW WITH A SADIST

"Then that should be your next step. Give him a call and see how he defines what the two of you did, and ask if he'd be bothered by you writing about all of your experiences."

"I can't ask him that."

"Why the hell not? He already made you come. There shouldn't be anything you're too embarrassed to discuss now."

"I don't know," I say, giggling. "I just don't think I could bring myself to do—"

Before I can finish, the sound of my office phone ringing cuts me off. The number on the display looks fairly familiar, but I'm not quite sure if I recognize it, so I answer with genuine curiosity while Octavia waits patiently.

"Hello?"

"Bree," Nolan's voice croons into my ear, sending me reeling. My eyes bulge as I look at Octavia.

"Nolan?" I say, and Octavia immediately sits up straight.

"Yeah, it's me," Nolan says in my ear. "How are you?"

"I'm good ... great, actually," I say. "How about you?"

Octavia motions for me to put the phone on speaker, but I ignore her. I don't need the entire office listening to this conversation.

"I'm good, but I could be better," Nolan replies. "I know we're a little unsure of where your story on The Black Collar will end, considering how things went in my office the last time you were here. But, I was wondering if I could see you again."

I raise my eyebrows and fight back a smile. "You want to see me again? To finish the story?"

Nolan chuckles. "My interest *isn't* in the story, Bree. It's in you. The story is completely secondary to me now."

I freeze in place as everything in my office ices over—my entire world frozen in time while Nolan continues.

"There was something about what we did in my office

that stuck with me," he says. "*You* stuck with me, Bree, and if it's okay with you, I'd like to explore that a little further. Actually, that's a lie. I'd like to explore it *a lot* further—with your consent, of course. So, are you free for dinner tonight?"

"Dinner? Tonight?" I repeat, saying it out loud so Octavia can hear it and I can believe it's true.

"Yes. Are you free?" Nolan asks, and I can no longer hold back my excitement.

"Yeah, I'm definitely free for dinner tonight," I say, and Octavia raises her hands in silent celebration like we're in the middle of a sermon.

"Good. Just tell me where to pick you up," Nolan says.

We exchange cell phone numbers and I give him my address.

"Okay, so I'll see you tonight?" I say, just as Octavia puts a hand on my shoulder, waiting for the call to end so she can exclaim.

"Absolutely," Nolan says. "I'll see you soon. Bye, Bree."

"Bye, Nolan," I say, and the second I hang up, Octavia shrieks, squeezing my shoulder.

"Oh, my god, you're living a fucking rom-com!" she says. "A dirty, kinky rom-com. It's so cute and hot."

All I can do is smile as nervousness and giddiness combine to form an unnamed chemical that makes my heart hammer. Nolan wants to see me again, and he sounded intent on taking our budding relationship a bit further. *A lot* further, in his words. My desire to feel pain explodes to life like a nuke in my chest, and I can barely contain myself.

"Well," Octavia says, trying to calm herself but failing. "Here's your chance to ask him how to finish the story."

"Oh. Yeah, I guess so," I say, suddenly bombarded by how annoying reality is.

As much as I want to, and as thrilled as I am about having dinner with him, I can't just focus on what I want with

Nolan. Not yet. There's still work to do. I still have a story to write. So, I try to suppress the swelling of eagerness in my stomach and the tingle between my legs. I have to focus because the work isn't done yet. After tonight, I'll know for sure what's next.

Chapter Twenty-Three

My nerves are fire beneath my skin as I look out the window of my apartment, waiting for Nolan to pull up. I don't know what kind of car he'll be driving, but I watch with a held breath as vehicles drive past my street. When a black Lexus pulls up to the front of my complex, I turn to stone waiting for the door to open. My barely-blinking eyes widen when the driver finally steps out wearing black pants, brown shoes, a cream sweater, and a long plaid jacket that incorporates all of the colors of his outfit. His brown skin ties everything together, and as he leans against the car door with his phone in hand, he draws the attention of multiple women walking on the street. They stare, but he doesn't acknowledge them at all. He keeps his head down, his eyes glued to the phone. I watch him in awe, and only the sound of my text notification breaks the spell.

Nolan: *Hey. I'm here.*

. . .

A smile forces its way onto my lips as I read the message, because while women were checking Nolan out, I was the one he was texting. I fight the excitement away and look in the mirror at my outfit. With him down there looking so good, my attire has to be on point, too.

I do a full inspection from the front, nodding my approval at the black knit tee paired with a black and white Bodycon skirt that stops in the middle of my thighs, before spinning around and making sure everything still looks good from the back. I'm tempted to swap out my necklace and earrings, but I fight the urge since Nolan is already waiting, and I step into black heels. After a final check, I let out a deep breath and head down.

Nolan turns to the sound of the door opening, and the second he sees me, his smile reaches his eyes as he looks me up and down. I watch as he takes in my entire outfit from bottom to top, shaking his head in obvious disbelief.

"What?" I question, descending the stairs and reaching him as he steps onto the curb.

"You never miss, do you?" he asks, still looking at me like he's taking inventory of everything I have on.

"What do you mean?"

"You look incredible, Bree," he says. "*Beyond* incredible. If you keep this up, you're going to make a few enemies on this block. People don't like being embarrassed like this, but here you are—killing them all."

My heart somersaults behind my ribs, making my knees weak and sending flutters to both my stomach and pussy. I have to focus and clear my throat just to keep it from showing.

"Thank you," I reply. "*You* look amazing. I love this color on you."

"I did my best," he says. "You ready to go?"

"Absolutely."

"Good. How does Ocean Prime sound?"

My eyebrows raise. "Ocean Prime? That place is expensive."

Nolan chuckles and shrugs. "So? Let's go."

He spins around and opens the door to the Lexus before extending his hand for me to take. Nolan gently guides me into the seat, closes the door, and walks around to the driver's seat looking like a million dollars personified. Once he's in the car, the engine roars to life and we're off to start the night.

The drive to South Fifteenth Street isn't long, and when we pull up to the restaurant, we're greeted by a valet who takes the keys to the Lexus with a smile, while a hostess escorts Nolan and I to our seats in the massive dining room. The entire place is accented by gold features, including golden tiles on the ceiling and lights behind the expansive bar. We weave through the traffic of seated guests until we reach our table, which is adorned with crystal wine glasses filled with water and empty gilded flutes awaiting champagne. The hostess is replaced by the server—a blonde woman with a skinny face and radiant smile—and our flutes are filled with a champagne I can't pronounce while we look over the menu. It's all quite the spectacle, and while I'm impressed with the elegance of it all, it's Nolan who steals my attention.

When we're finally alone, he watches me with impatience in his gaze. There's something about the look in his eyes that tells me he's happy to be out with me, but what he really wants is to get me alone. I've never met a man who can intrigue me so much without saying anything. When Nolan stares at me, I become desperate to know what he's thinking. What kind of wild thoughts run through the mind of a sadist?

"Can I be honest with you?" he asks, lifting up his glass of water.

"Of course," I answer.

"You look fucking *delectable*," he says, pinning me to the seat with hunger in his eyes. "The moment we shared in my office has had my mind locked up since you left that day. I haven't been able to think about anything else. I've never had that happen before."

My nerves become a raging inferno as memories of being bent over on Nolan's couch push to the forefront of my mind. The room is suddenly much hotter than it was when we first walked in.

"I'm not sure what to say to that," I reply, clutching my flute like a security blanket. "It's been on my mind a lot, too. It has honestly kept me confused."

"Confused? Why? Was it not what you wanted?"

"It absolutely *was* what I wanted, but as incredible as it was, it also complicated my situation. I came to The Black Collar for a story for the Philadelphia Inquirer. I wasn't supposed to become enamored with the lifestyle that is BDSM. I didn't expect to see things that night in the club that would latch onto me and never let go, and I certainly didn't expect to discover anything new about myself. While I did have questions concerning who I was and why I felt the things I felt, I never—not in a million years—expected to find answers behind the doors of The Black Collar. Now that all of that has happened, I don't know what I'm supposed to do about the job I was sent there for."

Nolan furrows his brow. "I don't understand the complication. You have a job to do, and I never thought it would change after what took place on my couch. "

My eyebrows raise. "Really? You don't have a problem with me writing a story about you now that we've ... been intimate?"

Nolan chuckles. "First of all, we weren't intimate. What we did was a drop in the bucket of what I'm dying to introduce you to. It was a spark to a roaring flame, and as soon as I get the chance, I'm going to show you just how hot it gets."

I swallow hard, completely disregarding the fact that the table next to us definitely overheard everything he just said.

"Secondly, I'm not ashamed of anything I do," Nolan continues. "I always expected you to publish the stories I've told you, and to describe my club in detail. So, if you decide to add your personal experience with me into your story, that'd be fine, too. I'll support whatever you choose to do. Like I said before, I'm interested in you, not the story."

"That's the second time you've said that."

"Because it's true."

"Nolan, you own a BDSM club where you're practically worshiped like a god. I'm an investigative journalist—not exactly a world of wonders. What possible interest could you have in someone like me?"

Nolan picks up his flute of champagne and chugs the entire thing before pausing as if he's waiting for it to lower his inhibitions. After a deep breath, he leans forward with his arms on the table.

"Your purity," he says, and when he blinks, I see the change in his demeanor. He darkens—like a black cloud has just swept into the room and settled over our table. It's the sadist stepping to the front.

"Let me be frank, Bree. Don't let the sumptuous wardrobe or the kind words of my friends fool you. I'm a devil, and nothing would satisfy me more than wreaking havoc on you, an angel. You've had scattered thoughts of needing more, but you never let it out because you didn't know what it was you wanted. It has been lurking just beneath the surface, waiting for someone to define it, coax it out, and feed it. That's what brought you to me. I'm meant to feed it. I'm meant to show you what you've been missing all this time. I'm meant to ruin your immaculacy, stain your whiteness, paint your flawless skin with colors of red, blue,

INTERVIEW WITH A SADIST

and purple. You're my blank canvas, and I'm meant to be your dark artist."

The blue in Nolan's eyes sparks to life, locking me in a trance that turns everyone else in the room to mist. They all disintegrate and float away, leaving me alone with my beautiful devil as my hunger for exploration grips me.

We lock eyes again, and my curiosity takes over. I want to know everything, starting with how he felt when our spark was born.

"What were you thinking when you had me on your couch?" I say, just as wetness reveals itself between my legs, forcing me to cross them.

Nolan shifts, pinching his lips together before answering. "Your skin was so perfect. Not a single blemish or scratch. Flawless. It took everything in me not to test the boundaries and press my fingers against your ass until the color of your skin changed, but I knew it was coming. I conjured up as much patience as I could manage as you bent over and pressed the wand against your clit, and the moment the flogger hit you, I knew I was addicted.

"Your skin came to life with red streaks that quickly vanished and hid from me—teasing me, telling me to hit you again if I wanted to see them. Each whip of the flogger was a gift, and the moans that escaped your mouth were a symphony to my ears. I swam in the sound, never wanting it to end. I wanted to show you exactly what you asked to see, and also so much more. I wanted to break you into a million shattered pieces so I could put you back together again, and there has never been a time in my life that my cock has been harder. That's what I was thinking."

My world spins as I look at Nolan, seeing the sadist in him take over at the table. It's like talking to a completely different person, one who's capable of casting spells on me with nothing more than gestures and sentences. The yearning in his eyes scares me and makes me want to give myself over to him simultaneously.

"And what are you thinking about right now?" I ask.

"That what I'm hungry for can't be satisfied by anything in this restaurant. The moment I saw you open the door to your apartment complex, I was ready to cancel dinner. I managed to resist my desire and make it here, but I'm afraid I've gone as far as I can. I'm ready to leave."

"But we haven't even ordered our food yet," I say with a pounding heartbeat that rumbles my entire body.

Nolan slowly shakes his head. "So?"

Before I can think straight, I nod to him. My ability to manage my thoughts is overtaken by this new part of me that craves to be on the receiving end of Nolan's sadism, and I stand up before he does. I watch him toss a hundred dollar bill on the table before he takes me by the hand and leads me through the maze of tables and chairs again, desperate to get me alone.

Outside, our valet looks at us like something is wrong before scurrying to have Nolan's car retrieved and handing over the keys when it is. Nolan guides me in again and walks calmly to the driver's side. The second his door is closed, heat envelopes the inside of the car.

"Fuck," he whispers before leaning over, grabbing me by the throat, and pulling me into a passionate kiss that makes me gasp.

In front of everyone outside, our tongues collide and fall into a rhythmic dance that warms us both, fogging the windows of the Lexus. While our mouths are joined, Nolan's fingers slowly squeeze, increasing the pressure on my throat and cinching my airway. My entire world tightens around me as tension builds in my head, but I don't want him to stop. There are gasps and exclamations from outside the car, but we ignore it all as we fall into each other. It's the most terrifyingly passionate kiss I've ever experienced, and by the time Nolan pulls away, I want to climb on top of him, audience be damned. My lungs clamor for air, sucking in gulps at a time, and I'm suddenly fucking turned on.

Nolan is breathing heavily when he puts the car in gear and pulls away, and he places a hand on my knee as we hit the road.

"Where are we going?" I ask, still panting.

"I want to take you to my place. Are you okay with that?"

"Of course," I say.

"Good," he answers as he steps on the gas, zooming the luxury car forward without regard to anyone's safety. "Everything I want is at my place."

"Everything you want?"

"Yes, Princess," Nolan responds. "Everything I want to use on you."

Chapter Twenty-Four

~ NOLAN ~

There's something about Bree that I can't resist. I've been trying—fighting myself internally every time she has come to the club—to free myself from her gravitational pull, but the more she's around, the closer I get, and the closer I get, the more impossible it becomes to pull away. Her presence grips me by both my heart and my cock—my heart flutters, my cock throbs—and having her around has become the most intense experience I've had in a long time. Considering who I am and the things I've done, that's really saying something.

In the restaurant, I didn't intend to lose my cool. I wanted to treat Bree to a nice dinner in one of my favorite places, and show her a good time before even thinking of anything sexual. But it's the way she talks to me. It's the fucking blue in her eyes that draws me in, setting a trap for me and once I'm in range, she ensnares me.

She asked me what I was thinking when I had her on my couch, and the memory was vibrant and vivid. While sitting in a crowded restaurant, my mind traveled right back to my office and saw her bent over with her bare, unblemished, immaculate ass in the air. The thought alone had my lungs clawing for oxygen. I went feral at the table, losing my sense of calm as the sadistic thoughts I'm usually able to keep at bay came speeding forward. I've lost all control now, and I won't stop until I have Bree bare in front of me again—until I can hit her, hurt her, hear her screams, and make her come all over me. I watched her explode last time, this time I want to be covered in it.

When I pull into the parking garage of my apartment complex, everything in the car is quiet. I'm sure she's thinking about what's about to happen just as much as I am, and we rush to exit the vehicle and make our way inside to the elevator. The second the doors close, Bree scrambles over to me and slams her mouth against mine. We kiss feverishly, our tongues clashing violently as we breathe into each other's mouths. We're engulfed by lust and adrenaline, and the more we kiss, the more I lose myself. I want to slam her against the wall and slap her. I want to see her cheek bloom with red before I wrap my fingers around her throat and fucking squeeze. I want to bend her over right here in the elevator and fuck her like a caveman until her pussy can't handle it anymore. I need to hear her scream for me. I want to chain her to the handrail in the elevator and slap her face with my cock until it starts to feel like a sledgehammer for her. I want to tear her apart with my brutality.

Fuck.

I push her back just before the doors open, fighting away images in my head of Bree crawling on the floor next to me like a good little slut. We're not at that stage yet, but that doesn't mean I don't crave it. Nonetheless, I block it out as we walk hand-in-hand to my apartment. The moment we're inside, Bree jumps onto me, literally wrapping her legs around my waist and forcing me to hold her up. I'm not the only one who has been waiting to let go. Bree is like an animal being released from her cage for the very first time. She's mad with lust, desperate to feel what she has been bottling up her entire life. But animals must be broken and tamed if you wish to keep them.

I carry Bree into the living room, kissing her the entire way, until we fall to the floor in between my couches and fireplace. She claws at my back, constantly pulling me closer like she can't control herself. She yanks my jacket off, tossing it to the side before tearing at my sweater next, clamoring to get her hands underneath so she can pull it off of me. She has lost all sense of direction and control, and I realize she needs me. Bree was a captive inside her own mind and within the walls of her upbringing. She was locked away, and now that the lock has been removed, she doesn't know how to act. She wants it all at once, and she needs me to show her the way. She needs me to tame her or she'll be lost for good. She is new to this world, but I'm not, and I will show her.

As she tugs at my sweater, I take hold of both her wrists and slam them on the floor above her head. She gasps, and my cock jumps at the sound, pushing against the fabric of my pants with an intense desire to break free. Bree looks at me, still breathing hard and heavy, ready to go berserk if I let her go.

"Listen to me," I say, staring her straight in the eyes. I let the darkness within me build to a crescendo and takeover, erasing everything sweet and humble Bree is used to. "Stop fucking moving right now."

Her body stills, but her eyes continue to scan my face. She searches for signs of the nice man she has been interviewing, but she won't find him.

"You are not in charge of anything here," I say. "I'm not one of your old boyfriends who couldn't control himself and thought it was hot when you couldn't either. Here, I'm in control. I own everything in this room, including you. Here, there is only one boss, one Master, one Dominant, and that is me. Do you understand?"

Bree's blue eyes finally settle and lock onto mine. "Yes," she says, and I want to choke her for not adding sir onto the end, but again, we're not there yet.

"Without moving, tell me what you want from me, Bree," I demand.

"I want it all," she answers. "I want all of you—all of the pain, all the pleasure, all the dominance inside you. I want it all."

"You don't know what you're asking for," I reply, scowling.

"Yes, I do."

"You *don't*," I bark. "You want me to hit you?"

"Yes."

My cock jumps again, my balls tightening at the admission.

"You want me to choke you?" I ask.

"Yes."

"You want me to hit you with more than just a flogger?"

"Yes."

"You want me to spit in your mouth, drag you across the floor, wrap your hair around my fist and pull until your neck feels like it might snap?"

Her eyes widen. "God, yes."

"You want me to fucking hurt you?"

"Yes, *please*."

I raise one of her arms and slam it against the floor again. "Goddamn it. You don't know what you're saying, Bree."

"Then fucking show me," she bellows, causing me to freeze, a deep furrow in my brow as I'm overtaken by shock. "I don't want to hold back anymore. I don't want to hear anymore. You want my consent? You have it. You said you owned everything in this room including me, then fucking own me. Do it, Nolan. Show me everything and let me decide for myself if I can't handle it. I don't know why I need the things I'm craving, but I know you're the only person I trust to show me what this is. I don't want to meet another supposed Dom and spend time figuring out who they are and if I trust them. It's *you*, Nolan. I want *you* to do it, and I don't want to wait another fucking second. Please. For the first time in my life, I'm able to be honest with myself and say this out loud—I need it, Nolan. Whatever *it* is, I *need it*. All of it."

My heart pounds so hard it rattles my insides. Blood rushes through my veins, filling my ears with noise as I stare at her. She's so fucking beautiful, so new, so delicate. I could break her if I do too much ... and she wants to be broken. No, she wants *me* to break her. She has chosen me. *Me*—the monster, the Dominant, the sadist.

So be it.

Chapter Twenty-Five

~ NOLAN ~

With Bree's hands pinned above her head, I let down any remaining walls I still had raised before this moment. Hearing her tell me she made a choice about who she wants to introduce her to pain crumbled every barrier I had left, and now my desires are free to reign. Now I no longer have to think. There is no plan that gets hammered out before I act—no, I'm my best when I improvise.

I let my eyes roam over Bree's body, taking mental snapshots of the places on her that I want to touch—the places I want to turn red. Her black shirt is still intact, blocking my view, and I've never hated fabric more. I need unfettered access to her skin, so I bring her hands close together above her head so I can hold both of them with one of my hands, while I use the other to tear at her clothes. Adrenaline fills me to the brim as I untuck the shirt from her skirt and pull it up enough to finally see her navel.

"Fuck," I whisper. Her skin is so beautiful it hurts me to

see it. My desire to mark her becomes so intense that it's actually a pain in my stomach that pulls a groan from my throat.

I pull Bree's shirt up until it bunches underneath her chin, before snatching her bra off, the fabric tearing in multiple spots as the clasp goes bouncing somewhere unknown. She lets out a yelp from either excitement or fear, and I slam the torn bra over her mouth.

"Don't say anything," I command, leaning forward until my mouth is directly next to her ear. "I'm only going to say this once, so don't forget it. Your safe word is and always will be *goddess*, just like last time. Nod if you understand."

She nods, and I sit up, straddling her. "Good girl," I say, before I reach back and slap her across the chest, instantly reddening her exposed breast. Bree chirps behind the makeshift gag of her bra, and I close my eyes to soak it in. The sound of her fearful moan excites me in a way I can't explain. I'm an addict gifted with a fix after far too long without it. My entire body comes to life as the fog of Dom space entangles me, giving me the ultimate god complex.

"You are music to my fucking ears," I say, before slapping her chest again, hitting both tits with one swing this time. Bree chirps again, but this one sounds more pleasure-filled, which makes me even harder.

"That's it, Princess," I say, staring down at my prey. "Embrace it. Let the pain consume you. Give in to it. Bathe in it and let it soothe you. Relax and trust me. Your body is mine and I will make sure the bruises remind you tomorrow."

I smack Bree across the chest a third time, and when she screams, I lunge forward and press my mouth against hers, swallowing the sound escaping her throat through the fabric of the bra in her mouth.

"You taste so fucking good," I whisper into her mouth, the bra working like a filter to my words. "I've wanted you since the first second I ever saw you, and now I'm going to show you who I am, Princess. Stay here and don't move. Do you understand?"

"Yes," she replies, her words muffled by her bra, but I don't remove it as I get up and walk into the bedroom, leaving Bree on the living room floor with her shirt under her chin and her bra in her mouth.

I walk into my closet and head straight for the cabinet inside, where I grab a condom, nipple clamps, handcuffs, and a wand vibrator, which has become my favorite tag team partner. Real men understand that toys are not your enemy. When your ego is removed from the equation, sex toys are the enhancement of a lifetime, because no matter how much I wiggle around, my cock can't vibrate. But, it can fuck with every thick inch I've been gifted with while this wand massages her clit without needing to catch its breath. This wand is my best friend, and when I combine it with toys that cause pain, there's no stopping us. My toys and I are the most awesome gang in the world, and we're about to cause chaos once again.

When I step back into the living room, I'm ecstatic to find Bree in the exact same place I left her—her hands still above her head, her bra firmly in place between her jaws. She's obedient, and I fucking love it. I kneel next to her, pulling her up with one hand and removing the bra with the other until she's sitting upright, staring at me with hunger in her blue eyes. The look on her face has a stranglehold on me, and I end up kissing her without intending to. The softness of her lips and the warmth of her mouth send me reeling, making my cock ache with hardness.

"God, what is it about you?" I ask once we pull away. She doesn't respond with words, but I feel the passion floating off of her, combining with my own. I kiss her again, but as our mouths dance this time, I use my hands to position her arms behind her back, where I secure the cuffs.

Part of me expects her to pull away when they click closed, but she doesn't. Bree simply watches me, trusting my every move and waiting patiently. She may have gone her entire life without acting on her desires, but she was made to be a submissive. It's stitched into the fabric of her skin and shows itself in the way she looks at me—waiting, wanting.

Bree sits with her hands fastened behind her back, watching me as I manage to remove her shirt and slide her body back until she's leaning on the couch. Once she's shirtless, I pull her skirt off and toss it next to the fireplace, before removing my own shirt and setting my toys on the end table next to the condom I intend to fill. I grab the nipple clamps from the table and dangle them in front of Bree's face.

"Do you know what these are?" I ask, and Bree nods. "Good," I say before placing a clamp on each of Bree's nipples. She sucks in a breath each time, and I lick my lips, my hunger for her growing with the sound.

Once the clamps are secure, I focus on the small dials on each one. Starting with her right nipple, I turn the dial until it clicks once, tightening on her hard bud, and Bree sucks in another breath. I watch her face intently as I copy the action on the left nipple, and she winces again.

"Does it hurt?" I ask, smirking.

"Mm-hmm," she responds through pinched lips.

My smirk evolves into a smile. "Good."

I use both hands and turn the dials again, sending Bree's head slamming back against the couch. I watch the muscles in her chest, neck, and stomach tighten as she tries to breathe through this new sensation of pain.

It's easy to fantasize about something, but experiencing it is different. Feeling pain is nothing like imagining it, but through it all, I don't see any sign of regret in Bree's face. She leans back with her eyes closed and mouth open, and I search her expression for signs of discomfort and disappointment but find none. The pain she is feeling doesn't cause anguish that makes her want to shout her safe word, but instead forces her mouth open as if she's pleasantly surprised by how good it feels. Slowly, the tension in her body dissipates, melting off of her like wax, and she lifts her head to look at me, waiting for more.

"Holy fuck," I whisper to myself, but it comes out much louder than I expected. "You're fucking incredible. You like it."

Bree raises an eyebrow and nods. "Yes ... I love it."

"Oh, my god," I say, shaking my head. "I'm fucking obsessed with you. Open your mouth."

Bree does as she's told as I begin to unbuckle my pants in front of her. Her eyes never leave mine as I pull off the rest of my clothes and step forward until I have a foot on each side of her legs, looking down on her with my cock directly over her face. Her mouth stays agape all the way up until the moment I shove myself between her lips.

I grab both side of Bree's face and begin slowly fucking her mouth like she's another member of my toy collection. I start gradually at first, using every inch of my dick—pulling all the way out until the tip of my cock dangles on her bottom lip, before pushing all the way in until I reach the back of her throat, only stopping when she gags.

"Your mouth is so perfect," I tell her between moans, and I mean every word of it. "It's so good I could come in an instant."

I have to force myself to pull out because I know I'll come if I don't. I take a step back and look at Bree, taking in the dazzling sight of her sitting there completely nude with nipple clamps attached to her tits. She's fucking stunning, and my cock throbs with anticipation as I step forward and turn the dials on each clamp again, maxing out their pressure. Bree moans as she slams her eyes shut, but I don't give her a second to recover before I shove my cock inside her mouth again.

This time, I'm not gentle. I grip the sides of Bree's face and fuck her mouth relentlessly. Each thrust is powerful and made to wreck her, but she doesn't fight it. With her hands still bound, she accepts it without tightening a single muscle in her neck. I fuck Bree's mouth until I'm on the verge of coming again, before pulling out and slapping her across the face. She moans with the slap, eyeing me with a look of unburdened desire instead of fearful anticipation. I can barely believe it, but she loves it, and it seals the bond between us. I'm completely captivated by how she responds, and my body reacts without thinking.

I grab Bree by the waist and lift her body until she's on her back on the couch with her legs in the air. Her pussy is delectable in front of me, and even though I didn't intend to taste her, I dive forward, my mouth blanketing her entirely. Bree is wetter than I ever could've imagined, and I drink all of it down like I'm trying to prevent dehydration.

"Goddammit," I exclaim. "How do you taste so good?"

I clamp my mouth on Bree's pussy again and lick until my tongue tires. I suck her clit into my mouth as I lick it, and give my entire mouth a workout until Bree's body tightens and she explodes, blessing me with more of her wetness to gulp down. She quivers above me as her legs squeeze against the sides of my head while I finish her off, licking her clit with my entire tongue until she comes down from heaven.

"Oh, my fucking god," she says, her eyes rolling back in her head momentarily. "You're so incredible, Nolan. It's so good."

"I know, Princess," I reply, wiping my mouth as I reach for the wand and plug it in. "I know."

I turn on the wand, and the instant it buzzes to life, I press it against Bree's clit. She jolts from the shock, then releases a drawn-out gasp as I slide my newly-sheathed cock into her pussy and begin fucking her. Her body rocks back and forth as I pound her hard, but the spin of the world accelerates when I grab the tiny chain connecting the nipple clamps and pull it, using it as leverage while I fuck her, still holding the wand against her clit.

"Fuck!" Bree exclaims as she's tormented by the pain of the clamps and utterly destroyed by the sensations on her pussy and clit. It all mixes together, creating a chaotic pleasure that Bree has never experienced before. She writhes like a woman possessed, taking every inch of me without ever trying to back away. She takes it all like my perfect good girl until she's ready to fall into bliss a second time.

"Fuck, I'm going to come again" she screams, surprised by the emergence of a second orgasm.

"Yes, give it to me!" I bellow. "Come on me while I come in you."

Just as Bree's orgasm storms to life, I yank the chain, snatching off both nipple clamps at the same time and sending a lightning bolt through Bree's body.

"Fuck! Oh, god!" she screams at the top of her lungs.

"Fuck yeah!" I yell as it all culminates into a body-wrecking tsunami of bliss, and I explode, filling the condom to the brim.

Both of us scream profanities into the air as our bodies ignite with pleasure at the same time. Bree shakes until she nearly slides off the couch, and I quiver until my knees buckle. We end up on the floor next to each other, panting and sweating as we slowly descend from the summit of pleasure, perfectly shattered.

Chapter Twenty-Six

~ NOLAN ~

I feel heavier than usual, as if Earth's gravity has increased from the damage we've done in this room. My lungs sting with fire as I breathe in deeply, my throat tight as I stare up at the ceiling with Bree next to me suffering from her own destruction. This is heaven blended with hell—the best feeling in the world that we all chase when given the chance. This is what we hope for when we think about sex in its truest form—no quickies, no man coming in two minutes while the woman can't even get close, no awkwardness, no regrets. Just this—annihilation and the carnage left behind when it's over.

After a few minutes of recovery, I finally manage to pull my head up from the floor and look around. The condom is still on my dick, my couch has moved back a few feet from how hard I was thrusting into Bree, and my toys are scattered —nipple clamps by the fireplace, the wand somehow under the couch like it's hiding, and clothes disorganized and spread all over the place. We really made a beautiful mess, and I smile as I lift myself up and look at Bree.

She lies on her back with her eyes closed and her chest rising and falling as she sucks in air. One arm is stretched out to her side while the other has settled over her face, covering her eyes. Bree looks like she really has been through something traumatic, and I love it. Her face is red around her mouth from my cock slamming into it, her entire chest is flushed, and both nipples look raw and red, the victims of torture and passion. From here, she looks overwhelmed, and I know what the effects of Sub Drop can have, especially on someone who is new to being a masochist and submissive. Soon, she will become consumed by emotions she can't explain, as her body comes down from all of the adrenaline, dopamine, and endorphins she was just flooded with. Her mind and body will have to reboot, and it won't feel good. She doesn't know it's coming, but I do.

Sucking in a deep breath, I pull myself together and get off the floor. Bree, on the other hand, doesn't move, which is perfect because I don't want her to. She has done enough by giving herself over to me. Now, it's my turn to give back.

"Hey," I say as I crouch down next to her and place a hand on her ankle. "You okay?"

Without moving, she replies, "Yeah. I just ... I don't even know."

"It's okay," I say, positioning myself closer to her. "I got you. Just hold on."

Slowly, I wriggle my arms underneath her knees and back, and scoop her up into my arms.

"Oh ... what are you doing?" she asks, finally looking at me and letting me see the redness in her eyes.

"Sshhh," I respond as I stand up and set my sights on the bedroom. "Let me take care of you, Bree."

I walk with her in my arms, carrying her like a new bride

over the threshold of my bedroom, and when we reach the bed, I set her down gently, pulling the covers halfway up her tattered body so she's not cold.

"Stay here," I command, and although she doesn't say anything, I see her muscles relax as she settles into the soft mattress.

I step into the bathroom and clean up—discarding the condom and washing myself off, before slipping into basketball shorts and exiting. While she waits for me, I walk back into the living room and quickly piece it back together—picking up our clothes and folding them into two neat piles on the couch, collecting the toys I used on Bree and placing them on the counter to be cleaned and sanitized later, and fixing the position of the couch so it's back in its normal spot in front of the fireplace. After everything is in order, I go into the kitchen and grab two wine glasses, a towel, ice, and a bottle of white wine, taking the entire trove back into the bedroom and setting it all on the side of the bed opposite Bree. Her eyes stay glued to me as I slide into bed and begin to pull her close.

"Nolan, what are—"

"Don't talk," I say, cutting her off. "Just come here."

Bree lets out a nervous giggle as she allows me to pull her body over until she's between my legs with her back to me, and the two of us lean against the headboard together. The back of her head rests against my chest as I grab the towel next to us and drop the ice cubes into it.

"Nolan," she starts again, but I stop her.

"Sshh." I place the towel on the bed and pick up the wine and a glass next, filling it up and handing it to Bree. "Sip this."

I see the smirk on her face as she takes it, but she doesn't say anything, finally getting the picture. While Bree sips her wine, I grab the towel and slowly bring it to her red chest, rubbing it gently against her right nipple. She hisses and I reduce the pressure, stroking down her sensitive flesh slowly until I sense her tension easing. She takes another sip of wine, and I move over to the other nipple, repeating the process. We spend the next twenty minutes this way—Bree sipping wine while I carefully caress her body, doing my best to soothe the wounds I caused.

"You don't have to stay the night, but you're welcome to," I say after another few silent minutes. "When you're ready, the shower is there if you want it, and your clothes are in the living room, neatly folded and waiting on the couch."

Bree shifts her position just a bit, raising her head so she can look up at me with a soft, gorgeous smile.

"Thank you," she says. "I think I'll stay like this just a little while longer."

We lock eyes for a moment, and I grin as I place the towel on the nightstand and wrap both of my arms around her, bringing us as close as humanly possible.

"Good," I reply, and we happily return to enjoying the silence.

We spend the next hour together, sipping wine while I massage the beautiful skin on Bree's naked body. The concept of time evaporates and neither of us thinks about anything but the moment. It's ours, and we settle into it like we've been doing it for years. The back of my hand rubs a trail down her chest and stomach before my index finger traces circles around her navel, and we share a laugh. Neither of us wants to move and disrupt the moment, so we stay in it together, and the Sub Drop I was expecting to ravage her never comes.

Black Friday

Chapter Twenty-Seven

When I wake up Friday morning, I feel like I exist in a world that is tilting. A rush of emotions sweep over me as I sit up and take in my surroundings, and find Nolan in the bathroom with his back to me, wearing black shorts and nothing else. The muscles in his back flex and twitch as he finishes brushing his teeth and putting cocoa butter lotion all over his body, and just watching him feels like a dream has been pulled out of my mind and placed right in front of me. Even from the back, the man is beautiful, and memories of last night are vividly in the front of my mind. My heart races watching him, but then the other side of my emotions comes to life and everything stills.

I'm not supposed to be here. It's Friday morning and I have to work, so the fact that Nolan drove us here reminds me of the fact that I don't have access to my car. In a panic, I shuffle out of bed to look for my phone, only to find that I'm still naked. I quickly pull the covers back over my exposed body. The shock comes with a nice, pounding headache that reminds me how much wine I drank last night as well. Not to mention I have a sore chest, and my pussy and clit are both feeling extra sensitive.

"Shit," I mumble as I hang my legs off the side of the bed.

"Good morning. You okay?"

Nolan strides into the room, and it's obvious from his severe case of being hot as fuck and moving swiftly that he's not being bogged down by a hangover. As he approaches, I can tell he's not wearing underwear beneath his shorts, because the outline of his cock is as clear as day, and I suddenly remember how I felt when I saw it for the first time last night.

He released it as I was sitting against the couch, right before he fucked my mouth. I don't know how it's possible for someone to be born with every inch of them sculpted so perfectly, but Nolan is flawless. Most of the time I think dicks are ugly. Even though I love them, they're not the most attractive things in the world—but Nolan's cock is somehow an extension of the man himself. It's thick, with a pen-sized vein running down the shaft, and it looks just as dominant and beautiful as he is.

Why am I still thinking about his dick?

I clear my throat and place a hand over my eyes, blocking out the light and hiding my embarrassment. "Umm, yeah, I'm okay. Apparently I have a bit of a hangover."

"Oh, that sucks," Nolan says as he stops next to me and crouches down. "Can I get you anything? Coffee, water, ibuprofen?"

"Those last two would be great, but I also need my clothes. What time is it?"

"Quarter to seven," Nolan answers.

"Shit. I have to be at work at nine. I'm so screwed."

Nolan places a hand on my knee and squeezes it gently, sending a shockwave up my leg. I pinch my lips together and look at him to find blue eyes staring back at me.

"Hey, I got you. I'll get your clothes and some medicine, and as soon as you're dressed I'll take you back to your place. Don't worry, I won't let you be late to work. You trust me?"

Looking into his eyes makes me think about every kinky thing that happened last night, and I'm suddenly ready to skip work.

"Yes," I say, grinning as he flashes a complete smile before standing up and walking away.

When Nolan returns, he's carrying my folded clothes in one hand, and a glass of water and two pills in the other. He hands me the water and pills first, then places my clothes on the bed.

"Take these, and make sure to drink all of the water," he commands. "Then, get dressed and we'll go."

Don't ask me why I like him commanding me to take care of myself. I just do, and I have to use every muscle in my face to keep from smiling as my heart flutters like moth wings. Nolan walks away to finish getting dressed while I take both pills and down the glass of water. I slip back into my shirt and skirt from last night, run my fingers through my hair in a futile effort to look decent without a comb, and wait by the bathroom door for Nolan to finish buttoning up his shirt. In just a few minutes, he has made himself look incredible once again, while I feel like a total bum waiting for him. Nonetheless, when he turns around, he steps up to me and softly places his lips against mine.

"How are you so beautiful first thing in the morning?" he asks, stepping back to look at me.

I scoff. "You're kidding, right? I literally look like a troll right now."

"If *this* is what trolls looked like, there would be so many people trying to fuck trolls," he says, and we both laugh at the same time. "There would be an entire category on Pornhub for troll porn if trolls looked like this. First thing in the morning, lunch time, late at night—it doesn't matter,

INTERVIEW WITH A SADIST

Bree. You're stunning. I've never been a big believer in any gods, but I don't know how else to explain you walking into my club for an interview. It must've been a gift from *somebody*."

I stand there with a stunned expression as Nolan leans in to kiss me again, before walking by as if he didn't just floor me. He clears his throat and goes to the bedroom door.

"You ready?"

I have to shake my head to snap out of the trance he put me in. "Yeah, I'm ready."

On the drive back to my apartment complex, I look out the window as I'm overcome by thoughts of what led me to this insane point in my life. Nolan drives silently while I think about all of the boyfriends I've had and what being with them was like. How could I compare them to Nolan while also acknowledging that there is no comparison? However, is that what Nolan is? My boyfriend? We haven't defined anything or said that we are exclusive, so I don't actually know what this is. All I do know is that I've never done anything like this in my life, and I fucking love it so far. It's all been so incredible that I know something must be on the other side of the horizon. The other shoe has to drop soon, because Nolan is what people mean when they say something seems too good to be true.

"You're in your head again, Princess," Nolan says, just before reaching over and placing a hand on my knee. "What's on your mind?"

Looking down at his hand, I answer, "Everything. All of it. Everything that's happened since we met."

"What do you think about it?"

"It's a lot. It's sort of staggering how much things have changed since I met you. It's like I have a whole new brain that thinks and feels things I never did before."

"Do you like it?"

I smile, looking at him while he keeps his eyes on the road. "Yes."

He turns to me as the car veers toward the highway exit. "Good."

Nolan weaves through traffic with ease, and pulls his Lexus up to the front of my apartment complex, stopping directly next to the curb. Before I can reach for the handle to exit, he places a hand on top of mine and doesn't let go.

"Bree," he says. "Listen, I just want you to know that while you're thinking about everything that has happened since we met, I'm enamored by it, too. I think you're incredible, and that includes more than just your jaw-dropping beauty. I love your personality and passion, and I'm infatuated with your sense of adventure and ability to open your mind when that's not what you're used to. I've loved our time together, and I desperately want to see you again.

"It's not even about the sex, although you were unbelievable last night. It's about more than that. We don't even need to have sex the next time we're together. I just want to see you again as soon as possible. So, I know you're about to rush inside and get ready for work, and I don't want to be disruptive to your day, but I definitely want to talk to you again soon. Cool?"

The smile that takes over my face is one I can't control. It's wide and reaches up to my ears, but I'm unbothered because the happiness and excitement I feel is genuine.

"Cool," I answer, just before Nolan leans his entire body across the car and kisses me. My heart races into a frenzy that makes me lightheaded as our tongues embrace again and heat explodes from one end of my body to the next. I quickly fill with lust that I have to ignore because I'm pressed for time, and somehow manage to pull myself away and get out of the car.

Nolan watches me until I reach the front door before

INTERVIEW WITH A SADIST

driving away, leaving me beaming on the top step of my complex. I smile again, although no one is around to see it, and all I can think about is the next time we'll be together. I know I'll be consumed by thoughts of last night for the entirety of our time apart, and I'll use it as fuel to get through the day. Somehow, the sadistic owner of Philly's new BDSM club has climbed into my life and filled it with passion and lust that makes my entire world seem brighter. I'm fucking obsessed and desperate for more.

"Bree?" a voice says, cutting right through my morning happiness and sending me reeling.

I startle, jerking my head around and finding Melissa staring at me from the bottom of the steps.

"Melissa," I say, stunned by her arrival. Where the hell did she come from, and how long has she been there?

"Hi," she says, before frowning and tilting her head to the side in confusion. "So, who was that guy you were kissing?"

Chapter Twenty-Eight

Old Bree stirs to life in my stomach. I feel her shifting as Melissa's voice works its way into my ears and sinks down into the depths of my very being, reawakening the version of me I worked so hard to eliminate. She wants to answer. She wants to lie and say that Nolan is nobody—just some random guy I met and brought me home, and certainly not the new man in my life that I love spending time with, who's also the owner of a BDSM club. Old Bree wants to deflect and say whatever is necessary to convince her old friend that everything is just as it was, but I refuse to allow her to have the chance. I swallow hard and push her down deeper than she was before.

"What are you doing here, Melissa?" I ask, instead of answering her question. She's used to being the person in charge of our friend group. Whenever she asks a question, Teagan and I are expected to answer, because Melissa is the one with the husband. She's the one who managed to put her life in order before the rest of us, so we're following her lead and she knows it. She is our commander, and we're the troops. Well, fuck that. She can answer my questions now.

Melissa steps onto the bottom stair with her flowing

blonde hair blowing in the breeze, and her hands in the pockets of her white trench coat. Her pants are light gray, as is the shirt beneath the coat, but her look is very angelic. The glow of white accented by the gold of her hair—the proverbial halo—makes her look as though she could never do any harm. She stands across from me while I wear last night's date outfit, looking a tad bit homeless with my disheveled hair, ruined makeup, and grocery-sized bags under my eyes. I can only imagine what judgmental people like Teagan would think seeing us standing together, yet somehow, of the two of us, I'm the better person.

"I was hoping we could talk," Melissa says. "We were angry at lunch the other day, and I didn't really like the way things ended between us. We're friends, so I thought we should talk it out, and I wanted to catch you before you went to work. I just didn't expect you to be getting home at this time."

"Whether I'm getting home at this time or not, you still came over without texting or calling first, so I would've been caught off guard either way."

Melissa flinches, doing her best to keep her anger at bay, but I see it. I recognize the simmer in her eyes.

"True," she forces herself to say with a playful giggle. "So, can we talk?"

"I have to get ready for work, so you'll have to come in," I say, before spinning around and opening the door.

I hold it for her and watch as she climbs the stairs with her eyes on me. Once she's in, the entire journey to my apartment is silent until we're inside with the door closed. She follows me into my bedroom and sits down on the bed, nervously shoving her hands underneath her thighs.

I refuse to start this conversation. If she came over—without any notice—to apologize or work something out between us, I intend to give her time and space to do it. So, without saying a word, I step into the bathroom and begin removing my makeup with a wipe. I feel her watching me until I look at her through the mirror, and she flinches as if I startled her.

"Sorry," she says, clearing her throat. "So, like I said outside, I didn't really like the way things ended between us at Starbucks. We've been friends for years, and we shouldn't let a disagreement break up what we've had all these years. I think you being more open-minded is a good thing, actually."

I stop mid-wipe. "You do?"

"Yes," she answers. "It's good to be impartial and receptive, especially in your line of work. You're just doing what you've gotta do to be good at your job, which you always have been. You're a great journalist, Bree. I don't think I could do what you do."

I finish wiping my face and take off my shirt, leaving my bra on as I turn around to face her. "I appreciate the compliment about my job, but I'm not being more open-minded for work. Meeting Nolan just happened to open my eyes to a lot of things, and I realized I was wrong to prejudge people. Nolan was the icing on the cake."

"Nolan is the club owner right?"

"Yes, and he's the guy I was kissing just now," I admit with my head high. Melissa's eyes widen momentarily before she realizes her reaction and stops herself.

"Oh," she says with a bit of a chuckle. "So, you're dating him now?"

"I don't know what we're doing, exactly," I confess, as much as I hate saying it out loud, especially to Melissa. "But I know we're having fun, and I feel like everything has changed for the better since I met him."

"For the *better*," she says, but it's not a question. As much as Melissa is trying to wear a mask to hide who she really is and how she truly feels, it's not comfortable for her. The mask

INTERVIEW WITH A SADIST

slips every now and then, revealing the true bitch she is. "But, we had a bit of a falling out recently. Surely, not *everything* has been *better*."

"No, literally *everything* has been better," I tell her, and I'm not sure I've ever felt more powerful in my life. I watch Melissa as she sits on the bed, and this is the first time I've ever looked down on her instead of it being the other way around. She was always the example—the lead I wanted to follow, but now I see her as a complete fraud who can't handle not getting her way.

"Wow," she grumbles. "That says a lot about how you felt about our friendship. I thought you would at least be a little upset about what happened the other day."

"I *was* upset, just not in the way you were expecting. I was more upset at the fact that I'd tried to be just like you for so long. I was upset that I never noticed how ridiculous Teagan is because she's trying to be like you, too. I was upset that it took me so long—it took me meeting Nolan to see the error in my worldview. But mostly, I was upset that my friends wouldn't support me if I changed my attitude for the better. That was the most hurtful part, but I got over it."

"You mean you got over *us*."

"I got over the bullshit, Melissa. All of it."

"All because you started *screwing* the owner of a BDSM club?"

"You see, *there* it is," I say, pointing a finger. "There's the *real* Melissa. Unlike you, the change I made when I realized how wrong I'd been was real. It's permanent. You coming over here this morning and acting like you're ready to be somebody different was all bullshit. You're still the same Melissa from Starbucks that afternoon. So, I don't even know why you came over here."

Melissa stands up and slams her hands onto her hips. "I came because I thought I could mend our friendship. I thought what we've had since college was stronger than that, but I see Teagan was actually right. You've changed too much. You've had the wool pulled over your eyes, and now that you're fucking the *subject of your interview*, I know it's over. You've become the devil's whore, Bree, and there's no coming back from that."

Melissa stares at me, fuming—her mask having finally fallen off to reveal who she has always been, and all I can do is laugh.

"Thank fucking goodness," I bark, chuckling. "Thank you for the big fat reminder that I made the right decision to walk out of Starbucks. God, Melissa, all I wanted was for my friends to be supportive. That's it. You guys act like I'm participating in human sacrifices. It's just kinks and sex."

Melissa's eyebrows rocket to the top of her face. "Just kinks and sex. Wow. You're truly gone. It's depravity. It's immoral. It's *wrong*, Bree! So, is that where you were coming back from this morning? You stayed the night at his house?"

"Yes, I did, Melissa—and what do you have to say about it?" I snap. "Go ahead, be the great, supportive friend you've always been, and tell me what you think about me fucking the BDSM club owner. I had a great, kinky time wearing nipple clamps while Nolan fucked my face like it was his personal cock sleeve. I came all over his cock, while you were probably lying on your back in the world's most standard missionary position, while Andy humped you until he moaned and grunted in your ear five seconds later.

"Instead of telling me how wrong I am, how about you tell me when was the last time Andy made you come. When was the last time you had an orgasm that you didn't give yourself? Tell me you've never had a single thought about wanting more. Tell me if you're even happy looking down on the world from your fucking high horse. Tell me all of that, and as soon as you're done, tell me 'bye' and get the fuck out of my apartment, because I have to shower before I go to work. I'm still all sweaty from being the devil's whore."

The tension in the room makes the air unbreathable as we glare at each other. There's no coming back from this. We're simply too different now, and Melissa isn't the kind of person who's capable of opening up and putting in the work to be a better person. I can't be friends with someone like her.

After a huff, Melissa turns on her heel and heads for the door, but before she reaches it, she turns around.

"I hope you're happy," she says.

"Sure you do," I snip, but she goes on.

"I hope your new friends, who engage in all the kink and think it's okay, support your new way of life. Because I don't, and I never will. I tried to mend things, but only a whore would fuck the guy they're supposed to be interviewing."

"No, Melissa. Only a whore would allow herself to be fucked by a guy who can't even satisfy her, just to keep up the appearance that she has the perfect life."

I see the venom of my words spread through Melissa's body, but she refuses to acknowledge or accept it. Instead, she spins around and walks away, never looking back. I stand in my room and watch her until the door to my apartment closes behind her, but I don't linger there. I never needed Melissa to come by and try to heal anything. I was fine before, and I'll be fine now. There are a lot of people in the world, and I don't need to be friends with any of the ones who won't have my back just because I enjoy something that they don't. So, I finish taking off my clothes and turn on the water to the shower, because before I go to work, I intend to wash off any last remnants of Melissa and Teagan.

Chapter Twenty-Nine

My mood is sour when I walk into work. The dumb ass, unnecessary conversation with Melissa seems to have placed a dark cloud over my head, and it feels like it's starting to drizzle as I step off the elevator and stride inside.

After last night, I expected my mood to be running at peak efficiency. I thought I'd be bouncing around all day, filled with the excitement of what just happened twelve hours ago, and all it took was Melissa's annoying voice to bring it all down. Now, it wouldn't matter if there were birds chirping at my desk, or if there was a giant rainbow stretching across the office and lighting up the entire space.

I'm annoyed, and when I sit down, I realize that the last thing I want to see is my computer screen. It stares at me, its face dark and ominous, reminding me that I still have a story to write about the man I'm ... seeing? Somehow, I'm supposed to come up with the words to describe exactly what's happening at The Black Collar, and who the man is that built it to be the success it has become.

How do I describe Nolan without confessing my attraction to him? How do I tell the city of Philadelphia that Nolan

Carter is a mysterious man with an affinity for kinky behavior and a love for what is deeper than the surface? He's a good-looking man who cares about his patrons and the reputation of his establishment ... who I've fucked once and am desperate to fuck again as soon as possible. He's passionate and humble ... and hot and sadistic with a huge cock. Philly, this man is not the monster you all think him to be. He's the monster I didn't know I wanted—the monster I want to tear me to shreds while he fucks me hard with a hand over my mouth. So fuck you, Philly, he's mine.

"Bree?" I whirl around in complete shock as the sound of Chase's voice cuts through my imagination. I'm so startled my heart is racing and I'm breathing heavily. "Oh, sorry. You okay? Did I scare you?"

"Shit. Umm, yeah ... no, I'm fine," I stammer, shaking my head to knock away the embarrassment. "How are you, Chase?"

He runs a hand through his gray hair and gives me a warm, but obviously forced smile.

"I'm good," he says, before motioning toward his office. "You got a second? Let's talk."

"Oh, of course," I answer, standing up with dread in my chest as Chase turns around to lead the way to his office.

Shit. What is this going to be about?

Chase takes his seat behind the desk while I claim mine in front of it, and once we're comfortable, he stares at me with a furrow in his brow. If he's trying to hide the giant question mark on his face, he's failing miserably. His expression is so intense, it actually makes my face scrunch up.

"You okay, Chase?" I ask.

"How are you, Bree?" he counters. "I feel like you haven't quite been yourself lately."

My eyebrows raise. "I haven't? How do you figure?"

"Well, usually I don't have to seek you out for updates

about a story," Chase says. "I know you never really wanted this story, Bree. I know you're a more conservative woman, and I know the subject matter was a bit much for you. So, I just wanted to make sure you weren't having a problem completing the assignment."

"Absolutely not," I fire back quickly. "Chase, this story has been ... life-altering."

"Life-altering?"

"Yes. Nolan is amazing, and seeing everything that goes on in the club really opened my eyes to things I would've never considered ... *learning* about before. It's been out of this world."

Chase pauses, that old look of confusion coming back full force, and I wonder if I may have said too much. My excitement about Nolan and learning I'm a masochist has me spilling information I should be keeping close to the vest, and I wish I could pull every word back and swallow them down again.

"That's *interesting*," Chase says, sinking me even further into my seat. "How's the story coming along then?"

If I sunk any lower, I'd be sitting on the floor.

"Umm ... the story is going ... you know, it's *going*. Sometimes stories go, you know? Go here, go there. Stories can go all around whenever they get to going—"

"Bree, stop. Why haven't you submitted a draft for this yet?" Chase asks, dicing through my bullshit. "This is what I mean when I say you haven't quite been yourself. I didn't expect a draft the next day, but it's been over a week, and I haven't seen anything on it. I want to publish this while the interest is still high. So, what have you got?"

Explicitly detailed memories of what I've done with Nolan flood my mind and threaten to steal my focus. What have I got? I've got the experience of bending over on Nolan's couch while holding a wand to my clit, while he

INTERVIEW WITH A SADIST

flogged me to an orgasm. I've got a sore chest from him slapping me last night, and I've got the memory of him caressing my skin and taking care of me after we were done. I've got an attraction so strong that I can't even begin to explain it.

"Bree, you okay?" Chase says. I shake my head again, realizing I just lost myself inside my own mind. Nolan has that effect, but I still don't know how to write about it.

"I'm fine, but the truth is that I have nothing right now, because I haven't written anything," I admit, because it's easier than coming up with a lie on the spot. "I've recorded a ton of Q&A, but I haven't dissected it and written anything down in a manner that would substantiate a draft for the story. I'm sorry, Chase, but I'm on it, I promise. I just need a little more time."

He pauses to glare at me again, and I realize I have a new pet peeve.

"Are you sure you're okay?" he asks, frowning as he tilts his head to the side like a confused puppy.

"Of course. Why wouldn't I be?"

He pauses again, and I let out a loud exhale to let him know that it's annoying.

"Don't get lost in it, Bree," he says. "It's best to just keep a story a story—*separate* from your life."

My heart drops into my feet.

"Of course," I say weakly, my voice sounding like a scared teenager who knows she's caught but won't admit it until all of the evidence is on the table—too ashamed to tell the truth.

"Okay," Chase says. "I want a draft by the middle of next week."

"Right. Yes. Absolutely," I say, nodding my head.

"All right," he says. There's a brief pause between us before he nods toward the door. "You better get back to it then."

"Right. Yeah. Thanks, Chase," I say, before scurrying out of the office with my tail between my legs.

I slam myself into my seat once I'm back at the desk. I should've known from the moment I saw Melissa standing on the sidewalk that today would be trash. It seems she has cursed the entire thing, because now I've embarrassed myself in front of my boss and committed to a deadline I probably won't be able to meet. Chase has given me less than a week to turn it in, but I still don't even know where to begin. The cloud above my head grows darker and it begins to pour.

When my cell rings, I think about not answering it. With the way everything has been going today, I figure it's probably just Teagan taking her shot at trying to mend things between our friend group. But then I remember she's a complete bitch, and there's no way she would call without Melissa's blessing, which I'm sure Melissa isn't giving after our convo this morning. So I pick up the phone and am pleasantly surprised to find Nolan's name on the display.

"Hello?" I answer, getting my first taste of happiness since I left his house this morning.

"Hey. You okay?" he asks immediately.

"Why does everyone keep asking me that?" I question aloud.

"You just sound a little off," Nolan informs me. "But I really wanted to check on you after last night, plus I saw that girl standing outside your apartment building looking like she was trying to ambush you. I saw her speak to you as I was driving away. Everything good?"

"Ugh," I groan as I spin around and place my head down on my desk. "That was Melissa, my *ex* best friend. She's become such a *see you next Tuesday*, and I'm pretty sure I've lost a friendship I'd had for years. This morning has been a nightmare, if I'm being honest, which really sucks because

INTERVIEW WITH A SADIST

usually I would vent to my friends about how trash the day has been."

"I'm sorry to hear that," Nolan replies. "Sounds like you could use some friends."

"Yeah, but new ones. My old ones have proven themselves to be very shitty people."

"Okay, so why don't you come hang out with me and my friends for lunch today? My treat."

Even with my face pressed firmly against the desk, I smile. "Really? You don't mind having me around again?"

"Bree, I never wanted you to leave," he says, making my heart explode. "I'm going to order in from The Capital Grille. You should join us."

"Who's us?"

"Myself, and E and J."

"E and J?"

"Ethan and Jackson."

"Oh, okay. Yeah, they're awesome."

"So, you'll come?" Nolan asks, and I nod.

"Yeah, sounds good. I'll be there," I reply, and the cloud slowly begins to dissipate.

Chapter Thirty

"Hey."

"Hey," Nolan says as he opens the door to The Black Collar, taking my hand as I step inside. He looks me up and down without saying anything, and while it's a little embarrassing to be gawked at, it feels good when it's Nolan. His blue eyes shine when he sees me, even in the dimly lit hallway of the club.

"You look amazing, as always," he says, grinning at whatever devious thoughts are running through his sadistic mind, and forcing a smile onto my face.

"Thank you. So do you. I wish I felt a bit better."

"Yeah, I feel you. I'm really sorry about whatever is happening with your friends. I hope it all works out."

"I'm not so sure I even want it to anymore," I admit, and I'm not sure how it makes me feel. I'm so sick of Melissa and Teagan's shit that it's easy to forget how long we've been friends. Maybe it's easier to take because I have Nolan right now, but there are no guarantees that our situation will ever develop into anything more than just a *situation*. If it ends, I'll be wishing I had those two bitches around. Or would I?

INTERVIEW WITH A SADIST

"Hey, I see you all in your head again," Nolan says after I go a few seconds without speaking. He steps closer and grabs both of my hands in his. "Don't think about it right now. We're here, we're hungry, and best of all, we're together. So, let's enjoy it. Come on. E and J are waiting."

Nolan grips my hand and leads me down the hallway of the club. The curtains are back in place, darkening the entire space until we emerge from the black and step into the dancefloor and bar area. I look up at the empty cages above the dancefloor as we walk past the bar and head upstairs to the VIP section, where Ethan and Jackson sit at a circular table in front of large trays covered by stainless steel tops.

"Hey," Ethan calls to me, dragging out the word and filling the air with the excitement of a family member who hasn't seen me in months. He gets up from behind the table and walks over to greet me with a hug.

"Oh, hey," I say, a bit startled by the gesture, but enjoying it nonetheless. "How are you?"

"I'm good. Hungry as hell. It's good to see you again," Ethan says, smiling from ear to ear as he looks back and forth between Nolan and I.

"Don't make it awkward," Jackson says as Ethan steps out of the way to reveal that Jackson has materialized behind him. He practically pushes Ethan out of the way and gives me a soft hug that's short and sweet. "How you doing, girl? It's nice to have you back here keeping Nolan in line."

"Oh, is that what I'm doing?" I ask as he backs away and the two beautiful men look at me with smiling faces.

"Child, please. You don't even know," Ethan says. His bald head glistens beneath the lights as he spins around and motions to the trays of food. "I'm too hungry to stand here talking to y'all. Let's eat. If this food gets cold, I'm gonna be mad if I gotta put it in the microwave."

"Word to Baby Boy," Jackson says as he follows his

203

husband chuckling. I don't understand the reference, but I smile and follow them anyway.

The four of us sit down at the round table with E and J on one side, and Nolan and I on the other. When Ethan lifts the covers from the trays, I'm shocked at the display of food before me. One tray has four New York strip steaks, all separated by dividers just big enough to fit each cut of beef. Another tray is covered with jumbo shrimp, while another is stacked with salad. Smaller containers of dressing, steak sauce, and cocktail sauce adorn the table, and there are four glasses of water to go with it all. It's quite the array, especially for ordering out.

"That's what I'm talking about," says Ethan, just before he grabs a ceramic plate from the center of the table and lifts a piece of steak from the tray.

"Damn, bro. What happened to ladies being first?" Nolan asks with a look of bewilderment on his face.

E freezes. "Oh ... uhh, you want this particular steak?" he asks me.

I nearly erupt into laughter. "No, I'm good. Thank you," I say, as I reach for a plate and use the silver tongs to cover it with salad.

"Girl, all you're going to eat is a salad?" Jackson inquires.

"Hell no," I reply. "This is my warm-up. There's no chance I'm not going to eat some of those jumbo shrimp."

"That's what I'm talking about," Jackson replies. "Don't be holding back because you're in front of Nolan. He's ugly anyway."

I try to answer, but end up laughing instead.

"Boy, I know you're not calling *me* ugly," Nolan fires back, before pausing to glare at me. "Wow, him calling me ugly seems awfully hilarious to you, Bree."

Everyone laughs except for Nolan, who twists his lips together, jokingly upset.

We spend the next few minutes getting our plates together and diving into our food. Everything tastes incredible, and I realize the cloud that was above my head this morning has completely vanished thanks to Nolan and his friends. I hadn't even thought about Melissa's morning drama, but then Nolan asks the question.

"So, did anything get worked out with your friend this morning?"

The three of them continue eating, but I stop chewing altogether, immediately reaching maximum annoyance.

"Umm, no," I answer. "My ex friend had nothing to say that I wanted to hear. So, I think we might be done being friends."

"Damn. What happened? If you don't mind me asking," Ethan asks, never taking his eyes off the last bit of his steak.

"My friends are a bit closed-minded," I reply. "They don't like anything different from them or their way of thinking. So, when I was assigned the interview that brought Nolan and I together, they gave me a lot of shit about it. They had some disparaging things to say about BDSM, Nolan, and this club —all without having ever stepped foot in here. It rubbed me the wrong way, and now that I've met you all, I feel even stronger about it. So, the three of us might not be able to be friends when it's all said and done. Plus, things between Nolan and I ..."

I stop talking when I realize what I'm about to say, but E and J are already smirking.

"Oh, you don't have to pause," Ethan says.

"Yeah, we recognized that immediately," J quips. "Not to mention that Nolan never talks about the people he's seeing, but he can't seem to shut up about you. So, E and I already know what's up, and we think it's awesome."

The warmth that erupts inside me spreads through my limbs and finds a home in my heart. I love how calm and accepting they all are. It's like talking to people I've known my entire life even though we barely know each other at all.

"Well, I appreciate the support," I say, partly to myself.

"You know, it's sad how people can be like that," Ethan says. He sets his plate down on the table and leans back against the plush, black cushion. "This world is full of people who are different, and that's what makes us beautiful. Why the fuck would we all want to be exactly the same?"

"Boring," Jackson agrees with an exclamation.

"And the thing about the people who want us to be the same as them," Ethan goes on. "They're the ones who tend to be the most hostile. Meanwhile, the people who are different and enjoy being who they are—we're the peaceful ones."

"I think it's because we're actually happy with who we are," Nolan chimes in. "We're happy being who we are and doing what makes us happy—loving who makes us happy. Other people are unhappy with who they are inside, so they get this weird jealousy for people who are happy because they can't attain it themselves. They can't find in themselves what we've found in ourselves."

"That jealousy is a bitch!" Jackson shouts.

"Fucking haters everywhere," Ethan says.

"They're on the outside mad as hell, while we're on the inside having a blast," Nolan says with a shrug.

"Sucks to be them," says Ethan.

"Sucks to be plain, bland, and boring as fuck," Jackson agrees.

"Fuck them all," says Nolan, and the other two join in.

"Fuck them all!" they shout together, before all three burst into laughter. You would think the three of them had been drinking, but there isn't any alcohol around. This is just their usual banter, and it makes me wonder if I was ever really friends with Melissa and Teagan, because we never had camaraderie like this.

"Don't worry about it, Bree," Ethan says, still chuckling to himself. "We got your back. If you need friends, we got you."

I smile wide and proud, but before I can respond, I'm cut off by the sound of feet stomping up the stairs. All four of us watch the top step, waiting for whoever has entered the club to emerge, and I swear, all of the joy is sucked out of the room when we see Maddy come into view. She's dressed for work, wearing all-black, with her blond hair hanging down in tight curls. She's truly a beautiful woman, but she looks miserable all the time, and when she sees me sitting next to Nolan, she stops at the top step and just stands there.

"What's up, Maddy?" Nolan says, greeting her because no one else had.

Maddy's eyes stay on me for far too long before she finally tears them away to look at Nolan. When the two of them lock eyes, her demeanor noticeably softens.

"Hi," she says to Nolan and to Nolan only. "Can we talk?"

Nolan keeps his eyes on Maddy. "Is it about business?"

Maddy pinches her lips together.

"Business," she says, before pointing to the group of us. "Is *this* business?"

Nolan sighs. "Maddy, I'm having lunch with my people."

"Yeah? Then what's *she* doing here?"

Everything stills, ice forming all over the furniture just from the coldness in Maddy's glare.

"What's the matter?" she goes on, and for the first time, I hear the pure rage in her tone. There's something inside Maddy that I've never seen before, but I get the feeling everyone else in here has, and they're doing their best to avoid it. "She doesn't have enough info for her little article?"

"Why does it matter, Maddy?" Nolan asks, and it's

obvious he's the designated spokesperson for the group when it comes to dealing with Maddy.

"Because she's here ... in my VIP section ... and it doesn't look like there's an interview going on," Maddy snips. "It looks like she's having lunch with you all—something *I've* never even done. Not to mention I could hear all of you whooping and hollering from downstairs. Sounds like the four of you are just having a good old time. The happy couple of E and J, and now Nolan ... and the journalist."

"Maddy, you don't know what you're talking about," Nolan says, but Maddy seems to know more than he cares to admit.

"I don't? Have you fucked?"

The ice that was forming before explodes into a giant ball of freezing snow that sticks to all of us. My heart begins to race a million beats per second as I'm overcome with anxiety, because Maddy looks furious when no one answers. Her face twists into a glare of both anger and pain as she eyes Nolan, but the pain melts away when her eyes shift and she gawks at me.

I gasp, flinching as Maddy stares daggers at me. If looks could kill, they'd be planning my funeral right now, and from the way she's staring, I'm not sure Maddy isn't already planning it for real. The look on her face terrifies me to the point of shock, and all I can do is stare back. My lungs stop working as I hold my breath, but she doesn't turn away.

"Maddy," Nolan barks, and the sound of his voice finally breaks the trance.

Maddy looks at Nolan for a second, and I sense the pleading in her eyes before she whirls around and walks back down the stairs. We listen to her stomp all the way toward the exit and slam the door shut behind her.

"Damn, is she okay?" I ask, my heart still pounding from the most intense stare down I've ever had.

INTERVIEW WITH A SADIST

"She'll be fine," Nolan says, but from the look on his face, I know there's no confidence in his words.

Chapter Thirty-One

I don't know what to think about Maddy. Although we didn't talk about her almost at all after she stormed out of the club, she never left my mind. While I obviously don't know exactly what's going on with her, I'm not an idiot. Either she and Nolan were once a thing, or she's fixated on him and doesn't want anybody else getting close.

I didn't want to bring it up in front of E and J, but seeing as how Nolan invited me back to the club tonight, I need to know the details about Maddy if he and I are going to continue down this path. I can tell from the way Nolan deals with her that he's used to doing it, so if he knows what's up, I need to as well, because she doesn't seem to be getting any better. As for Nolan's invite, how could I possibly turn it down?

This week has been nothing if not chaotic. I have new feelings popping up and poking holes in my life, causing leaks all over the place that have made me feel lost at sea. Sometimes I'm floating on my back with my face to the sun, other times I'm face-down on the verge of drowning from the onslaught. It all came to a head this morning when Melissa decided to

INTERVIEW WITH A SADIST

show up to my apartment and cause another leak, flooding my life with an overload of emotion and frustration. So, when Nolan asked me to come to the club, I jumped at the opportunity to blow off some steam. Nolan is the best thing in my life at the moment, plus this gives me another chance to go into the club to see how it operates without looking at it like a journalist. Let's face it, tonight's visit is not going to be about my story in the Inquirer. Tonight is about me.

After struggling to choose an outfit, I decide to settle on something sexy and comfortable at the same time—something that will help me fit into the dark atmosphere of the club. I go with an all-black lounge set, with a high split top that opens above my navel on one side, and tight leggings. Black and gray heels button up the outfit, and after getting my hair and makeup perfect, I step out of the apartment and start my trip to The Black Collar.

The entire drive over is filled with excitement and anxiety. The last time I was at the club, I was doing my best to document what I was seeing so I could describe it to the Inquirer's readers. I wanted to see every corner, and breathe in the atmosphere of the place so I could represent it honestly as a journalist. Now, as I park my car, the glowing sign above the door is completely different. I'm here as a guest of the club and of Nolan, but I'm also a participant in the lifestyle. I'm not just here to view it, I'm here to take part in it. I'm here to live it, and by the time I reach the bouncer, I feel like I'm looking over the side of a high bridge, my stomach in knots and my mind racing too fast for me to settle on anything.

Music blares from inside the club as I reach the same bouncer I met the first time I was here. He speaks into a radio on his shoulder just as I step up to him, and before I can say a word, the door to the club opens and out steps Nolan. The small line of people trying to get in without filling out the online questionnaire grows silent as Nolan walks up to me wearing black pants and a black, quarter-zip polo shirt. The torso of the shirt is black, but the sleeves and collar are black, white, and gray plaid. As usual, he looks phenomenal and sucks up all of the attention on the street.

"Hey," he says, greeting me with a hug and soft kiss on the neck when he leans in.

I shiver and push away a strong desire to beg him to bite me in the same spot. "Hey."

"You look incredible," he says, and I can't help but fixate on the fact that he's not trying to be quiet. It doesn't matter to him that we're in front of his bouncer and an entire line of people trying to get into the club. He compliments me without regard to anyone else. It's like he's claiming me.

"Thank you," I answer, smiling. "So do you, which is nothing new."

"Thanks. You ready for your second dose of this place?"

"You have no idea."

"That's my girl. Let's go."

Nolan takes me by the hand and leads me away from the gawking crowd, and we step into the atmosphere of The Black Collar. The curtains are up and the doors are open, giving a full view of all of the dark rooms brightened by bouncing lights of varying colors. Bass from the music resounds inside my body, making my heart feel like it's giving off extra beats, and the smell of leather and perfume fills the air.

This is it. This is the life inside a BDSM club, and I breathe it in. The sound of cracking whips snapping against exposed flesh consumes me, making me jealous of whoever is enduring the pain, because I now know what it's like to be hit. I understand the sensation of beautiful agony, and I want it again. Even with my nipples still sore from last night, I'm ready for more. I want the sting of a flogger on my ass again.

As Nolan leads me down the hall on our way to the bar, I glance inside each room as we pass them. My heart flutters when I see men and women strapped to the St. Andrew's Crosses in the impact room, and I yearn to experience their pleasure. Unlike last time, I'm not seeing all of this for the first time and wondering how it makes me feel. I know how I feel, and what's more is that I know how it feels. By the time we reach the dancefloor I feel swamped by my desire to play. It's new to me and I can barely believe it, but just walking through the club has made me horny as fuck.

When we finally reach the bar, I find myself biting my lip as I look up at the cages above the dancefloor. Nolan orders us a bottle of Cristal from Ethan, but my eyes stay locked onto the man and woman in the center cage. The two of them put on a fabulous show—the woman dancing with her back to the man as he flogs her over and over again. Just seeing the toy in his hands mesmerizes me. I want to be her, and I want Nolan to be him.

"Hey, you good?" Nolan asks, trying to pull my attention from the cage.

"I'm fine," I answer.

"Take this."

I turn around to find Nolan holding a double shot of a clear liquid in front of me.

"What is it?" I ask as I take it from him.

"Just vodka," he answers. "It's to jumpstart the night, then we sip the Cristal."

Nolan knocks back his shot, and I follow his lead, feeling the burn of the vodka as it sloshes down my throat and heats me up from the inside out. We follow that up by taking a big enough swig of Cristal to cut our glasses in half, and the concoction in my belly quickly mixes with my desires, multiplying the feeling of lowered inhibitions in an instant.

"Fuck," I say aloud, although I intended to whisper it, and Nolan laughs.

"What's up? Are you okay? You seem ... *different* tonight."

"What is it about this place?" I ask, turning around to look out onto the dancefloor and up at the cages filled with happy, sexy people. "I couldn't see it before, but I understand it a bit more now. There's electricity in the atmosphere, and I don't know if I've ever felt this alive in my entire life." Nolan looks at me with a flirtatious smirk. "What?" I say, smiling back.

"Freedom looks good on you," he replies before taking another swig of Cristal.

"Freedom? Freedom from what?"

"From the closed-mindedness you were raised with. Freedom from being jailed inside your own judgment of yourself and others for anything outside the norm. This is freedom to be who you truly are, and to understand that wanting to feel pleasure doesn't make you wrong, it makes you smart. Life is short, and it'll be over before any of us know it. What you're feeling now is the understanding of how short it all is, and that it would be such a waste not to enjoy it—not to do what makes you happy. I see the realization on your face, Bree, and it's fucking beautiful.

"You understand that as long as your desires don't cause harm or trauma to anyone, then doing what you want isn't wrong. I've watched you go from closed off, to curious, to open, to informed, to understanding, and tonight you're at the final part—appreciation. I've witnessed a metamorphosis in you, and through each stage of it, you've only become more beautiful to me. The fact that you didn't fuck with any of this before you met me makes it even better, because I know your feelings about it are genuine. You're not trying to impress me. You just *are* impressive. It's been a gift to watch you change for the better, and I feel privileged to have experienced it with you."

A flood of raw emotion washes over me as I realize this is the first time in my life I've ever felt acceptance like this. From the time I was a child, there has always been judgment hanging over me from either my family or friends. I've lived inside a box, and not only was I not allowed to break out of it, I wasn't even allowed to question why I was in it, or acknowledge that there ever was a box. I was expected to sit inside my prison and feel grateful for its existence, because the box was supposed to be my guide to the perfect life of white picket fences and pristine kitchens for me to stand barefoot in, while I waited for my white-collar husband to come home from work. That was always supposed to be my future, and anything off that path was simply a distraction and wrong. What I *wanted* was wrong. What I *felt* was wrong. *I* was wrong, and I never had anyone around to tell me different until I met Nolan. With him, I feel seen. He truly sees me for who I am, and he doesn't judge me for it. He accepts me and welcomes me to new and open thoughts. He wants to watch me grow, and I never knew how good it could feel to be free to do it.

My thoughts swarm me, making me feel dazed and exhilarated, and before I can think better of it, I grab Nolan by the shirt and pull him into me. We kiss in front of the bar with music filling our ears, alcohol flowing through our veins, and freedom shrouding us like a protective blanket. We make out in front of everyone, and although I can feel the stares of those around us and I can hear the whooping and hollering of Ethan from behind the bar, Nolan is my only focus. Our tongues fall into a rhythmic groove that adds an immeasurable amount of fuel to the growing fire inside me, and the rest of the world washes away. I no longer see or hear them, I only feel Nolan, and I want to feel more than just a kiss.

When we pull away, my senses kick back in and the world returns like I've emerged from under water. The music of the club blares, but it's nothing compared to the sound of my own heartbeat.

"Thank you," I tell Nolan.

He frowns. "For what?"

"For accepting me," I say, before giving him another peck on the lips.

He smiles. "That's not something you have to thank me for, but it's my pleasure."

We lock eyes for a moment as my thoughts run wild. I just got here, but all I want is to be alone with him. I came out so I could blow off the steam of my shitty day, but I didn't know that all I really needed was Nolan.

"I'm so glad I met you," I tell him. "Now take me to your office."

Nolan's head tilts to the side. He heard me, but he wants to hear it again, and it's obvious from the devilish grin on his face. "What?"

"Take me to your office ... and fuck me ... Sir," I say for the very first time in my life, and my entire body reacts to it. I don't know where it came from, and I have no idea why I say it, but it feels like saying the one word I was always meant to say.

I remember Nolan describing the encounters he'd had with the woman he called his Little One. Back then, I didn't understand why anyone would want to call someone Sir, but I get it now.

It's simple. He's not my boss in a company. This isn't the military, and he's not my strict father who asks me to say "Yes, Sir," and "No, Sir." But, he's the man I want to give myself over to. I *want* to submit to him. I want him to have high expectations of my submission, and I want to reach them. I want to call him Sir because I want him to own it. I want him to own me. I want to be his—to be under his control and under his protection. I don't have a kink for being a little girl, but I do want to submit to him wholly and completely—for him to be my guide, my savior, my tormentor, my punisher, my protector, my god. He is my Sir.

"Take me to your office," I repeat as he pulls me closer until we're centimeters apart. "And fuck me, Sir."

Horns practically grow from Nolan's head as he looks at me, his face darkening with a satisfied deviance that sends chills up my spine and wetness between my legs. His grip tightens around my waist, and I watch as he gives way to the sadist within him, letting him have free rein.

"You want to give yourself to me?" he asks in nearly a growl.

"Yes ... Sir," I reply, emphasizing the last word—the one I know he wants to hear most.

"You want me to own you?"

"Yes, Sir."

"Are you mine?"

"Completely, Sir. Do with me as you please, just do it *now*."

Nolan's grip tightens so much it hurts as he struggles to keep himself bound together. He's ready to lose control, and I'm ready to let him.

"Say no more, Princess," he says as he kisses me again, before turning toward the stairs. "Come with me."

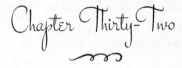

Chapter Thirty-Two

Our worlds collide and explode when the door closes. Before the lights are even flipped on, Nolan has his mouth pressed against mine and my back pinned against the wall. He smothers me with his passion, kissing me lustfully as he holds my face in the palms of both his hands. The erotica in the room is turned all the way up until there's no room left. Nolan locks the door and flicks the light switch behind me, but even when the lights come on, none of it matters. There is no desk, couch, or decor. There is only he and I, our bodies intertwined, our hearts beating in sync, and our desires to dive into our kinks as the driving force for it all.

"How is this possible?" Nolan asks, pulling my face away from his so he can look at me. "How's it possible for you to be so perfect?"

Infatuation and craving roar to life in my chest, but I don't know how to respond. How does one reply to such a question? I have no idea, but Nolan doesn't give me time to answer anyway. He's back on me in a flash, our tongues caressing each other until I pull away a second time.

"Give it to me," I command. "You know what I crave.

Please give it to me, Sir."

"Tell me again that you're mine," Nolan says. "Say it again so I know you won't leave once I hurt you."

"I'm yours, Sir. You introduced this world to me. I belong in it because of you. I'm not going anywhere."

Nolan smiles as he takes two steps back. "Good girl. Now, on your knees."

Adrenaline pumps through my veins with the force of an engine as I swallow hard and slowly do as I'm told. Nolan stands back and watches me, his face devoid of all emotion as I lower myself to the floor. Once I'm down, his figure becomes so much more imposing. He grows to twice his size as he menacingly looks down at me, and I feel powerless below him —exactly how I like it.

I place my palms on my thighs and go still, waiting for Nolan's next command.

"Good. Now don't move, and don't speak," he says, before turning around to walk to the cabinet in the corner. I watch him open it and pull out a black ball fastened between two leather straps. A ball gag—something I've never experienced before. My heart quickens just looking at it.

"Open," Nolan says when he reaches me. He holds the gag in front of my mouth, and when I part my lips, he shoves it in, fastening the straps tight behind my head. Once it's on, he steps back and looks at me. "God, you're so fucking beautifully disgusting it makes my cock throb. You make me want to skip everything and get right to fucking you until you shatter, but I'm a Dom after all, and I'll be patient. We'll take our time, Princess. You will answer with a nod of your head when asked a question, otherwise, you'll be silent. Do you understand?"

I nod my head and bite down on the ball so I don't smile behind it. Who would've known that I would fall in love with sexual acts of this nature? In two seconds flat, I went from no experience with a ball gag to absolutely loving the feeling of one in my mouth. Drool pools around my tongue and I can't do anything to stop it from leaking out. It falls to the floor in a string of spit, but I'm not disgusted. I *want* to be distasteful and nasty, as long as it's for him.

"You're so fucking incredible," he says as a puddle of spit forms on the floor beneath me. He's not turned off by it. Somehow, he likes it and it drives me crazy.

Nolan quickly makes his way behind me and crouches down at my back. He ties my hair into a ponytail for me, then wraps the hair around his fist and uses it to lift me to my feet. Pain screams from the back of my head down my neck, but it's not torturous. I'm aroused by it, and I moan as he uses my hair to guide me back to the wall directly next to the door.

"You're my perfect little slut, aren't you?" he asks as he tears at my leggings, forcefully yanking them down until they're at my ankles.

I nod my head, and Nolan slams a hand onto my throat as he slaps my pussy with the other hand. I squeal and squirm beneath his touch, and he tightens his grip around my throat. As the air to my brain is cut off, Nolan holds his grip, watching as my face fills with tension and I know I'm changing colors.

"Yes," he says, smiling like the devil himself. "That's it, Princess. Brighten up for me. Look how beautiful you are."

Nolan lets go of my throat, and just as I'm about to suck in air, he slaps me across the face, not hard enough to knock me over, but enough to give me a perfect stinging cheek.

"I want to fuck you so bad, Bree," he says as he uses the hand between my legs to rub my clit. My knees wobble beneath his touch, but his other hand keeps me standing. All I can do is moan behind my gag.

"Look at this perfect little pussy." Nolan says as he looks down. "Goddamn, every inch of you is a work of art."

Nolan reaches back and smacks my clit the same way he just slapped my face. The pain radiates from my pussy to each of my limbs, and my moan pushes its way past my gag until it reaches the rest of the office. My legs shake under my weight, and just when I stabilize myself, he does it again. The sound of the slap echoes and bounces off the walls of the office, sending stinging tears to my eyes.

"Yes, Bree," Nolan says, enjoying every second of the torment. "You're such a good girl for me. I fucking love it."

He reaches back and slaps my pussy again, and I nearly collapse from the pain, but before my body can go limp, Nolan drops to his knees and clamps his mouth on my clit, licking it over and over again.

"Oh, fuck," I mumble behind the ball gag, my words never actually leaving my mouth. Instead, only spit escapes and falls down onto Nolan's shoulder, but he's too busy eating me out to notice.

I wrap my hands around his head and pull him forward, encouraging him to keep going as I feel myself careening toward the edge of an orgasm. I press my back against the wall and push my hips out so I can grind against his face, and he moans into my pussy, loving it all.

"Yeah?" he says, looking up at me. "You want to fuck my face?" he asks, before slapping my clit again with perfect aim, making it sing with pain and pleasure.

I nod my head, and he slaps me again, jolting my body.

"You want to fuck my face, you little whore?" he says, and I nod eagerly. He slaps my clit again and I cry out. "Yeah? Then do it, and don't stop until you give me all of you to drink. Do it. Fuck my face, Bree."

Nolan slaps my clit one last time, before lunging forward and sucking my clit into his mouth. Like a fucking madwoman, I grab the back of his head and hold on as I grind myself against his face with absolutely no mercy. I know it must hurt to have a grown woman press down with all of her weight, but I don't fucking care. I squeeze the back of Nolan's head and fuck his face until sweat beads through my clothes. I fuck until my lungs are on fire. I grind until the orgasm I'm craving finally sweeps over me in a fury, and I burst like a pipe into Nolan's mouth.

My screams are too strong to be held back by the gag this time. Every decibel squeezes its way past the ball and fills the room as I press Nolan's mouth against my pussy until it's all over, and I'm left a trembling mess on weak legs. Nolan stands up and slams his wet mouth against the other side of the ball gag, kissing me without kissing me, and I kiss back. Sweat, cum, and spit soak our mouths and fall down in long strings to our clothes and the floor. Neither of us is concerned because this is heaven, and there are no worries in heaven.

"You taste so fucking good," Nolan says, backing away enough to unfasten his pants. "Now I'm going to ravage that dripping wet pussy of yours until your legs don't work. You're going to have to fucking crawl out of this room tonight. Are you ready for my cock, Princess?"

I nod my head as Nolan removes his belt. He reaches into his pants, and just as he's about to pull his beautiful cock out for me to see, there's a knock at the door.

We freeze, both of us with bulging eyes as we wonder who the hell it could be. I panic, but Nolan shakes his head and raises a hand. He's calm as he clears his throat and speaks with a deep, confident voice.

"Yeah?"

The sound of the door knob rattling sends a spike of fright through my heart, but luckily Nolan locked the door.

"Hey!" Nolan shouts, stepping closer to the door. "Who the fuck is it?" he barks, and the response stops us both dead in our tracks.

"Nolan, can I come in? It's Maddy."

Chapter Thirty-Three

~ NOLAN ~

"Nolan, can I come in? It's Maddy."

With my cock as hard as a rock and stretching the fabric of my pants, I freeze in place with my eyes as large as saucers. My heart hammers, the blood in my veins rushes like a waterfall, and I can feel the burning sensation of Bree's eyes as she stares at the side of my face, wondering what to do.

How did it come to this? Fucking Madelaine ... Maddy. Still not able to move on after all this time, and somehow still capable of ruining things for me. While I stand in front of the door with a look of trying to remain calm, she jiggles the knob again, trying her best to get inside because I almost never lock the door to my office. This is out of the norm, and she knows it. She also knows something is brewing between Bree and I, and while I never thought it would affect her, it obviously has.

Madelaine has started to fall apart—showing up late for work, doing a piss poor job when she does manage to make it in, and butchering every relationship she enters. I can see it all crumbling around her, but it's not my place to be her savior. Not anymore.

I glance over at Bree, and she looks so delicious next to the door with the ball gag in her mouth. I have half a mind to ignore Maddy's pleas and simply bend Bree over in front of the door instead. Her leggings are down at her ankles and there's wet spots on her clothes from all of the drool, and while the sight of her makes me want to forget the entire world, I have to focus. I have to get Maddy out of here.

As quickly as I can, I button up my pants and straighten out my shirt to the best of my ability. I can't dry the wet spots from Bree's saliva, but I can try to hide them. So, I take a deep breath and step toward the door holding a finger to my lips so Bree knows to remain quiet while I handle this. When I open the door, I only open it enough to stick my head out— another major departure from the norm, but I have no choice.

"What is it, Maddy?" I say with a deep furrow in my brow. I want her to know how much she's annoying me right now, and it's not like I have to lie. Bree's bare pussy is only inches away, and not being able to taste her feels like the worst kind of torture.

Maddy stands outside my door in her usual black-on-black work clothes. Her hair is tied into a ponytail and her makeup is flawless, somehow making her blue eyes pop even more. After all the time I've known her and learned about the kind of person she is, Maddy is still a beautiful woman, and while I don't feel responsible for her, I also don't want to see her hurt.

"Hey," Maddy says in response, but her eyes shift to the small gap in the door above my head. She tries to look at me, but her eyes keep bouncing back and forth as she talks. "What's going on? I haven't seen you all night. You okay?"

I frown so hard it makes my head hurt. "Am I okay? I'm

fine, Maddy. What's up? You knocked, and tried to open the door, so I figured it was something urgent."

She tilts her head to the side trying to see in, but the only open space is above my head. "Umm ... it's nothing too urgent, I guess. Can I come in for a minute? I just need to talk to you in private."

"If it's not urgent, then why do you need to talk to me in private?" I ask, my brows still furrowed.

"Why can't I come in?" Maddy fires back with each of her words dipped in accusation.

"Because I'm fucking busy, Maddy. It's not a good time right now, and I'm not in a good mood, so if it *isn't* urgent, then I'll have to get with you later."

Maddy scoffs and shuffles her feet in frustration. "Wait. There's a guy out here who's trying to get into VIP without a reservation."

"Are you kidding me?" I snip as my annoyance reaches new heights. "Maddy, VIP is your section, and this kind of thing is something you've handled on your own a million times. Take care of it, and if you have any trouble, you get one of the bouncers to handle it. Why are you acting brand new?"

"Why won't you let me in?"

"Because you're full of shit right now, and this looks an awful lot like a familiar road I don't want to go down with you."

She flinches, apparently feeling physical pain from my words, and I recognize the moment the fight leaves her body. Maddy looks down at the floor for a moment, obviously distracted by her thoughts, before she looks up at me, nodding slowly.

"Okay, Nolan," she says, all of the determination having left her voice. "I'll take care of it. Go back to *whatever* you were doing. Bye."

I think about responding with words that would lessen

the blow of my rejection, but Maddy is gone before I can put a sentence in order. Through the gap in the door, I watch her walk down the hall and disappear into the thick crowd of people in the VIP section, never turning around once.

The second she's gone, I close the door and turn my attention back to Bree, who's still cemented against the wall next to the door with her pants down and the ball in her mouth. I see the apprehension in her eyes, and the last thing I want is to remove the gag from her mouth and have a conversation about Maddy. Maddy's actions are making it to where Bree and I will eventually have to talk, but not today. Not right now.

"I'm sorry about that," I say, hoping to erase the puzzled look on Bree's beautiful face as I step close to her. Her body heat alone makes my cock instantly hard again, but I don't dive right in. I can see she's concerned, and I'd be an asshole if I ignored that and just took what I wanted. So, I exhale and do the right thing.

"I want you to know something, Bree," I begin, looking her directly in the eyes. "Looking at you right now, seeing you standing there with your leggings at your ankles, your knees apart, and your mouth agape as drool rolls down your body makes my cock hard. I want to fuck you right now, without wasting another second. However, if our brief intermission has made you want to stop, all you have to do is shake your head from right to left. Simply shake your head, and I'll remove the gag. Otherwise, I'm going to finish what I started in this room tonight. Now's your chance."

I watch with a pounding heart as Bree glares at me. There is no doubt that questions are flowing through her mind, wreaking havoc on her comfort with me. Questions without answers can be unbearable, and I wouldn't hesitate to stop if she said so. I'm on pins and needles as a full minute ticks by without movement or a single sound. The two of us look at

INTERVIEW WITH A SADIST

each other in silence, and while Bree is obviously marred by curiosity, she doesn't shake her head.

I take a step closer to her, and she doesn't move. I place a hand on her hip, and still, she doesn't move. I lower myself back into a crouching position, my mouth only inches from her glistening pussy, and she remains still. Bree doesn't move a single muscle until I use two fingers to lift the tiny hood over her clit, and run my tongue over the exposed nub. Her movement is not a head shake, it's a writhing release of tension as she relaxes her body and gives herself to me once again. In an instant, Maddy is gone, and there is only us.

"Fuck," I mumble between licks. "A single second away from you is too long."

Bree moans above me, and I look up to find her eyes closed. Her hands grip the sides of my head again as she embraces me, enjoying our reentry into erotica. While still holding her clit hood up, I slowly insert two fingers into her pussy and curl them up toward her stomach from the inside, desperately searching for her G-spot as I finger her and lick her clit simultaneously.

"Fuck," she tries to say, but it comes out as a muddled, incoherent moan, which only spurs me on.

Over the span of a few minutes, I work myself into a rhythm, pumping my fingers like a piston while I suck her clit and glide my tongue up and down. Bree's breathing becomes cadenced as sweat begins to bead on both of our foreheads, and I don't dare stop. I know she's on the verge of a second orgasm, and second orgasms take time and patience, so I hunker down and commit to reaching the finish line. My mouth aches and my arm quakes, but I continue because giving her the orgasm she deserves is what it's all about. If my cock stiffened anymore it would cripple me, but I keep going until the familiar sound of an oncoming orgasm climbs from behind the ball gag.

"Come on, baby," I whisper as I dig in and work for what I crave. "Give it to me. Be my good girl and come in my mouth."

"Shit," Bree tries to yell, just as my hard work pays off and she detonates. Her body erupts into a frenzy of convulsions as she struggles to keep herself standing, and I keep going until she finally comes back down to earth.

Bree breathes heavily, panting hard as she struggles to suck in enough air, but I don't wait for her to gather herself. I've waited long enough, and I can't manage it another fucking second. I have to be inside her here and now.

I stand up quickly like there isn't enough time, like I don't know if another asshole is going to knock on my office door, and I grab Bree by the throat. She moans beneath my grip as I squeeze her airway just to make her face change colors one last time, before I spin her around and slam her against the door. I don't give a fuck if the entire club is listening now. I'm too hard and I want her too badly. Only the signal of her shaking head—only the safe word could stop me now.

I'm so fucking riled up by the sight of her, I don't have the patience to wait once she's in position. Forcefully, I bend Bree over just enough to give me access to her pussy, and I slide my cock all the way inside. I'm pleased to find that she's absolutely soaking wet, and I use it as motivation to fuck her ferociously.

I grip her hips so tight that I know she'll bruise, and I use every inch to shred her, pounding in and out of her pussy with forceful, savage strokes that would slam Bree's head against the door if she wasn't using her hands to brace herself. She moans behind the ball gag, her volume rising higher and higher with each stroke, culminating in a blaring squeal when I slap her ass and leave a beautiful, deep red handprint. Her sounds and the sight of my mark on her send a gallon of blood surging to my cock and I'm immediately bowled-over.

"Ah, fuck," I growl, still pumping. "Yes, I'm going to fucking come! Yes!"

Just as I'm wrecked, I snatch my cock out of Bree's pussy and use my hand to stroke out thick, white strands of cum onto her ass. My knees wobble as I jerk myself, coming harder than ever while I stare at my handprint on her pristine ass cheek. Her ass and my cum is the perfect combination, and I collapse onto the floor in complete satisfaction.

Still panting, Bree kneels on the floor next to me and I use the last bit of my energy to sit up and detach the ball gag from her face. Once it's gone, I toss it onto the floor as she wipes away spit and wiggles her mouth around to loosen the muscles in her face. I watch her and smile, tickled by the sight of her trying to bring sensation and life back into her red cheeks. When she sees me watching, she stops moving her mouth and begins to laugh. That's when I reach out and pull her body down onto mine, and we lay on the floor together like two kids too overtaken by lust and infatuation to need a bed for affection.

We lay on the floor of my office giggling together, and I'm not even sure what we're laughing at. Is it the fact that we had to stop because of Maddy, or because my cum is now smeared across my floor? Perhaps it's because Bree looked funny swaying her jaw back and forth after I removed the ball gag, because she's not used to wearing one.

Our laughter could be for a multitude of reasons, but none of them really matter. All that matters is that we have laughter in common. We have a sense of humor in the middle of the craziness that has become our lives since we met, and from my experience, I know how important that is.

I may not know the future or how the past will affect us, but I can recognize a perfect present when I see one, and this is it. Right here. Right now. Just me and Bree.

Fade to Black

Chapter Thirty-Four

"Goddamn it. I can't stand when the mall is packed like this. You know I hate people."

"Actually, I didn't know that, but it's nice to learn something new about you, Octavia."

The two of us stand in the middle of the food court with our hands on our hips, watching a violent sea of teenagers and families stride by on their way to one of the many stores in Philadelphia Mills. We should've known better than to come here on the weekend, but Nolan is occupied with meetings today, and Octavia's husband, Mike, is having a boy's day. So, it's just us ladies at the jam-packed mall, with gossip to spew and money to spend. Now that I think about it, it's the perfect way to spend my Saturday evening.

It has been a few days since I've had time to sit down and talk to Octavia. In our line of work, we spend plenty of time outside the office on assignments, and sometimes our schedules don't line up enough for us to be in the same place at the same time. While all of my life-changing events with Nolan have been taking place, Octavia has been out and about. So, we've got a lot of catching up to do, and I can already hear the expletives and exclamations before I even begin.

The first store we enter is Barnes & Noble, because ... of course. There's no way I'm going to come to the mall and allow myself to be swarmed by all these people without at least giving myself something to look forward to when I get home, and everyone loves a great book. I mean, who the hell doesn't?

Unlike the rest of the mall, B&N actually isn't filled to the brim with people, although I am immediately shoulder-checked by a curly-haired blonde on our way in, who doesn't even turn around after she hits me. While our society needs more people to read, everyone would much rather be chained to their cellphones, scrolling TikTok and leaving bookstores to rot and die. Today, however, I'm grateful that the place isn't packed, because I don't need tons of people around when I start talking to Octavia about my sex life.

As we enter the bookstore, Octavia trails close on my heels as I quickly make my way inside and head straight for the escalator to the second floor. I dodge the counter and do a spin move to avoid a collision with a woman clutching a stack of books, and step onto the moving stairs like a true B&N professional.

"What are you, a running back?" Octavia says, giggling as she steps on behind me. "You're out here dodging tackles and stiff-arming children like you're getting ready for the combine."

I chuckle as I turn around. "I didn't stiff-arm any children. That kid was at least a teenager."

Octavia, with her black skin glistening under the lights, laughs. "You're a mess. Are you looking for something in particular? You aimed straight for the second floor like you already know what's up there."

"I do," I admit as the stairs reach the next level and we step off. "I'm actually interested in this new book that just came out. I hear it's incredible, and this author has become a huge deal lately. Here is it."

I pick up the hardcover and hand it to Octavia, who looks it over.

"*Right of the Slash*," she says, reading the title before turning the book over and checking out the back. "By Nasir Booker. Oh, he's cute, too. What does he write about?"

"BDSM," I tell her, and her eyes quickly shift over to me a little wider than they were before. "Ah, so *that's* why you're interested. All right, since you brought it up, go ahead and spill the beans."

"Spill the beans? People still say that?"

"Don't you dare deflect, Bree. You spill those beans right now or I'm walking out of here."

I take the book back from her and open it, glancing at the inside flap to read the blurb. "There's not much to spill. We've been hanging out a lot and having a great time. He's incredible, and the people I've met from hanging out with him have been amazing, too. His friends, E and J, are super cool."

"Ah, unlike those two stiff bitches you were hanging out with before?"

"Hey, those stiff, stuck up, judgmental, bratty bitches were my friends. Well, at least I thought they were, and yes, E and J are much cooler than Melissa and Teagan. So, I've upgraded my life in all aspects."

"That's great, Bree. I'm really happy for you," Octavia says as I tuck the book under my arm and pick up another by Nasir Booker. "So, is it safe to assume that you're now very comfortable with the owner of the BDSM club? Are you guys officially dating?"

"Umm," I begin, still unsure how to answer that question. "Yeah, I think we are. We've done a lot since I told you about the time he flogged me on the couch in his office. We've been out to dinner ... sort of ... I've even been to his house since then."

"Oh, you two are dating big time. You've been to his house? Wow. Did you guys watch Nutflix?"

"No, we definitely didn't watch a mov—wait, what?"

"Did you role play? Did he turn you into Princess Bubblecum?"

"Octavia!" I blare as I burst into gut-wrenching laughter. I laugh so hard I have to place my hand on the shelf to hold myself up. "Nutflix and Princess Bubble*cum*? What is wrong with you?"

"Don't laugh at me. I bet you'd get an Oscar for that role. Anyway, keep going. Besides the kinky sex that now has you ready to purchase books by Nasir Booker, how is he? Did he turn out to be a good person? As much as I care about the sex being great, what I really want for you, Bree, is to be happy. So, is he a good guy?"

As I manage to pull myself together and stand up straight, I think about everything I've learned about Nolan since we met. He has always been polite, even when he's being sadistic. He has always cared about honesty and love, and I've never heard him be an asshole to any of his friends or employees.

"To be honest," I start, grinning with pride as I think about him. "Nolan has done nothing but impress me. Yes, the sex is out of this world and he has shown me things I never would've dreamed I'd experience, let alone enjoy, but we have a connection that resonates with me. We laugh a lot, which I'm not used to with a guy. Most men who are as sexy as Nolan *know* they're sexy, and they try too hard to fit that image. They're always smoldering and licking their lips."

"God, I hate that shit."

"Right? So annoying. Anyway, Nolan doesn't do any of that. Fitting the female gaze is just part of his personality—the way he dresses, the cologne he wears, how humble he is in a world where he's revered, all of it is perfect. I actually find myself being envious of how well he and his friends get along. They're all so cool, funny, and accepting. The whole thing has been a dream. I don't know, maybe I got lucky and stumbled into *the* one."

"All from an assignment that you didn't even want," Octavia says, beaming as she listens. "Look at God!"

I scoff and chuckle. "Please. Unless your god is into watching me squirm from nipple clamps and drool from a ball gag, I'd say this isn't divine intervention."

Just as I finish talking, I turn to find an old woman standing directly behind me. She looks at me with wide eyes, obviously having overheard what I said about clamps and gags. She speed-walks away from us, and the second she's out of earshot, Octavia and I burst into laughter again.

"Well, I just ruined her day," I joke, still chuckling.

"Or made it. You never know. Don't let that gray hair fool you," Octavia quips.

After we pay for four books between the two of us, we spend the next hour roaming around the mall, talking about everything and nothing at all. While I'd like to get home and give Nolan a call, it's actually really nice just to spend time with Octavia. After everything that happened between my college friends and me, it's great to have her around, and part of me wishes I would've been spending my time hanging out with her instead of wasting it on those two. Nonetheless, we're here now, and our trip to Philadelphia Mills has been a tremendous, hilarious success.

With multiple bags in both of our hands, we finally decide to make our way out to the parking lot. Unfortunately, that means we have to leave the way we came in, which is through the food court. We parked where we did because it was close to Barnes & Noble, but now that we have to exit through the massive crowd of people searching for a place to eat, it feels

INTERVIEW WITH A SADIST

like we've made a mistake. So, we put our heads down and try to make a straight line for the exit.

We pass most of the crowd and walk past B&N again, which is only a few feet from the mall exit, and I glance over my shoulder at a group of people in the center of the court. Somehow, in the middle of all those people, I manage to catch eyes staring at me. A blonde with curly hair stands next to one of the many tables, and she's staring directly at me, unblinking. My feet slow down all on their own as my heart begins to race.

Is that ... Maddy?

"Hey, you good?" Octavia asks, just as a large family walks past us and directly into my line of sight, blocking the woman from view as Octavia and I step outside. The automatic doors to the mall close behind us, and we're finally underneath the sky and clouds, but my mind is consumed by the woman.

"Umm," I start, unsure of whether I saw what I think I saw. "I just thought I saw someone."

"Who?" Octavia asks, but instead of responding to her, I follow my feet as they lead me back through the doors of the mall.

I scoot past people and say, "Excuse me," more times than I can count, but by the time I make it back inside, the woman I thought I saw is gone, replaced by two teenagers making out like they're not in public. I look around to see if I can find her, but it's no use. Whoever I thought I saw is no longer there.

When I return to Octavia, she frowns. "You okay? You look like you just saw a ghost."

"I'm good," I answer. "I think my mind is just playing tricks on me."

"Oh, okay. What do you say we get something to eat before we end our evening?"

"Yeah," I say, still struggling with the image of the woman in the mall. "That sounds good."

Chapter Thirty-Five

"Okay, this is your last chance to make it as clear as possible, because today's the day I start writing this story. Final warning, Nolan," I say in a joking voice as I secure the final button on my blouse.

I only have until Wednesday to get a first draft to Chase before he loses it and burns my career to the ground. Missing deadlines is not an option with Chase. I've never done it before, and this story won't be my first time. So, when I woke up this morning, the first thing I did was call Nolan to let him know that this was it. I have no choice but to start, and if he wants to take back what he said about me writing whatever I want to write about him, now is the time to tell me.

"Nothing has changed, Princess," he says, making me smirk as I do one final makeup check in my bathroom mirror. "I'm not ashamed of my club or anything I've done, and I'm certainly not ashamed of you. You're a part of my story now, so whatever you choose to write about is up to you, but I'm good—just the devilish BDSM club owner who met a journalist and grew a very serious attachment to her. Unfortunately, in this shitty society we live in, *I'm* not the one who'll be judged if you decide to write something about us in your story. That's the part you have to think about."

"Sadly, that's very true," I say on an exhale. I approve of my makeup job and leave the bedroom on my way to the kitchen. "But, one of the many things I've learned from you is that the truth is the only part of the narrative I can control. How people react to the truth isn't my responsibility, so I can't let that decide my path for me. All I can do is inform them. After they have the info, the rest is up to them."

"Ah, so you actually were listening during our Q&A," Nolan jokes.

I scoff. "Of course. What did you think I was doing?"

"Fantasizing about bending over my couch."

I suck in a breath as a smile completely takes over my face. "Oh, well you got me there."

The two of us laugh as I finish my morning routine in the kitchen. I fill up a small travel mug full of coffee and grab a banana on my way out, before stepping out of the apartment and striding down the hall.

"All right, I've got to go now. I'm about to get in the car," I tell Nolan.

"Okay," he replies. "I'll call you later. Please drive safe."

Again, another smile. "I will. Talk to you later. Bye."

"Bye," Nolan says.

I hurriedly drop my phone into my purse and head for the exit. The second the door opens, I nearly fall down the stairs from utter disbelief and shock.

Maddy stands at the bottom of the steps with her hands in the pockets of her black hoodie. The makeup around her eyes is smudged like she's been crying, and her curly blonde hair is in tatters. She looks like she just dropped out of bed and drove here without a single care about her appearance.

I think to call her name, but it gets lodged in my throat as I stop at the landing and look at her. She glares at me, her face devoid of all emotion but her eyes blazing with intensity. Men think that enraged women are frantic and emotional, but the truth is that a woman with bristling rage in her gut looks exactly the way Maddy does right now—frighteningly calm.

It takes a while before I'm able to bring myself down the stairs. With each step, thoughts form in my head and burst like bubbles all around me. The last few times I've been around Nolan, Maddy has been trying to talk to him about something, but he hasn't done it. It could be about work, but the look on her face would suggest otherwise, and being denied access like that can lead to a problem. Also, Maddy's hair reminds me of what I thought I saw as I left the mall this weekend. That curly blonde hair stood out to me in the middle of the food court, and looking at it now only makes the memory clearer.

It was her, wasn't it? But that doesn't make any sense, because how would she know Octavia and I were going to the mall? How would she know we were going to Barnes & Noble? As much as I want the question answered, it still makes no sense, leaving me flustered as I reach the bottom of the steps and come face to face with her.

"What are you doing here, Maddy?" I finally force myself to say. I clear my throat and speak again, hoping my words don't sound so petrified this time. "Better yet, how do you know where I live?"

"I followed you home from the mall," she answers as nonchalantly as if she'd just told me the sky is blue. She has no shame or concern that I'd freak out about the admission. There isn't an ounce of care in any of the pores on Maddy's face.

"You *were* at the mall. I knew it," I snip, and the fact that I was right satisfies me and fills me with terror.

"Followed you there, too," Maddy goes on without moving any part of her body other than her mouth. She's a

INTERVIEW WITH A SADIST

robot in a trance. "I've been following you since you left the club on Friday night—you know, when you spent all that time in Nolan's office. Yeah, I knew you were in there, and I've practically been outside your apartment since you came home from the mall. You didn't leave yesterday, staying in to enjoy your Sunday while probably sexting Nolan all night. I only left to get food and come back. Even slept in my car last night."

My eyes bulge. That explains why she looks so distraught right now. This woman has been sitting in a car outside my apartment since Saturday night like a detective on a fucking stakeout. My heart begins to pound like a drum, but I'm also quickly filling with anger that fuses with my fear.

"What the fuck is wrong with you?" I bark, stepping back like a weapon just suddenly appeared in Maddy's hand. "Why? Why are you stalking me?"

"Not stalking," she says, still so calm it's baffling. "I just wanted to talk to you, but it took me some time to build up the confidence to do it. I don't know you, and I imagine your impression of me isn't good, seeing as how you came to the club at a time when I was beginning to struggle with the fact that Nolan and I wouldn't be getting back together. That realization has been hard, and done things to my state of mind that I never thought could happen to me, yet here I am. Nolan broke me, and trying to recover from that has been harder than I ever imagined."

The alarmed look on my face suddenly shifts to one of confusion. I furrow my brow and tilt my head. "What do you mean he broke you?"

Maddy's eyes drop down to the ground, where they remain as she relives whatever memories are flashing before her eyes.

"Nolan has always been the perfect combination of good guy and bad boy. He's chivalrous and kind while also being brutal. As I'm sure you've learned by now, he loves to cause pain, and I used to love letting him inflict it on me. I didn't do it because I'm a masochist. I did it because I loved that he enjoyed doing it to me. It gave me immense pleasure to know I was giving him the thing he wanted, which was to make me bleed and leave me writhing in agony every day. He loved hurting me, and I loved him for it, but he couldn't give me the thing I actually did want."

"Which was?" I ask, suddenly hooked into her story.

"To be public," Maddy admits. "He had no problem doing what we did in private, but when I wanted him to admit to the world that I was his woman, he suddenly lost his voice. I wanted him to be loud about me, and I wanted him to do it in the place where he's revered most. The Black Collar. In that club, Nolan is a god. His ability to bring people in and accept who they are, while also running the place with an iron fist has made him the leader and advocate for the life-style we've all wanted. He's our best representative, and everyone who goes to the club knows it. Every woman there wants him, and every man wants to be like him."

"I highly doubt that. It's possible to appreciate someone without wanting to sleep with them," I argue, but Maddy slides right past me.

"I wanted them all to know," she says, her jaw suddenly tightening. "It wasn't enough that Ethan and Jackson knew how he fucked me behind closed doors. I wanted our world to know. I wanted to be front and center at the place we loved most, and he wouldn't do it, so I threw myself at him even more. I thought that if I gave him more, he'd want me, and my way to do that was to feed his sadism. I cut myself for him. I bled for him. I asked him to cut me, to torture me until I cried, to hang me until I passed out at the bottom of the rope and resuscitate me afterwards. I told him to break one of my fingers or toes, or to hit me until he knocked me unconscious—whatever it took to make him happy. I asked him to go all out, but suddenly I was doing *too much*. All of a sudden, I was taking things *too far* for him. Him! A fucking sadist!

"I was only doing it because I loved him so much, and he abruptly didn't want anything to do with me. He told me I scared him. How? He was the one who'd caused *me* so much physical pain. He wasn't afraid of me, he was scared of how much I loved him, and he broke it off with me while I was at the peak of that love.

"How did he think I would respond? Of course I showed up to his house after that. Of course I snuck into his office, stripped off my clothes and cut my palms so they would bleed onto his floor. He loved my blood before, but not now? Bullshit! I bled for him, and he wouldn't even tell the world he was with me. How fucking unfair."

Tears form in Maddy's eyes, and I can tell she's not putting on an act for me. The way she feels about Nolan, regardless of how extreme it is, is very real to her. A tear dives to the ground, and when she sees the wetness on the floor, she sniffs and looks up at me, finally coming back to the reality around us.

I'm not sure what to say. Hearing about her relationship with Nolan wasn't how I planned on starting my morning, but learning just how far she was willing to take things has me reeling. She asked him to hang her. That's a level of dedication, commitment, and ridiculousness I've never heard of before. It's no wonder Nolan ended it, but when someone is willing to go that far, you have to consider how they'll react if you break it off. Obviously, Nolan hasn't thought enough about it, because keeping her employed at his club was a terrible idea. She already thinks every woman in the place wants to fuck him, and adding me to the mix could certainly be the straw that breaks the camel's back.

"Maddy," I try to begin, but the rest of the sentence evades me.

"He's going to break you, too," she suddenly says. "It probably feels great right now, doesn't it? Him, dragging you upstairs to his office, knowing it's in the back of the VIP section where I work every night. Rubbing it in my face. You love it, don't you? Fucking him in the same office I fucked him in so many times? The way he hits you? The way he degrades you and makes you feel powerful at the same time? It's intoxicating, isn't it? Well, if you think it all feels intense now, just wait until you realize he doesn't actually care about you. Wait until it finally hits you that he doesn't give a fuck, and that he'll always keep you hidden from that precious little world he created. You just wait, Bree. If you don't get out now, you'll end up just like me. Broken."

I swallow hard, inadvertently pushing all of my responses down into the pit of my stomach. Anxiety bubbles up in my belly until it comes up in my throat and gives me heartburn, making me feel sick with tension and fear. Maddy, on the other hand, looks satisfied that she has affected me. She finally smirks before wiping it away and clearing her throat. She straightens up her stance and looks me in the eye.

"Maybe I'm wrong," she says, slowly turning on her heel. "Maybe you and Nolan will work out just fine. If that's the case ... at least I know where you live."

With that final veiled threat, Maddy turns around and walks away.

Chapter Thirty-Six

When I pull up to the club on my lunch break, Nolan, Ethan, and Jackson are walking inside without a care in the world. The club was closed last night, and the three of them enjoyed a day of football and drinks together, before having a relaxing evening and waking up to a quiet morning with birds chirping and the sun shining. None of them had a crazy stalker sitting outside their apartment, sleeping in the car like a complete psycho. They laugh together as they saunter toward the door, unlock it, and step over the threshold into their world of safety. It must be nice to be so carefree, and not be threatened first thing in the morning.

I spent the entire morning fuming about what happened with Maddy. As I sat at my desk, my coffee got cold and my stomach rumbled while Chase eyed me from his office, wondering why I wasn't working on the story that's due in forty-eight hours. Even as I felt the burning sensation of his eyes peering into me, I still couldn't bring myself to think about what to say about Nolan, because his ex was just standing at the bottom of my steps and reminding me that she knows where I live.

How do I write about how awesome Nolan and the club are when I've just been told that he will leave me high and dry? Where do I find the words to write an amazing story after the morning I had? So, I just fucking sat there thinking about all of it, glancing up at the clock every few minutes, and counting down the seconds until my lunch break just so I can get to where I am right now—speed walking through the unlocked doors of The Black Collar with fire spewing from my eyes.

When I get inside, the boys are seated on the stools around the bar. Ethan has the drawer from the register displayed on the bartop, counting money as Jackson reviews receipts and Nolan scans a large stack of documents. They seem to be in business mode now, and it doesn't look like a good time to interrupt what they have going on, but I'm too pissed to think straight.

"Nolan," I bark, and all three heads snap over to me as I stomp down the hall and into the expansive room. "Why didn't you tell me about you and Maddy? Why didn't you warn me?"

Nolan doesn't move a muscle. He doesn't even put the stack of papers down, choosing to look at me over the top of it instead, which only makes me madder.

"Bree?" he says, obviously confused by my presence. "What are you talking about?"

"Don't play stupid with me, Nolan," I snap, pointing my finger directly in his face as I step close to him, completely doused in rage and fear. "You could've told me that you and Maddy dated, and that it didn't end well. You could've told me that she was in love with you, and you broke it off with her when you knew she was showing signs of being out of her fucking mind. You could've told me she was unstable."

Nolan clears his throat and finally places the stack of papers down on the bar, while E and J look on in silence. I don't bother to glance at either of them, because I can see them both staring at me with wide eyes out of my peripheral vision. When Nolan turns back around to face me, he doesn't look angry or defensive. He's calm and collected as usual, with obvious concern in his eyes.

"I hear what you're saying," he begins. "The only problem is that I don't know what you're referring to. I *do* understand that Maddy has some issues that she needs to work out, and I've been trying to help her with that, but she doesn't want my help in the only way I can give it to her. She wants it in ... *other* ways—ways that are unacceptable to me. So, since she won't accept the counseling I told her I was willing to pay for, I won't attempt to force it on her. That's where I stand with Maddy right now.

"As for the relationship we had, I didn't tell you because it's been over for months. I've moved on, and I hoped she would, too. I don't have any lingering feelings—bad or good —and I'm not the kind of person who likes to talk about the people I used to be with. I wasn't going to talk shit about my ex to you, Bree, so I chose not to say anything. That's my explanation for everything you just said. Now, I need you to explain what happened that made you burst through the door with your hair on fire."

My frustration threatens to deflate because of how calmly he provided an explanation, but the experience was too intense to let it go just like that.

"She came to my apartment, Nolan," I inform him, and the blood in his face drains completely.

"Right after we got off the phone, I opened the door to leave and there she was, standing at the bottom of the steps like she knew I was coming. When I asked how she knew where I lived, she admitted she'd been following me since *Friday*, and that she knew I was in your office that night. She's fucking crazy. She even told me she'd slept in her car just to confront me this morning, and before it was all over, I'm pretty sure she threatened me. It was fucking scary."

Nolan suddenly gets up from the table and pulls me into a hug. I'm angry enough to push him away, but my fear needs the comfort and I end up putting my arms around him, too.

"I'm sorry, Bree," he says, his voice deep with worry. "That's crazy, and I'm so sorry that happened to you. I'll talk to Maddy."

"How you gonna do that?" Ethan says, finally chiming in. "She hasn't shown up to work since Friday night."

"I don't know, but the shit she pulled is unacceptable," Nolan replies, just as I take a step back.

"Wait, she hasn't been to work since Friday?" I ask.

The three men look at each other, and I can tell they've already talked about this.

"No," Nolan says. "I haven't seen or heard from Maddy since she came to my office on Friday. She hasn't shown up to work or answered her phone at all."

"Well, that's a fucking bad sign, isn't it?" I snip as a heavy dose of fear returns to my bloodstream.

"Hey, I'm going to find her, and I'll talk to her," Nolan says, but it does nothing to make me feel better. "I won't let anything happen to you, Bree. I promise. Maddy's situation is partly my fault, and I'll take responsibility for it. Trust me."

I pause a moment to look at Nolan, and I can see that he's being genuine. I see how much he cares and I believe he'll do whatever he can to find Maddy and talk to her, but that doesn't mean I'm not still worried. He didn't see the look in her eyes. He didn't see how robotic she was, and how placid her demeanor was when that tear fell down her face. A woman *that* upset and calm is terrifying, there isn't anything Nolan could say that would erase the memory of what has happened over the last couple of days.

"She followed me everywhere I went this weekend," I say.

My anger at Nolan becomes completely diluted by my worry, until anxiety is all I feel. "I went to the mall with my friend and Maddy was there, standing in the food court just watching me. This is serious, Nolan."

"I know," he says, pulling me in again.

As we hug, I look at E and J, and see the seriousness on their faces as well, but instead of finding comfort in their sympathy, it only makes me more afraid. Their look isn't one of empathy. It's apprehension. They're worried for me.

"Listen, I won't come to work tonight," Nolan goes on. He takes a step back but keeps both of my hands in his. "E and J can run the club tonight, and I'll go by Maddy's place to talk to her."

"What if she's not there and you can't find her?" I ask.

"Then I'll come by your place to make sure everything is good. I can even stay the night if you're comfortable with that. Whatever it takes to make sure you're safe, Bree. Okay?"

I don't know what else to say. It's either this, or stay home alone, worried to death that Maddy will find a way inside. So, I guess I have no choice but to accept this and hope for the best.

"Okay," I reply, but nothing about how I feel is okay.

Chapter Thirty-Seven

The knock at my door startles me, and as I rise from my couch, I walk to it in a sour mood. I can't even relax in my own apartment without jumping at the sound of a knock at the door. Unfortunately, my building isn't one where someone outside has to be buzzed in before they can come inside, so any stranger on the street can wander into the building and rap on any door. It's nerve wracking, but the sound of footsteps and whispers in the halls never bothered me before. Ever since Maddy showed up this morning, I've been a nervous wreck inside my own home.

When I reach the door and open it, I breathe a sigh of relief even though I knew it would be Nolan. He texted me that he was coming over forty-five minutes ago, but my anxiety still had me on edge while I waited for him. He steps over the threshold wearing an all-gray sweatsuit from top to bottom. Everything is form-fitting, and his black shoes match the black logo on his hoodie. Even when he's not dressed to impress, he still manages to awe me, but I'm dealing with a crisis right now, so I try to ignore it.

"So?" I say, slamming the door shut and making sure to

lock it behind us. Nolan walks in and stands in the middle of the living room, his hands shoved inside the big pocket of his hoodie.

"Well, like I said on the text, she's not home," he responds, and I somehow manage to deflate even more. I walk past him and plop down onto the couch as a feeling of hopelessness cascades onto me from the ceiling.

"I can't believe this is happening to me," I mumble. I mean for it to be to myself, but Nolan overhears and sits down next to me.

"Hey, nothing is happening to you," he says, trying to reassure me of my safety. "Yes, Maddy was completely out of line for following you like that, and it's weird and scary as hell to wake up with a stalker standing at the front of your building, but nothing is going to happen to you, Bree. I promise. I will find Maddy eventually, but until then, I'll do whatever it takes to make you feel safe. You have my word. Nothing is going to happen to you."

Nolan relaxes next to me and places an arm over my shoulder, pulling me into a comforting hug. I place my head on his chest and listen to the sound of his heartbeat. Somehow, hearing his helps to calm my own.

"Do you want me to stay for a while?" Nolan asks.

I immediately nod. "Yes. It doesn't have to be all night. I'm sure you'll want to check on the club, or you've got stuff to do in the morning. Just stay for a while. Maybe have dinner and help me calm my nerves."

"Ethan knows how to take care of the club. I'll stay as long as you want me to. I got you, Bree."

I pull myself up and look into his beautiful blue eyes.

"Are you sure?" I ask. I don't want him to feel obligated to stay just to make me feel secure.

"Of course I am," he says, before smiling and adding.

"Now, what do you have here to eat? The Maddy manhunt has made me hungry."

For the first time since I talked to him on the phone this morning, a smile finally forms on my lips. "Follow me into the kitchen. I'm sure we can rustle up something for you."

"Oh, not the *rustling*. I'm sure it'll be something spectacular if you're *rustling* it. It's not everyday someone *rustles* something for me. Lead the way, *Rustle* Simmons."

I force a frown, trying to control the smile overtaking my mouth. "I know you didn't just say that."

Nolan and I laugh together as we get up from the couch and head into the kitchen, where we open the pantry and refrigerator to find tonight's dinner. It isn't until we've been standing there staring at nothing that I realize I need to get groceries. Nolan, however, finds a frozen lasagna and points to it.

"How about this?"

"That?"

"Yeah, why not? You don't like lasagna? That'd be weird, considering it's in your freezer."

"Of course I like lasagna," I reply with a giggle. "It's just that it's you, and it's frozen lasagna. I'd rather make something fresh for you."

"What? Girl, you better get this oven fired up and make this *fresh* frozen lasagna," Nolan quips, chuckling to himself as he pulls the box from the fridge and inspects the image on it. "Look at how good this looks. Why wouldn't I want to eat this?"

I snicker and take the box from him. "You don't want something a little more special?"

"First of all, all the *special* stuff is obviously still at the grocery store," he jokes.

"Hey!" I bark, still smiling.

"Secondly, I'm in *your* apartment, in *your* kitchen, and that's as special as I need it to be. I'm good, Bree. Let's get it."

My mind takes a few seconds to soak Nolan in, smirking at the fact that a man who looks like him is as sweet as he is. Not that I condone anything that Maddy has done, but I understand why someone would get stuck on Nolan. He's otherworldly and hasn't stopped amazing me since the moment I sat in his office the very first time.

"Okay. It takes an hour to cook," I say, setting the box on the counter and opening it at the end. Once it's in the oven, I go back to the mostly-empty fridge and grab a bottle of wine. "You want some wine? It's Port."

"Port? That's literally my favorite wine," Nolan says. He walks to the counter and stands shoulder to shoulder with me.

"Is it?" I ask. "Mine, too. I love it because it's inexpensive and hits like liquor."

"All facts. See, I knew there was something I liked about you—you and that good taste of yours."

I pour our wine and we move into the living room to watch TV on the couch. I put on something from Hulu and we make ourselves comfortable, laughing at the comedy. After a few minutes, my wine glass is almost empty and I'm feeling good.

"You want some more wine?" I ask Nolan as I stand up, who's finishing the last drops from his own glass.

"Definitely," he replies, standing up to meet me. I turn to walk into the kitchen and he grabs me by the hip, following me as I go. When I reach the fridge, Nolan sets his glass on the counter and wraps both arms around my waist, pulling me as close to him as possible while I try to pour.

"You're distracting me," I tell him as I struggle to get the wine into the glass. I spill some on the counter and have to put the bottle down as Nolan nuzzles my neck.

"That's what I'm here for, right?" he says, the warmth of

his breath heating me up. "To distract you from all the bull-shit going on. There is no world but ours. It's impossible for me to be close to you without fantasizing about being inside you. I've fought it all night because I didn't want to be rude, but I think a distraction is the best way to forget about it all. So, let me distract you, Princess."

"Fuck," I whisper as I he licks my neck, reminding me of what his tongue is capable of and making me wet. I didn't invite him over for this, but no part of me wants to say no. The angst I feel about Maddy is nothing compared to how much Nolan makes me want him.

"What about the food?" I whisper as my eyes close and I begin losing my grip on my restraint.

"There's forty minutes until it's done," Nolan says. "I guess you better hurry up and come in my mouth then if you want to eat on time. Right now, I only want to eat you."

I gasp as Nolan uses my hips to spin me around, and the moment I'm facing him, he drops to his knees and begins to unfasten my pants. All of my worries evaporate as he pulls them down, kissing around my pussy as he snatches the pants off completely and tosses them aside.

"On the counter," he demands, and I jump, wasting no time to do as I'm told. As a result, Nolan wastes no time clamping his mouth on my pussy.

"God," is all I can think to say as the same tongue that felt great on my neck feels like utter magic on my clit. I've never known a man in my life who enjoyed eating pussy as much as Nolan does. Considering he's a sadist, I'd think he's only into causing pain, but that's what I get for thinking I know every-thing. While I throw my head back in stomach-clenching plea-sure, Nolan proves that a sadist is much more than someone solely focused on pain.

For ten blissful minutes, Nolan eats my pussy without taking a break. On his knees with his neck arched back to hit

INTERVIEW WITH A SADIST

the right angle, he continues to suck and lick my clit rhythmically until I begin to see white specks at the edge of my vision. My fingers squeeze the back of his head as the orgasm draws near, and right before I go over the event horizon, he backs away, leaving me panting.

"Not without my permission," he says, smiling sinisterly as he stands up and places a hand around my throat. "Now, get down and follow me. Tonight, you'll learn to ask for permission before you come. Let's go."

With his hand still around my neck, I hop down from the counter and let Nolan guide me into the living room, where he forcefully throws me down on the couch and sits next to me—one hand on my throat, the other on my pussy.

"I don't need a single toy to own you, Princess. This pussy belongs to me."

Nolan squeezes my throat until I can longer suck in air, while rubbing my clit with perfect pressure. In a flash, my orgasm appears again, ready to unleash itself on me, but Nolan watches me closely. He keeps his eyes on my body and somehow notices the tension in my legs, the redness in my chest, the curling of my toes. He lets go of my throat and stops rubbing my clit before I can come, and it makes me weak.

"Oh my god," I say, exasperated, breathing heavily.

"Do you want to come?" he asks rhetorically.

"Yes. Please let me come, Sir," I beg, and Nolan responds by choking me again as he rubs my clit.

"You'll have to earn it, baby," he growls, totally focused on me and my body without any regard to his. I'm astonished as another orgasm reaches for me, and Nolan stops before it can take hold.

"Fuck," I bark, desperate for the release.

"Who do you belong to?" he asks.

"You, Sir," I reply.

"Who does your pussy belong to?"

"You, Sir."

"Who does your cum belong to?"

"You, Sir."

"Good fucking girl."

For the third time, Nolan wraps his fingers around my throat and squeezes. My face reddens as the tension builds inside me and I'm forced to hold my breath while Nolan massages my clit again. After all of the edging, I'm already on the verge of overload once again, but my body is weak from the lack of oxygen, and I'm shocked by the appearance of stars in the corners of my vision.

I feel my clit being pleasured, but darkness begins to squeeze the sides of my eyes as Nolan continues to choke me. He doesn't let go as an orgasm sparks in my stomach, and I'm ready to give myself over to it, but before I can tumble into ecstasy, the darkness overtakes my vision and I fall into the pitch black as everything goes silent.

Chapter Thirty-Eight

~ NOLAN ~

Bree lets out a soft moan just as her body goes limp. I release my grip on her throat and her head rolls to the side, eyes closed. Her breathing becomes heavier as her lungs work to wake her back up, and even in this unconscious state, she's as gorgeous as ever, and I'm the one with their breath taken away.

I didn't mean to make her pass out, but I'd be lying through my teeth if I said seeing her this way didn't make my cock throb with anticipation. Bree is naked from the waist down, the skin around her neck red from my vicious grip, and somehow she's still angelic. I still want to fuck her senseless while also protecting her from everything in this world. This situation with Maddy has me ready to lash out and hurt someone, and seeing Bree this way reminds me of how much she needs me. She needs my protection from Maddy the same way she needs me to teach her about the lifestyle. I am the guardian of this beautiful jewel, and I'll be damned if I let anything happen to her. The only person putting their hands on Bree will be me.

Bree's head rocks back and forth as she begins to come to, and I take a step back, utilizing this moment to just breathe her in. She's so gorgeous it's ridiculous, and when she wakes, I don't want it to be a moment of questions. I want her to wake up to sensational pleasure so she knows it was my hand that gently placed her into unconsciousness and my tongue that brought her back.

Without another second wasted looking at her, I drop to my knees and push Bree's knees apart. She moans as her brain starts up like an engine, rumbling back to life as I cover her bare pussy with my mouth and begin to lick. The moans of sleepy confusion turn into growls of pleasure as she awakens to the sensation of me eating her pussy like I'm starved for it, and her hands instantly clamp down on my head, pushing me deeper and making sure I don't stop.

Bree is so perfect it should be a fucking crime. Instead of being upset about passing out from being choked, she dives deeper into it, clutching my face and grinding her body, somehow waking up hornier than when she went to sleep. My gut tightens at how much she turns me on. I've never been so in awe of someone in my entire life.

"I ... god, Nolan," she whispers above me, her hips still grinding as she presses my face into her. I use a finger to pull up the hood of her clit and position my mouth directly over it, licking softly as I suck.

"God," she moans, driving me mad with lust, and this time I won't stop. She passed out before she could come, and now I'm craving it. I need to feel her release every ounce of stress and tension directly onto my fucking tongue.

"Yes, baby," I say, before falling right back into rhythm.

"Oh, god," she says again, her mind going numb as her need to come reduces her vocabulary to only a couple of words.

"God," she repeats, gripping my face so hard it brings tears to my eyes, but I don't dare stop. She could draw blood and I wouldn't stop now. "Oh, my god. Oh, *god*! God, Nolan can I please come? *God, please*!"

Bree screams like she's dying, and I pull away just long enough to command her with three words.

"Come for me."

"Oh, my fucking god," she blares at the top of her lungs.

Her scream echoes throughout the room and has the volume to travel three floors above and below the apartment. Bree's body goes into a seizure of convulsions as she squeezes her eyes shut and succumbs to the most intense orgasm I've ever witnessed. Just watching her makes my cock drip precum, my heart racing with adrenaline as Bree is crushed beneath the weight of euphoria. The moment she comes down, I move forward, crawling over her limp body like a lion claiming its kill.

"I can't handle how fucking perfect you are," I tell her, breathing onto her neck before I lick the lobe of her ear. "You tear me into pieces and I don't know which way to go. Half of me wants to watch you. I just want to look at you and thank the fucking cosmos for granting me the gift of your presence. But, then there's the other half—the half that wants to tear you limb from fucking limb. I want to ravage you and watch you break apart beneath my touch. My brain is sliced in half every time you come around, and I don't know which half to listen to. You're perfect, Bree. Do you hear me? You are my perfection."

"Nolan," she whispers, before turning head toward my mouth and pressing her lips against mine.

This kiss feels deeper than any before it. It's filled with passion and fire—the kiss of two people who have long ago fallen off the deep end for each other. Is that what we've done? Have I fallen for her? Has she fallen for me? If this is what falling feels like, I don't ever want my feet on solid ground again.

We continue kissing, caressing each other until I lift myself into a seated position between Bree's legs, both of us panting hard as we meld into each other. I press the tips of two fingers against her clit, massaging it as I stroke my cock in front of her. It's so hard I could explode if I'm not careful. Usually, it takes concentration and effort for me to come, but Bree pushes me to the edge without even trying. She watches me, licking her lips as her gaze bounces between my eyes and my hand around my cock, and I can feel her getting wetter for me. When I finally position myself at her entrance, she's dripping again, making the moment I push into her even more blissful.

"Goddamn it, Bree. You're so fucking good," I say as I begin fucking her with long strokes.

Every one of these thick inches is intended for pleasure, and I use them all to plow into Bree hard. Too many men think sex is about speed, and too many men are fucking wrong. I pound into her with long, powerful strokes that have her fingers clawing the couch, trying to tear the fabric from the cushions.

"Yes, Nolan. Fuck me hard. Fucking break me," she says before falling into a chorus of moans that motivate me to work harder.

I fuck her hard enough to bruise us both. The sound of our bodies slamming together fills the air as the couch shifts from each stroke. I lift one of Bree's legs onto my shoulder while holding the other in front of my face. I suck one of her toes into my mouth, never missing a beat as I continue stroking, and she squeals with delight as I lick each toe before placing the leg on my other shoulder.

With her ankles by my head, I lean forward enough to raise her ass off the couch, giving me the perfect angle to plow into her G-spot. Both of us moan and scream as I fuck her hard, pounding that beautiful little pussy with everything I've got until fire starts to spread through my entire body. I close my eyes and keep going, refusing to stop until I explode like a fucking atomic bomb.

"Fuck, I'm going to come," I yell as I pull out and stroke my length in front of Bree, who immediately starts rubbing her clit furiously as she watches thick strands of cum shoot onto her stomach.

I grunt and grimace as I keep stroking.

"Fuck, I'm going to come again," she screams.

"Yes! Rub that fucking clit, baby. Come for me," I yell as I'm blessed with watching her body close in on itself once again.

Both of us yell up to the clouds before finally crashing back to Earth. The sound of our breathing drowns out everything else as the world stills. Bree lays on the couch, unmoving, while I lay on my back on the floor, completely spent. Neither of us says a word until the sound of the oven timer going off startles us both. The next thing I know, we're both laughing.

"How did you sync our sex with the timer?" Bree asks with a giggle.

"I have no idea," I reply. "But, I know I'm not getting up to turn it off. That's all you."

"What?" she fires back. "There's no way I can get up right now. You turn it off."

"What makes you think I can? *You* do it."

"Go turn it off, Nolan."

"It's *your* oven."

Bree and I burst into raucous laughter, but neither of us gets up. After a few minutes, nothing changes. From her position on the couch and my position on the floor, we continue laughing, and the timer keeps chiming until the sound of it fades into the background. Eventually we'll get to it, but not even lasagna is worth ruining this moment.

Chapter Thirty-Nine

I don't know what came over me last night, but waking up this morning feels like I got hit by a train. My pussy is sore, my neck is in agony, my legs feel like I just completed a 5K, and I'm pretty sure I'm a little hungover. Physically, I'm miserable. Mentally, I'm on cloud nine.

I've dated plenty of men in my life. The dating scene isn't new to me, and I've even been in some relationships that I thought might work out in the end. I've never thought about marriage or anything, but I've been in love before and even had thoughts about the possibilities of the future with someone. My ex from last year was named Jarred, and we got along very well, but the sexual connection just wasn't there. In hindsight, I now know my need for something other than vanilla sex was what slowly dragged us down into the mud, but that doesn't erase the fact that Jarred and I got along great. However, *great* pales in comparison to what Nolan and I have.

I've never thought about the importance of chemistry, because until you have an example of what it feels like, it's hard to know that you and your current partner don't have it as much as you might think. Fifty percent chemistry is better than none, and that's what I think I've had in the past. We would get along great, but the sex wouldn't be where I needed it to be, or the sex would be good, but the friendship wasn't there. At least one piece of the puzzle has always been missing, and I couldn't identify what it was until now.

With Nolan, we have everything I've ever wanted in a relationship. We laugh constantly and the sex feels like it's from a completely different universe. Nolan rocks my world into another dimension. He sends me into orbit. His gravity pulls me in and forces me to revolve around him. I'm floating amongst the stars when I'm with him, and I don't think I need to use any more space metaphors to make my point clear. The chemistry between us is unlike anything I've ever known, so waking up sore puts a smile on my face. I'll gladly hurt for joy like this.

After nearly burning the lasagna last night, we actually did end up eating and watching TV on the couch together. We shared another big laugh when Nolan sat down and soaked his pants in the wet spot I left behind, and then spent the next few hours watching *Abbot Elementary* on Hulu, which I hadn't even seen before, but Nolan told me it was a requirement to watch it. We spent the entire night laughing at the show while sipping port wine and cuddling. If I had to pick out what my dream night would be, choosing something other than what we shared last night would be a very tough task. It was perfect, and we ended it by laying in bed together and falling asleep wrapped in each other's arms. Last night, my apartment became nirvana.

As I slowly shift myself in bed, I slide my arm across the mattress to touch Nolan, but find that he's not there. I wake up to an empty bed every morning, but it feels much worse today knowing he was here last night. The brightness in the room forces my eyes to only open only halfway, but I can still

INTERVIEW WITH A SADIST

see enough to know that Nolan is not only gone from my side, he's nowhere in the room.

"Nolan?" I say, lifting myself up into a seated position. The apartment is completely quiet, but at the end of the bed is a small piece of paper that looks like it's waiting for me. It takes effort and resilience just to reach it, but I manage and find that it's a handwritten note from Nolan.

My Princess, you desperately need to befriend a grocery store. You were out of coffee, so I'm going to stop by the club and make sure everything is good, then grab us some breakfast and the most caffeinated drinks I can find. I'll be back soon.

Nolan

I smile like a kid receiving their first bike as I put the paper down and get out of bed. My head hurts a little, and I feel a bit unsteady on my feet, but I manage to happily force myself into the bathroom where I pull on a robe and make sure I don't look like a complete zombie. Now that I know Nolan is coming back, I want to make sure the place—and myself—is in decent shape. I don't know what our morning will consist of, but it's our first one together, and I want to make sure it's special.

Cinching my robe together, I keep thinking about last night as I walk into the kitchen. The pan of lasagna is still on the counter, as are our plates, wine glasses, and the empty bottle of port. I reminisce about our sex on the couch while I rinse out the glasses. I'm pretty sure I actually passed out last night, which is definitely uncharted territory for me. Everything was foggy by the time I came to and found Nolan's head between my legs, but it all felt too good to stop. I have absolutely no complaints, but passing out during sex is definitely a whole new level of kink for me, and I love that Nolan is my guide through this new world.

I move through the kitchen like I'm on autopilot, washing dishes while thinking about how amazing last evening was. I get everything completely cleaned up and set my sights on the couch. I grab a bottle of fabric cleaner and a rag, and begin scrubbing the area that I soaked last night, and I don't realize it until my face starts to hurt that I've been smiling the entire time. By the time I'm finished and ready to go back into the bedroom, the muscles in my cheeks are sore, and it dawns on me that it's Nolan who has put the smile there. He's the cause, and my sore cheeks, neck, legs, and pussy are the effect. Is being with him really this incredible? How is it that a man can make me feel this way?

Luckily, I don't have to wait long for Nolan to return, because before I can make it back into the bedroom, he knocks on the door. I grin to myself, imagining him standing in the hall holding bags of food and a tray of coffee cups, looking like a meal himself while knocking on the door with his elbow. I place the spray bottle and rag on the kitchen counter and can't get to the door fast enough. I'm actually excited to see him, and I yank the door open with a racing heart.

"Well, aren't you glowing this morning? You must've had an amazing night."

Somehow, my heart hammers faster and harder than it ever has, and I feel lightheaded as adrenaline and shock ignite like a firecracker, sending me reeling as Maddy steps forward holding something long in her hand. There's no time to understand or react, because she swings too fast and everything goes black.

Chapter Forty

The first thing that returns is my sense of sound. My air conditioner whirs, humming muffled in my ears as if I'm under water at first, before slowly clearing up and coming in sharp and crisp. Next is my sense of smell—the perfumes that have dripped atop my dresser over the years and left my room smelling fragrant and sexy. Lastly, I open my eyes and engage my sense of sight. Everything is draped in shadows, but they slowly rise and disappear into the ceiling, making way for the brightness of the sun and the shock of a lifetime, because I can finally see the person sitting in a chair in front of my bed with one leg crossed over the other. She's still wearing the same tattered appearance she had when she met me in front of my apartment yesterday morning, and the sun reflects in her eyes, making them glow as she peers at me holding a tire iron in her hand.

Maddy.

She glares at me with a menacing expression, her face blank but bristling. She's a river of lava that has crusted over. One false move and everything will come spewing out, and there's no telling what damage could be done.

I try to sit up and assess the situation, because I don't know how I got to my bedroom. I remember hearing the knock at the door and opening it. As soon as I realized it was Maddy and not Nolan, there was a jolt to my entire world and everything went dark. Now, I'm in bed and I don't know how or why. When I try to move my hand to wipe my face, it doesn't even come halfway. There's a metallic clank and an unbreakable tension locking my arm in place, and I look up to find that both of my wrists are cuffed to my bed frame, as are my ankles.

"Oh, my god," I whisper to myself, before the panic sets in and I scream it. "Oh, my god! What the fuck? What are you doing, Maddy? Uncuff me right now."

"Shut the fuck up," Maddy snips, her voice sounding exasperated as if I've been screaming for hours and she's finally tired of it. "You're not in a position to tell me what to do, and I don't have a lot of time to explain all of this before I do it. I read the cute little note that was on your bed when I dragged you in here. The one from Nolan. He never did that for me. No notes. No coffee in the morning. No breakfast. Nothing. He never even stayed the night at my place, but here he is doing it with you. How sweet. Did you know he used to call me Madelaine? He was the only one who ever did, but he stopped once we broke up. He started calling me Maddy just like everybody else, and I realized how much I used to like him calling me Madelaine. It's the little things, you know?"

"You can't do this, Maddy," I say.

My mind feels like it's short circuiting from how insane all of this is. If my fear won't convince her to stop this, maybe logic will. I try to think of everything I could say to make her stop what she has started, but my head hurts from being hit with the tire iron, so my thoughts come in slowly.

"I can't do it?" Maddy replies, standing up. She places the tire iron on the mattress and leans on it like a kickstand. "I've already done it, Bree. I'm here. I'm in your apartment and you're chained to the bed. It's done. All that's left is the finish, but we're building up to that. Don't you worry. I just need a second to gather my nerves. I've never killed anyone before."

My eyes widen to the size of dinner plates as my heart rattles my organs from pounding so hard.

"Wh ... what? You can't ... No ... Nolan is coming b—" I stutter, as coherent sentences evade me, but Maddy cuts me off.

"I know he is," she says, appearing morose as she looks down at the bed. "He's coming back with your coffee ... and finding you dead is exactly what he deserves to return to. It'll break his heart to find you dead in your bed after having what I'm sure was a wonderful night with you. Eventually, he'll get over it though, and when he does, I'll be there to comfort him. He'll never know the measures I took to bring us back together, but that's what love is all about. You do whatever you have to for the people you love, so I'll have to live with the guilt of being a murderer, but I can accept that. For him, I'll accept it."

"Maddy, stop it. You can't do this. Why are you doing this?" I bark, hoping someone in a nearby apartment will hear me, but Maddy raises the tire iron and steps closer to me. She doesn't have to speak the words for me to know it's a threat.

"Because he's ready to make you the one," she yells, slapping the bed with the tire iron. It lands with a thud and my eyes sting with tears thinking about the metal hitting my head. "He's ready to be public with you, and I can fucking see it. He's doing it right in front of me with the meetings at the club, and the fucking lunches with E and J, who never showed me the love they're showing you, by the way. Nolan likes something about you and I don't know why, but I'll be damned if I stand back and watch you take what was supposed to be mine.

"I was his Little One. I was the one who was willing to go to the furthest extreme to satisfy his desires. I dedicated myself to him completely, and he fucking turned me down. I don't understand it, but I can't allow it, because nobody is as passionate as Nolan.

"Out of all the guys I've allowed to fuck me, no one has made me feel the way Nolan did. All I cared about was pleasing him, and there was nothing better than hearing him say he was proud of me. I begged him to love me, but he was so caught up in the success of the club and whatever else he had going on in his life that he just couldn't do it. But he'll be able to now. Once you're out of the way—once he loses someone he cares about, he'll change. I can tell he has grown in the months we've been broken up. He's ready to commit now instead of being the god of that club, flaunting his sexual prowess in front of everyone like he used to. Now that he's ready to settle, it has to be with me."

"Maddy, you have to stop and think," I plead, hoping with everything in me that she'll listen, or that I can stall long enough for Nolan to return. "If you beat me to death with that tire iron, there will be blood everywhere, and I've already told people about you showing up to my apartment yesterday. Everyone will know it was you, and you won't even end up with Nolan because you'll be in jail. Think it through."

Maddy laughs beneath her breath as she shakes her head and looks at me.

"You think you've got it all figured out, don't you?" she says, glaring at me. "You think because you're some fancy journalist and I'm just some whore who works at a BDSM club that you're better than me? Smarter than me? Well, how's this? I'm not going to beat you with the tire iron. I only needed this to knock you out once I saw Nolan leave your apartment. It sort of puts dents in my plan because you have a knot on your head now, but with the way Nolan likes to fuck,

INTERVIEW WITH A SADIST

he'll just assume that was from him. So, no, I'm not going to beat you with this. I'm going to smother you with your own pillow, then remove the cuffs and leave you in bed for Nolan to discover as soon as he gets back from his little store run. When he finds you, he'll think you died in your sleep or something. I didn't sit outside your apartment the entire weekend plotting this out just to beat your brains in and leave evidence behind. I have a plan, dummy."

"He'll never fall for that," I bark. "He already knows you were watching my place. He knows you've been following me."

"Which I will apologize for," she says nonchalantly. Maddy shrugs as if she's talking about the weather, completely believing her own hype. "I know he's going to be upset, and maybe he'll even suspect me, but with no evidence and the passage of time, he'll get over you, and I'll be there to comfort him when he does. He's only known you a few weeks, Bree. The memory of you won't last forever, and your little story about the club will never come out. No one will have a leg to stand on when it comes to accusing me."

"Please stop this," I beg. "You've already admitted that Nolan didn't want you the way you wanted him, so why are you risking all of this for someone who doesn't want you?"

"Because he's the one I chose," she blares, slamming the iron down on the bed again. "It's something a little closed-minded bitch like you could never understand. I've been in the lifestyle since I was a teenager, dating asshole after asshole and never feeling like there was someone truly worthy of my submission. But that all changed when I met Nolan. He earned my trust and the depths of my soul over time, because he's a true Dom, not one of these boys running around thinking they're Christian Grey. Nolan is the last of a dying breed, and he's the one I picked. I can't go out and give myself to someone else just like that.

Choosing Nolan was the same as imprinting on him. I belong to him now, and you belong to no one. So, don't try to make sense of things you can't understand. I *belong* to him. Forever."

Maddy places the tire iron on the end of the bed and takes a step toward me. I yank my leg back trying to get away, but the cuff around my ankle snaps tight, keeping me stuck in place. There's nothing I can do but watch as Maddy stalks toward me, reaching across my body for the pillow Nolan went to sleep on last night. She clutches it tight in both hands, staring down at me with no emotion at all.

"Maddy ... *please*," I say, but I know it's no use. She's not going to stop, because it's all too far gone now. She plotted it out in my own parking lot, and she has already managed to get inside my apartment and chain me to the bed. There's only one more task on her checklist now, and she's in position to mark it off. It's over.

"It's really not your fault," she says as she slowly climbs onto the bed and straddles me. "You were just the wrong journalist at the wrong time, sent to the wrong club. There's a small part of me that's sorry it has to be this way, but there's a much bigger part that needs Nolan, and that part will do anything to have him. So, you have to go. Goodbye."

"Please," I say, but the rest of the sentence is snuffed out by Maddy slamming the pillow onto my face and pressing down with all of her body weight. I try to move my head to the side, but there's just too much pressure. Maddy secures the pillow directly over my nose and mouth, and just like last night when Nolan was choking me, I can't even get the smallest amount of air.

Maddy presses down on the pillow, and all of my panic fades away. I think about Nolan first, before my thoughts shift to Melissa and Teagan, who told me I'd regret succumbing to this lifestyle. I think about Octavia, and even Chase, who encouraged me to pursue the story but not to get too deep into it.

It's funny what pops into your head when you're dying, but as my world begins to fade away again, I find a sense of peace and acceptance. I stop thrashing my legs and arms, and let go. Hopefully, Nolan will be smart enough to know I didn't just drop dead the morning after he spent the night at my apartment, but that's out of my control now. This is it. Goodbye, Nolan.

"Maddy, no!" a muffled voice shrieks. The sound echoes in my head like I'm in an empty hall, and I wonder if it's even real. Have I died already? Where am I? What's happening?

Suddenly, everything around me explodes back to life as Maddy and the pillow are yanked off of me. Light bursts back into view just as Nolan jumps on top of me and begins hitting the cuff on my left wrist with the tire iron Maddy put on the bed. He gets in three thwacks before the cheap cuff opens and he's able to snatch it off and throw it to the floor, but as he moves to my right wrist, Maddy jumps onto his back and begins pummeling him in the head as she screams at the top of her lungs.

"Stop!" she bellows. "Leave her. She has to die. Fucking let me finish her. Stop it! This is for us!"

All I can do is watch as Maddy slaps and punches Nolan in the back of the head while she clings to his back like a monkey, shrieking in his ear as tears stream down her face. I'm terrified as the scene plays out in front of me because I'm helpless to do anything about it, and Maddy suddenly hops off Nolan's back and charges for me. She launches herself at the bed and I raise my one free hand to protect my face as she brings her fist hammering down on top of me.

"Die, you fucking cunt! Die!" she screams, but she only gets off two hits before Nolan's arms wrap around her waist and pull her off again.

The two of them stumble back, slamming against the wall and putting a hole in it as Maddy fights with all her might to get free. Nolan has no choice but to tackle her to the floor and drag her over to the other side of the room where a belt lies on the floor next to the radiator. He struggles to grab it because Maddy is fighting so fiercely, but she's not strong enough to stop him.

Nolan pins her down with a knee on her chest while he curls the belt into makeshift handcuffs with a loop on each side. He secures the belt around a bracket on the radiator and shoves each of Maddy's hands into a loop before cinching it all down. Maddy flails for a moment, until she finally realizes she can't get free because the belt is too tight. She would have to use her teeth to gnaw at the buckle in order to loosen it, but she isn't calm enough and doesn't have the energy. She stills, breathing heavily before she bursts into tears.

From the bed, I watch as everything finally calms down. Maddy sobs on the floor as Nolan gets up with worry and fear hanging from his face like a mask. He climbs onto the bed and places a palm on my cheek.

"Are you okay?" he asks, his eyes drowning in worry.

I shake my head. "No ... I mean, yes. Physically I'm fine, but ... I'm not okay, Nolan. It's not okay."

"I know. I'm so sorry," he whispers as he places his forehead on mine and closes his eyes. "I shouldn't have left you alone. This is all my fault and I'm sorry."

I don't know how to respond. All I can do is close my eyes and let the tears stream down my face. After a moment, Nolan kisses my forehead and gets up, returning to Maddy who has curled into the fetal position and is bawling on the floor. Nolan crouches down next to her and places a hand on her shoulder as she sobs.

"I'm so sorry it came to all of this, Madelaine, but at least now you'll get the help you need," he says.

Nolan stays next to Maddy as he pulls out his cell phone and dials 911. He tells the operator everything that happened, and it only takes a few minutes before we hear sirens approaching.

Although I'm still cuffed to the bed, I breathe a sigh of relief, because after everything we've been through, it's finally over. But, even with the end in sight, I'm too traumatized to think straight, and I don't know where Nolan and I will go from here. I don't know where I'll go. I'm just happy it's over.

Chapter Forty-One

~ NOLAN ~

It has been a week since I've seen Bree, but it didn't take me seven days to understand why she'd need time to herself. The situation with Maddy was traumatic to say the least, and I don't know how I could've been so stupid. I knew Maddy had shown up to Bree's apartment, and that she'd even slept in the parking lot over the weekend, but it never crossed my mind to search the parking lot for her the night I slept at Bree's place. Like an idiot, I had gone straight to Maddy's apartment, then straight back to Bree's. I was so hyped up about spending time at Bree's place that I never truly registered the threat that was Maddy. I didn't really think she would do anything violent, and in hindsight, I realize how dumb that was.

Maybe that's why the thought stayed in the back of my mind as I left Bree's apartment the day Maddy attacked her. That morning, I left with a satisfied smile on my face after a magical night of making her pass out and soak her own couch. I was riding high, but when I left to make sure the club was locked up and to get coffee and breakfast for us, there was a tickling in the back of my brain—a thought that I couldn't shake away as I drove from place to place. It sat in my gut like a rock, telling me that I hadn't been thorough in my search for Maddy. I didn't know what to make of the thought until I was parking my car in Bree's lot. Then it hit me right in the face as I was walking while holding our coffee in one hand, and a bag of food in the other. Instead of going straight inside, I decided to search the lot and only had to check one row of cars before I saw it. Maddy's car.

I dropped the coffee and food onto the concrete and darted inside to find the door was locked, which was weird. I didn't lock it when I left because I wouldn't have been able to get back in if I returned and Bree was still asleep. That was all the sign I needed, and I threw the entirety of my weight at the door twice to get it open.

Seeing Maddy on top of Bree with a pillow over her face sank my stomach to the bottoms of my feet, but I didn't have time to gawk. I acted as fast as I could and was lucky enough to save Bree's life, but the trauma had already been done, and saving her wouldn't erase it. She needed time after it was all said and done, so I swallowed my pride and desire to be with her every day, and gave her the space she needed.

When Maddy was charged with false imprisonment, assault with a deadly weapon, and attempted murder, I wondered if I'd hear from Bree, but she stayed silent for another few days. I didn't hear from her until this morning when I woke up to a text asking if I wanted to meet her at Fairmount Park. I could've jumped through the ceiling I was so excited, but I remained calm and typed out a relaxed, "Of course." Now, as I walk toward her sitting at a table in the park, I have to focus on keeping my cool again. Seven days without seeing her has been brutal, but I understand the seriousness of this moment and try to keep myself together.

Bree sits at the table wearing black pants and a white hoodie. Her hair shifts with each gust of wind and her makeup is subtle, but there's no stopping those blue eyes from being mesmerizing. They sparkle beneath the light of the sun, and she glows with no effort needed. When I approach, she gets up to meet me, pulling me into a hug that I wish would last longer and be followed by a kiss, but neither happens. We sit on opposite sides of the wooden table, our hands in the center, close but not touching. I want our greeting to be so much more than this, but she almost died because of me. I'll never forgive myself for that, so I understand if she doesn't forgive me either.

"Hi," she begins, looking a little sheepish as her eyes fixate on a splinter on the table.

She fiddles with it instead of looking at me, as if making eye contact will be enough to crumble the walls she has obviously built around herself.

"Hi. How are you?" I reply, noticing the splinter but keeping my gaze on her since she's the only thing in this park I want to see.

"I'm okay," she says. "Sorry I haven't texted or anything. It's been a pretty rough week."

"You don't have to apologize. I understand. I'm just glad you decided to today. Is everything okay? How's work going?"

Bree's eyes never leave the splinter. "It's fine I guess. I haven't been to work since ... it happened. After Chase found out what went down, he gave me an extension on the story. When I go back next week, he's going to expect the draft from me, and I don't know what to do about that, but that's my cross to bear. I'll figure it out."

I want to place my hands around hers, both for my comfort and hers. I want her to know that I'm here if and when she ever wants or needs me, but I don't know how to say that without it sounding like I'm disregarding her emotions and thinking about myself after the ordeal she just suffered. This is about me because it involves me, but it's not really about me or what I want. It's about Bree and how she feels, so I shut down my own feelings and try to figure how to help her find peace in hers.

"I'm sure Chase understands that you've been through something extreme," I say, trying to keep the topic centered around her work instead of us. "He'll stay patient and give you all the time you need. If he doesn't, just tell him we haven't finished discussing it yet. I'm sure he'll back off after that, and if he still doesn't, just let me know and I'll handle it."

"That won't be necessary," Bree snips quickly. "I can handle Chase. It's everything else in my life that I can't handle right now. Everything has felt so heavy since all of that shit went down. I can barely spend time in my own apartment because I keep thinking about the chain of events leading up to the moment your ex walked through the door and hit me in the head with a tire iron. Even now, when I'm trying not to get caught up in thoughts about that day, it still consumes me. I should've known I couldn't see you without being wrapped up in what happened, but ... I wanted to see you, so it was a risk I was willing to take."

"Do you regret it now?" I ask. Bree finally raises her eyes to meet mine, and we maintain eye contact. "Now that I'm here and you can see me, do you regret texting me to meet you?"

Bree sighs as her eyes fill up with tears that never fall.

"No," she says softly. "I've missed you, Nolan, but I feel lost after all of this. I was just a quiet little girl before, hidden safely within the walls of my cautious life. Sure, maybe I was closed-minded and miserable, but I didn't know it. I thought I was happy. At least until I met you. You swooped in like a gigantic gust of wind that rocked and rattled my life, knocking everything over and revealing my unhappiness. You showed me what was lying beneath my comfort, and I was never able to put anything back in its place. You fucking ruined everything, Nolan, and now I feel more lost than ever.

"Being around you and your friends showed me how horrible mine were, so Melissa and Teagan are out of my life for good. I still have Octavia, who's ten times better than anything I had before, but our friendship flourishing the way it is still feels new to me, too. Everything has been pulled up by the root, and there's no putting it back. I'm just floating in space with nowhere to go now."

The atmosphere is engulfed by silence after she gets it all out. It's difficult figuring out how to respond when someone tells you that you practically ruined their life. It hurts, but I deserve it.

"Look," she begins again, and I brace myself for the onslaught of emotions that are already threatening to ruin me mentally. "I didn't ask you to come here just to breathlessly tell you how much everything has changed since we met. I called you here because I desperately wanted to see you. I wanted to hear your voice and smell your scent. I just wanted to be around you, and I miss talking to you. I miss laughing with you. Even though we were having sex all the time, we also formed a friendship in our time together, and you want to rant to your friends, so that's what I'm doing. I apologize if it feels like an attack."

"It's fine. I deserve it, Bree," I say, and when she doesn't refute it, I know she agrees. "I should've been more cautious with the situation. You deserved to know that the person I was telling stories about in our first interviews was Maddy. I should've told you that we had been together and that it didn't really end amicably, and I definitely should've told you that she'd been trying to spark up a new flame with me at the time you showed up at the club. I was dumb, reckless, and selfish for keeping that from you. It almost cost you every-thing, and I'm sorry, Bree. Truly."

She stares at me, her eyes still misting over. "Yeah, it would've been nice to know that she was the Little One. Then again, maybe I should've put it together from the way she was acting. I was reckless, too, because I was so in awe of you. I disregarded Maddy, and if I regret anything at all, it's that I didn't recognize a woman in pain—a woman who deserved the time and space she needed to heal from whatever you two had before I showed up. I wouldn't have been in her face like that if I had considered that she was hurting. So, you're not the only one at fault. We both should've been more sensitive to her situation."

"Yes, you're right," I admit, before we're overtaken by silence again.

The breeze flows through Bree's hair, sweeping it up and forcing her to comb through it with her fingers. She looks so elegant performing such a minuscule gesture that it gives me chills. I've come to adore everything about her, and I know that leaving this park is about to be like jumping from a bridge without a bungee cord. I know I'm going to fall and hit the ground below, splattering my happiness all over the concrete.

"The last thing I want to do is make you have to relive the trauma of what happened," I say. I inch my hands closer to hers but don't let them touch. "So, please take all the time you need to heal, Bree, even if that means you never call me again. Yes, that would fucking suck, but I would understand and would have no hard feelings. No one should ever have to expe-rience what you went through last week, and I'm sorry it happened. If you ever want to talk to me again, just call me and I'll be there. No matter the time.

"I just want you to know that I have very strong feelings for you," I go on, finally feeling brave enough to reach out and wrap my hands around hers, cupping them inside of mine.

"Everything that I've never wanted with anyone else, I want it with you. I've always been about the lifestyle, embracing my kinks and focusing solely on them. I never wanted a public, affectionate relationship where we hold hands and kiss in front of people. With you, I want all those things. I want to flaunt you in front of the entire world and show them all that you're mine. I want everyone to know we belong to each other. We've been through a lot, and saying this doesn't help in any way, but I needed to say it. I'll give you all the time you need, but I had to say that first. Okay?"

The tears in Bree's eyes finally break through the dam and begin to fall, streaking down her beautiful cheeks as she takes a deep breath and lets it out.

"Okay," she replies, pulling her hands away as I stand up. I take a step back and start to turn away, before saying one last thing.

"Oh, and about your story," I start. "Tell it all. Tell the world how you met me, and how you met E and J, and how spending time with someone you had much different expectations for changed who you are internally. But, also tell them about the dark side of it all. Tell them about what happened last week, and tell them how you need time to deal with and heal from it. Just let it all out. Spill your blood on the page, and hopefully when you let it out, you'll feel better. At the end of the day, that's all I want for you, Bree. I just want you to be happy."

She doesn't say anything in response. Her eyes stay focused on me, and I know there are a million different things running through her head as she continues to wipe away streaking tears. There certainly are a million thoughts in my head, and none of them make me feel any better. None of them makes this any easier, but I don't expect it to be easy now. I've earned the difficulty, and I accept it. I'll take it all if it makes life for Bree even a little better.

The wind brushes across my face, Mother Nature herself kissing me on the cheek in an attempt to comfort me. I wish I could appreciate it, but I'm hurting too much as Bree's eyes go back to the splinter on the table, and I turn to walk away.

"Bye, Bree," I whisper, but the breeze takes my words and carries them off in the distance. She never hears them, and I leave without knowing if she would've responded at all.

Chapter Forty-Two

When I walk into The Philadelphia Inquirer for the first time since the incident, all eyes turn to watch me. Even though I lived through the ordeal, everyone at my job acts like they weren't sure if I was dead or alive, and they gawk at me like I'm an actual zombie strutting into the place with a desire to eat brains. My only actual desire is to make it from the elevator to my desk without feeling like the entire world is watching me.

Nonetheless, the eyes stay on me as I walk past the multitudes of people huddled up and whispering. I know they're just curious and want to ask questions but can't bring themselves to do it because they're either scared or not close enough to me to inquire. Instead, I only get their eyes fixating on me until I reach my desk and sit down, finally protected by the walls of the cubicle.

I almost didn't come in today. As the hours ticked down last night, I sat in my apartment wondering what it would be like to come back here after a couple of weeks off. I figured everyone would do what they're doing now, but it wasn't the stares that made me want to take an extra day, it was the fact that I would have to come in here and work on my story about Nolan. I've been trying to do anything but think about what happened, and that meant that I needed to dodge thoughts about Nolan, too.

After our brief meeting at the park, I told myself that I probably wouldn't be able to be with him after all of this, but my heart wouldn't let that thought hang around long. As much as I wanted to move on from the entire situation, memories of what Nolan and I had stuck to me like tar, and I couldn't shake him off no matter how hard I tried. Wherever I went, thoughts of Nolan followed like a poltergeist, whispering reminders of what we'd done together. Seeing him in my thoughts always started off fine, but eventually shifted into the vivid memory of what happened in my apartment.

Every time I thought of Nolan, I thought of Maddy, and it didn't matter that she was now spending her days confined to a jail. What she did latched onto my brain and hijacked my thoughts of Nolan until there was no him without her, and the last thing I wanted to do was walk into the Inquirer and be forced to think about Nolan and The Black Collar, because thoughts of Maddy would be an inevitability. The only reason I didn't go through with adding another day to my time off was because I reached my limit. I grew tired of having my joy stolen by what I went through, and the only way to reclaim my happiness would be to take Nolan's advice that day in the park. I needed to get my ass to this office, and bleed onto the page.

"You made it," Octavia says from behind me. I spin around and find her beautiful face lost somewhere between wanting to smile and looking worried. "Welcome back. How does it feel? You gonna make it through the day?"

Since she's obviously torn between smiling and frowning,

I let her know it's okay by smiling big. Once she sees me, she drops the anxious look completely.

"I'm okay," I say, leaning back in my chair. "I don't know if I'm going to make it through everybody fucking staring at me, but as far as my work is concerned, I'm going to make it just fine."

"That's great to hear. Have you talked to Chase about a new deadline yet?"

I shake my head. "No, and I don't really plan on it. I'm sure he'll come to me when he feels comfortable, but by the time he does, I intend to already be working on it."

"Oh, you figured out your angle on it?"

"Yeah, I guess you could say that."

"Awesome. So, how are you gonna do it?"

I look down at the floor in front of me as I remember what Nolan told me. "I think I'm just going to let it all out. I'm going to tell everything. If Chase ends up thinking it's too long, that's fine. I have to get it all out, so I'm not going to think much. I'm just going to type until I've got nothing left."

Octavia frowns. "And, Nolan's cool with that?"

"It's his idea," I say, a proud smirk tugging at the corner of my mouth.

"Oh, well all right then," Octavia says. She steps forward and leans in to give me a quick hug before backing out into the hall. "Well, I've got some work of my own to do, so I"m gonna let you get to it. Good luck, Bree."

"Thanks, Octavia." She walks away, making her way down to her own office, and once she's gone, I spin around to start up my computer.

I remove my digital recorder from the drawer, which contains all of the Q&A material I did with Nolan, and I set it on the desk next to my keyboard. If my memory slips and I can't think of specifics, I'll rely on the recordings from when

INTERVIEW WITH A SADIST

we first met, but something tells me I'll never have to press play. I open a Google Doc on my Drive, and center the cursor with a twelve point bold font in Times New Roman. Without a moment's hesitance, the title of the article comes to me, and I type it out.

Interview with a Sadist

As soon as I see it, I know what I'm about to do, and I know it's going to be out of this world. I place my fingers on the keyboard, and lower the filter in my brain that makes me think before I speak. I drop that filter all the way down to zero and begin typing without worrying about what I'm going to say.

I start from the very beginning, telling the story of the moment I received the assignment from Chase to interview the owner of The Black Collar, and I don't hold back when I describe how it felt when I first saw him. I tell the world how my mind slowly opened up to the idea that maybe the world of kink was where I belonged, and I type with no shame when describing the moment I told Nolan to flog me on his couch. I speak about a woman who worked at the club—a woman in considerable pain who I do not name—and how she was the personification of what my ex friends warned me about when I began this journey of self discovery and sexual freedom. I write about the laughter Nolan and I shared, and the feeling of falling down a rabbit hole of adventure and infatuation that left me feeling weightless. I put it all on the page, and do not hide the details of the morning the unnamed woman came into my apartment and attempted to kill me, only for me to be saved by the man I was falling for. I bleed it all out, and I cry when talking about my meeting in the park with Nolan.

By the time I'm finished, hours have passed, I'm exhausted, and my makeup is ruined from the streaking tears that have carved out narrow passageways in my foundation. I'm a complete mess, but I feel a million times lighter than when I first began.

I don't even take time to proofread it before I give Chase the permissions to read it and make edits, then I'm out of the cubicle and headed out. I wave to Octavia on my way, who smiles and waves back as I step onto the elevator and make my way toward the parking lot. Once I'm in my car, I sit inside of it for a moment, thinking about everything I just wrote for this story. I spilled my guts, and writing it all down seems to have been the cathartic experience I needed it to be.

In my front seat, I remember how it felt to be with Nolan. I remember all of the great times of laughter we had together, and the soul-crushing orgasms he gave me. I think about how happy I was when we were together, and how replacing him would be impossible. For the first time in weeks, I think about Nolan ... and *only* Nolan.

Every thought fills my stomach with rabid butterflies, and the memories of his face and blue eyes warm my entire body. My smile is uncontrollable, and I know that if I deny myself smiles like this one, I would be doing myself the greatest disservice and setting up the rest of my life to be a giant disappointment full of regret. I can't do that. I won't.

With my smile still lingering, I decide my next move with a fluttering heart and excitement coursing through my finger-

INTERVIEW WITH A SADIST

tips like an electric current. I feel the current all the way down in my bones as I stick my key in the ignition and start the car, on my way back to where it all began.

Chapter Forty-Three

When I park across the street from The Black Collar, my mind wanders right back to the first time I ever did it. I remember the nervousness I felt jolting through my body with every move I made. I remember stepping out of my car onto wobbly legs as I eyed the sign on the building, before walking across the street to be greeted by Maddy, who led me to the other end of the building where Nolan's office was. He looked so incredible the first time I laid my eyes on him, and I remember the revelation that his eyes were blue, which threw me for a loop right there at the door. The moment I spoke to him I knew I was a goner.

It's sad to say, but sometimes the perfect romance requires time apart. Not *a lot* of time, but some. I'm not a believer of the saying *absence makes the heart grow fonder*, but in most cases, a small amount of separation gives people the space they need to think about what they have with a clear head. For me, my two weeks without Nolan sent me on a rollercoaster. One minute I was high, missing him and remembering how amazing we were together. The next minute I was low, sad and filled with fear as I realized that Nolan entering my life also brought his baggage of Maddy and my near death experience. But, at the end of it all, I wrote the most therapeutic story of my career, and have the clearest mind I've ever had. My vision is no longer blurry, and I know what I want and need to do.

When I reach the door, I check to see if it's open before knocking, and I'm excited to learn that it is. I make my way down the hall, glancing at the curtains and closed doors of each room and visualizing what's behind them. The thought alone puts a smile on my face, and I realize that just being in the building and knowing what goes on here makes me happy. I like the idea of being surrounded by kinkiness, because kinkiness in a place like this means freedom. This is where people go when they're no longer shackled in place by the judgmental opinions of society. The only thing that matters here is consent, the rest is about being open-minded and enjoying life while you still have the chance to. I'd forgotten how freeing this place is. I'd forgotten that freedom is power, and I've never felt more powerful than I do when I'm here.

When I reach the big room with the bar and dancefloor, I pause at the entrance. Nolan, Ethan, and Jackson all sit at the counter doing their usual routine for this time of the day. Ethan is behind the bar fiddling with the register, while Jackson combs through receipts like a detective looking for clues, and Nolan sits at the end with a drink in front of him and a solemn expression on his face.

I'm not sure why he's a handful of seats away from the other two, but there's obviously no joy in him. It's like his side of the room is covered by a cloud that's invisible but still capable of casting a shadow, and he's the only one in the darkness. He looks miserable as he picks up the short glass and takes a very small sip of something dark. I usually wouldn't think twice about him or anybody else having a drink, but the fact that it's one in the afternoon sort of stands out.

He's dressed in all-black, funeral colors, and he certainly

looks as miserable as a widow as he scrolls through his phone, never taking a moment to stop and watch anything. He just flicks his thumb over and over again, flying past everything on the screen like none of it matters anyway. He's still as gorgeous as ever, but he's not the energetic Nolan I remember, and I'll admit that seeing him this way fills me with a combination of emotions, both good and bad.

I don't want Nolan to be hurt, but seeing him this somber says really did care about me. He wasn't using me, and he wasn't lying when he said he wanted things with me that he never wanted with anybody else. His feelings were real, and it didn't matter what Maddy said about his short attention span. He only had a short attention span when it came to her and other women before me, because after two weeks of us being apart, Nolan still looks just as sad as the day he said goodbye at the park, when he didn't think I heard him.

I'm not sure how to start. After thinking about it the entire drive over, I'm at a loss for words now that I'm here. I end up simply clearing my throat, and that's all it takes in an empty club. The sound echoes like I shot a cannon on the dancefloor, and all three men turn to face me. The second Nolan and I make eye contact, he puts his phone down and stands.

"Bree?" he says, automatically looking concerned. I haven't texted or called a single time since that day at the park, so he's probably wondering what might have happened that I would show up here unannounced. Ethan and Jackson don't say anything. Both of their bodies freeze in place while their eyes bounce back and forth between Nolan and me.

"Hi, Nolan," I say as I begin slow steps toward him and he does the same. "How have you been?"

Nolan lets out a long exhale. "Miserable without you," he replies, setting free a million winged creatures in my belly. "What are you doing here?"

"I don't know," I respond because it's the truth, but just like when I wrote the story this morning, I don't allow myself to think before I speak. I just let it all out. "I spent the entire morning writing the story I've been working on for so long, and once it was finished, the only thing I could think about was getting to you. I left my office without telling my boss where I was going, and I drove here without knowing what I would say when I saw you. I just needed to see you.

"I've missed you a lot. I miss the way you make me laugh, the way you constantly remind me that it's okay for me to be me—who I *truly* am. I miss the joy we bring out of each other. I miss submitting to you. I miss giving you control because I know I can trust you with it. I can trust you with my life, and we all know that's true because you literally saved my life.

"Nothing has been the same since the day I met you, and I'm so sorry if I ever made you feel like you ruined things for me in a way that I didn't love, because while my entire trajectory has shifted because of you, it has shifted in all the best ways imaginable. I honestly think you're the best thing that ever happened to me, and I'd be a fool to give that up just because someone tried to hurt me.

"Maddy loved you. She loved you so much that she was willing to do the most extreme thing to get you back, but what she couldn't accept was that you didn't choose her. You chose *me*, and it's not your fault that she reacted the way she did when she finally figured it out. What happened wasn't your fault, Nolan. You chose me, and I choose you. Right here, right now. I choose us."

I look into Nolan's eyes and to my utter surprise, they're filled with tears. I'm shocked into complete disbelief because he's a Dom. He's so masculine and in control all the time, I would've never thought that I'd ever see him cry.

He inhales deeply before letting it out and glancing over at his friends, who both have tears in their eyes as they watch us with smiles on their faces. Ethan reaches across the bar and takes Jackson's hand in his, and they nod to me, giving me their silent approval and praise.

Nolan quickly wipes away any tears before they can fall, and steps toward me with pure delight in his eyes. His cheeks come to life and he slowly morphs back into the happy, powerful man he was when I met him. He takes both of my hands in his and pulls me close to him.

"I would've waited forever for you," he says, placing his forehead on mine. "But I'm so fucking glad I don't have to."

"This may sound crazy," I say. "But I think I've fallen for you, Nolan."

He smiles the most beautiful smile I've ever seen as he replies, "You have. I know because I've fallen for you, too."

My face can barely fit the massive smile that takes over my mouth just before Nolan leans in to kiss me. Our lips touch as our tongues collide, and all the drama washes away.

I'm not here for work anymore. He's not talking to me in response to questions asked. We're together because we've chosen to be. We're here because our hearts refuse to be separate from one another, and every cell in my body knows I'll never go back to who I was again.

Old Bree is no longer in the depths of my stomach watching as New Bree takes over. Old Bree is gone for good, faded to eternal black, and all that's left are the best parts of me—the parts that desire nothing more than to be his.

Two Months Later

Epilogue

"It was so good seeing you guys again," I say as I pull Octavia into a hug in front of the restaurant, while her husband Mike talks to Nolan off to the side.

"Yes, you two are always a good time," Ocatavia says as we embrace. "I can't even tell you how happy I am that everything worked out with y'all. You guys are an incredible couple, and we love hanging out with you, so let's figure out what we want to do next weekend and make plans. Oh, and I know E and J are working tonight, but they need to come, too, so let them know."

"We definitely will," I reply just as Mike and Nolan shake hands and engage in that quick little embrace that guys do, basically just bumping shoulders.

"Okay. I'll see you at work on Monday, and congratulations again, Bree. You deserve it."

"Thanks, Octavia. I'll see you Monday."

Nolan and I split from Octavia and Mike, headed our separate ways to our respective corners of the parking lot. Nolan grabs my hand as we walk, and opens the door for me when we reach the car. I can't help the smile on my face as he

INTERVIEW WITH A SADIST

waits for me to slide into the passenger seat, before leaning into the car to kiss me. My palm finds his cheek and we sink into it, forgetting the car pulling up next to ours, and ignoring the stares of other patrons walking by. When we're together, it's just us. No one else matters in our world. We smile as we struggle to pry ourselves apart before Nolan closes my door and walks around to his side to start the car and whisk us away.

"I love hanging out with them," Nolan says as we hit the highway, headed for Center City. He reaches across the center console and blankets my hand with his.

"I know, right? Mike is cool, and Octavia has *always* been the best. She's so supportive," I say. "When you and I were first starting, she was the one who had my back. Hell, she even helped me realize how trash Melissa and Teagan were, which is why I haven't spoken to them in so long. I'm glad she and I have gotten so much closer over the past few months."

"Me, too. There's nothing like having true supportive friends. I never would've made it this far without E and J. They're the ones who anchor me. I would've floated away into oblivion a long time ago if it wasn't for them."

"Yeah, those two are awesome. I love how excited they were when we found out about the nomination."

"Well, it's not every day one of their friends gets nominated for a Pulitzer. You did such an amazing job with that story about how we met. You put yourself on the map big time and you deserve all the praise. We're all so proud of you, babe."

I smile from ear to ear just thinking about it. I may not win the Pulitzer Prize, but just being nominated for publishing *Interview with a Sadist* is enough for me. I knew the moment I sat down that the story would be phenomenal, but I didn't think it would take off the way it did. Even Chase said it was the most incredible story he'd ever read, and he was honored to publish it. I guess things are different when you're writing from your heart instead of your head. The personal connection I had with the story could never be matched, which is why the nomination is so important to me. I've known about it for a week now and it still feels brand new, even after celebrating tonight with two of our friends.

"Thank you," I say with a proud smile, just as Nolan pulls into his private parking space on the side of the club. The bright light from the sign shines into the car, making us glow.

"Now, are you ready to *really* celebrate?" Nolan asks.

I nod, grinning. "Absolutely."

We step out of the car and walk hand-in-hand into the club, where a sea of people and music flood our senses the moment the door is opened. Bass blares through the speakers from every corner as bright lights dance, jumping from wall to wall. The smell of perfumes and scented lotions fill the air as leather, latex, and bare skin cover the place from floor to ceiling. It's an adrenaline rush just to walk into The Black Collar, and for us, this is home sweet home.

Nolan takes my hand and leads me down the hall, where people talk and dance, grinding against each other as the music gives them endless energy. They all move out of the way so Nolan and I can have a clear path to the dancefloor and bar. Ethan serves drinks behind the counter, while Jackson looks down on us from the VIP section upstairs—his new domain since Maddy is awaiting trial and will never return. We nod to both of our friends as we walk past the bar and head for the darker section behind it.

Nolan high fives with the bouncer at the entrance of the main stage, and the two of us step inside the room that is completely full of people. They're broken into multiple groups, huddled up together like they're trying to keep warm around a fire, but they all stop what they're doing when we walk in. Their eyes find us and lock on, all of them in complete awe as we walk down the center aisle and ascend the steps leading to the stage.

The energy in the room shifts from admiration to exhilaration as Nolan and I stand center stage facing the crowd, and they silently take their seats in the auditorium. My heart thuds, making my knees weak as I turn my back to the crowd and take off my black jacket, revealing my bare back, just before I step out of my leggings, wearing nothing but lace underwear. I don't turn around and show them my bare chest, because although Nolan and I want to display our love on the biggest stage in the club, only he gets to see me naked.

Nolan removes his shirt and gives the crowd their first glance at the striated muscles in his chest and abs as he reaches into a large box next to me and pulls out our favorite toy, or as he would call it, his favorite *weapon*. The crowd murmurs as the long tresses dangle down to the wooden stage and brush across it while Nolan holds onto the shaft, flexing his wrist as he prepares to put the Cat O Nine Tails to use.

I look over my shoulder at the toy and smile to myself as I step up to the St. Andrew's Cross in front of me and position my limbs in front of the massive black X. Nolan hangs the tresses of the flogger over his shoulder, and steps behind me, locking my wrists and ankles in place before rubbing his hands up my back.

"You're so fucking perfect," he whispers, before kissing his way up from my shoulder to my ear. "Meeting you is the best thing that ever happened to me, Bree, and I can't believe I've found someone to share this stage with. You and I are the example of love in BDSM this world needs. We're the leaders they can follow. We are king and queen of this palace, and I'm so proud of everything you've accomplished. Thank you for completing me, Bree. I love you."

My heart warms, sending heat to the rest of my body as I smile. I can't believe I'm here. The Old Bree never would've thought doing something like this was okay, but Nolan made me anew, and belonging to him is my greatest honor.

I didn't want the assignment when Chase gave it to me, and if I never would've met Nolan, I'd probably still be stuck in a bad friendship and miserably closed-minded. I never would've known about this lifestyle, and I never would've known how trapped I truly was. He freed me, and the drama we've made it through together has done nothing but make us stronger. So, Nolan is right. We're the example he always wanted the world to see, and there isn't any other place I'd rather be.

Nolan kisses me on the cheek as I look over my shoulder at him, grinning devilishly. "I love you, too ... Sir. Now show them what love and Dominance truly look like."

Nolan's smile matches my own as he pulls the Cat O Nine Tails off his shoulder and grips it tightly. He takes two steps back and positions himself behind me as I look forward with excitement coursing through my veins, my skin vibrating with anticipation as I await what's coming.

"With pleasure, Princess," Nolan says, just before he flicks his wrist and the tails of the flogger crack in the air like a whip, striping my back with beautiful red art.

Acknowledgments

It's impossible to quantify how important 2023 is for me and my family, and Interview with a Sadist is a huge part of it. I started writing this book on the heels of Kingdom, which was the best release I've ever had, and there's a ton of pressure that comes with that. Kingdom spread my name to places it had never been before, and it's safe to say that more people know me now than any other time in my life, which means that Interview with a Sadist had to be flawless, or it all could come tumbling down like a house of cards. In this industry, one day you're up, the next you're bottoming out. It's scary, and when you add that to the fact that I intend to retire from the military next year, the pressure I've been feeling during the writing process for this book could easily form diamonds. So, with all my heart, I truly hope I hit the mark.

With success comes a little more attention and the need for a bigger support system, so my usually small list of people to acknowledge is actually bigger this time around. Not by much—I'm still an introvert with trust issues—but a little.

Let me start by thanking the one person in the world who I don't have trust issues with, and that's my partner in crime, my best friend, my business partner, and the love of my life. It's pretty incredible when all of that can be rolled into one person. To my wife, Isabel Lucero, thank you so much for all of your continued support. We have hours-long conversations every single day about our business and the industry, and I love you so much for being my sounding board and allowing me to be yours. So much of what I write is inspired by us, I think people would be surprised, and that just makes the entire process better. You're always my muse. I love you, baby, and no number of haters could ever diminish how brightly you shine.

A massive shout out to my agent, Ena Burnette, and SBR Media for all of your support and guidance. Our relationship is brand new but thank you so much for representing me. Your advice and support during the process of selling Kingdom was a huge deal to me, and we never would've gotten into audio if it wasn't for you. We have so much more work to do, and I know we're going to only get bigger and bigger. I'm trying to make both of us rich, so the manuscripts are going to be coming fast. Let's get it.

Robin Harper, we do not miss when we link up. Every time we do a cover, I think, "There's no way I'm topping this." Then we start on the next one and end up outdoing it. Every. Single. Time. I absolutely love this cover. It's so freakin' beautiful I could cry. Thanks for all of your patience. I'm pretty sure this is the most mocks we've ever had, so thank you for sticking with me through all the changes. On to the next one.

Shout out to Shauna Casey and Wildfire Marketing Solutions for all of the events leading up to this book release. I wanted to try something new this time around, and everything has been fantastic. Every event went off without a hitch, and now all we can do is hope it pays off in the end. Thanks for giving me a bit of confidence leading up to release day.

I have to drop a gigantic shout out to Kiuyana Pruden, Tiffanie Emans, and Megan Archibald. We didn't know each other before this book brought us together, and I appreciate all of your help and feedback while I was still in the writing process. It's strange, because I am full of confidence when I'm writing, and then it all starts to melt away when I'm done. Once I start editing, I have zero confidence left whatsoever, and I'd be drowning if it wasn't for your supportive words while we were in the beta phase. All of you made me feel like I had hit another home run, which was huge following the success of Kingdom, and now that it's all over and release day is looming, I feel really good about what's to come. Thank you all.

Shout out to Bookstagram and all of the Facebook groups that have shown me so much love leading up to this. But my biggest shout out has to be to BookTok. I don't know why 70K+ of you follow me, but I appreciate each and every one of you. If they ban TikTok, we will fucking riot.

Shout out to every person who has called themselves a fan of mine at any point in time. Look, I'm just a kid from Clovis, New Mexico. Although it will always be home and I will always love it, I was lucky to move away from there. I had to sell myself to the military to do it and being in the military when you don't want to be can certainly have its challenges. The point is, I was never supposed to be this. I was never supposed to become this, and I never imagined myself growing up to sell my writing and have a fanbase eager to see me and talk to me. My imposter syndrome is real, and I don't believe I deserve it all, but you do. You all believe in me and love my work, and I am forever grateful to my fans, which is why I have no problem hugging anybody or taking pictures when you come to see me at signings. I love you, and I couldn't do this without you. Because I'm a man writing spicy romance, I will always have to win people over, but my fans are out there fighting that battle for me every single day, and we're winning. Thank you all so much.

Lastly, I want to drop a bit of advice for anyone who may be trying to have a come up of their own. Life is hard, and it's a monumental challenge just to build up the confidence in yourself to pursue anything at all, let alone something outside the norm. In your pursuit of success, there will be people who claim to be your friends, who actually have no interest at all in watching you reach your goals. They will be close to you, acting like they're supportive up until the moment you reach a level they have yet to reach. They don't want to see you win because it makes them feel like they haven't accomplished anything. They view your victories as a challenge and your relationship as a competition. When you want to celebrate your accomplishments, they're fuming—doing everything they can to remind anyone who will listen that they have goals too, and their pursuit of those goals deserves more attention than your accomplishment. They can't be happy for you until they reach their goals, too. That is not friendship.

The hate may be low key, but it will be there, and you have to watch out for it. Not everybody wants to see you win, but you must stay the course, even if it means letting go of people you once loved and trusted. As humans, we crave socialization. We desire companionship and friendship, but it should never come at the price of diminishing yourself so someone else can feel good about themselves. Be who you are and pursue your goals with everything you've got. The real ones will support you, regardless of what they have going on in their own pursuit of success. The fake ones will out themselves and fall to the wayside. Don't let them stop you. Stay on your grind. They can either jump on the cape to go along for the ride, or fall the fuck off, but never let haters stop you from flying.

Until next time, Greer Mafia. Embrace your kinks.

From Isabel Lucero

When I met him, he was my savior—a hero swooping in to lend a helping hand. I didn't know he was actually the villain.

Liar
  Manipulator
  Murderer

Vicente Moreno embodies it all, but he casts a spell I can't escape. There are times I'm not sure I even want to, because with him, I feel alive, even as I teeter so close to death anytime we're together.

I made a deal with the devil for my own safety, but now I'm in his lair, and he's scarier than any threat on the street. It's wrong to want him the way I do, but I'll happily be consumed by the flames of hell if it means an eternity with the Prince of Darkness himself.

Because when his gravelly voice asks, "Who do you belong to?"

There's no hesitation when I reply, "You."

The Prince of Darkness is a dark, diverse mafia romance that features an age gap, degradation, praise, violence, and a variety of kinks found in the BDSM lifestyle. TWs can be found on the author's website.

The Prince of Darkness

The Prince Of Darkness
BY

ISABEL LUCERO

About the Author

WS (Will) Greer is the author of bestselling novels such as Claiming Carter (The Carter Series), Kingpin (An Italian Mafia Romance), and The Therapist (The Therapist Series). He's also a USAF veteran since 2004, and is still serving today, after 4 deployments to the middle east and countless assignments overseas.

WS prides himself on being a man who writes spicy romance with the absolute best of them, while also understanding and appreciating that he is a guest in the house of romance that women built.

WS grew up in Clovis, NM, and now resides in Delaware, where he lives with his wife--bestselling author Isabel Lucero-- and 3 kids.

Find WS on social media:
  TikTok: https://vm.tiktok.com/ZMe5RDsCD/
  Facebook: www.facebook.com/SuspensefulPen
  Instagram: www.instagram.com/author_wsgreer
  Twitter: www.twitter.com/author_wsgreer
  Amazon Central: http://amzn.to/2kztq7Z
  BookBub: http://bit.ly/2P6kzO8

More From WS Greer

Thank you for purchasing *Interview with a Sadist*! Please leave an honest rating and review wherever you purchased your copy. It'd be very much appreciated!

Check out these other titles from WS Greer

Frozen Secrets (A Detective Granger Novel)
Claiming Carter (The Carter Trilogy #1)
Becoming Carter (The Carter Trilogy #2)
Destroying Carter (The Carter Trilogy #3)
Defending Her
Kingpin (An Italian Mafia Romance #1)
Long Live the King (An Italian Mafia Romance #2)
Red Snow (A Detective Granger Novel)
Madman (Love & Chaos #1)
Boss
The Therapist (The Therapist #1)
Shameless (The Therapist #2)
The Fallout (The Therapist #3)

MORE FROM WS GREER

Toxic (The Therapist #4)
Kingdom

Want more from WS? Visit WS-GREER.COM for much more!

Printed in Great Britain
by Amazon